Starry-Eyed Love

ALSO BY HELENA HUNTING

HELENA HUNTING

ST. MARTIN'S GRIFFIN
NEW YORK

First published in the United States by St. Martin's Griffin, an imprint of St. Martin's Publishing Group

STARRY-EYED LOVE. Copyright © 2022 by Helena Hunting. All rights reserved. Printed in the United States of America. For information, address St. Martin's Publishing Group, 120 Broadway, New York, NY 10271.

www.stmartins.com

Designed by Devan Norman

Library of Congress Cataloging-in-Publication Data

Names: Hunting, Helena, author.
Title: Starry-eyed love / Helena Hunting.
Description: First edition. | New York : St. Martin's Griffin, 2022.
Identifiers: LCCN 2022000898 | ISBN 9781250624727
    (trade paperback) | ISBN 9781250861603 (hardcover) |
    ISBN 9781250624734 (ebook)
Subjects: LCGFT: Novels.
Classification: LCC PS3608.U594966 S73 2022 | DDC 813/.6—
    dc23/eng/20220111
LC record available at https://lccn.loc.gov/2022000898

Our books may be purchased in bulk for promotional, educational, or business use. Please contact your local bookseller or the Macmillan Corporate and Premium Sales Department at 1-800-221-7945, extension 5442, or by email at MacmillanSpecialMarkets@macmillan.com.

First Edition: 2022

10 9 8 7 6 5 4 3 2 1

For Deb.
I couldn't ask for a better friend than you.

So I'll trust *my heart, what else can I do?*
I can't live in dreams if my dreams are to come true.

—*Cinderella*

Starry-
Eyed
Love

1

THE GREAT DATE DEBATE

LONDON

"One more round?" I tap my empty margarita glass.

"Ohhh, London's cutting loose tonight!" Harley, my younger sister, elbows me playfully in the side, her dimpled grin wide and toothy.

Avery, our older sister, looks up from her phone, which she's been on for most of the evening and points a finger at me. "I'm not piggybacking you home."

"Ha ha. I'll be fine. We had all those apps." I motion to the nearly empty plate of spinach dip and the remains of our nachos.

Truth be told, I'm already feeling the first two margaritas, but I'm having too good a time to put a pin in it now. I'll take a couple of Tylenols before bed, drink a gallon of water, and be fine tomorrow morning. Mostly fine, anyway.

When our server comes around again, I order another margarita, Harley picks a sex on the beach, and Avery asks for a half-pint of light beer. While we wait for our drinks to arrive,

I arrange the paper stars I've amassed over the past couple of hours into a small pile. I'm a compulsive fidgeter, and I used to pick my nails. It's a nervous habit, and one I've had to learn to curb. Now instead, I make origami stars. I've made about two dozen since we've been here, which has helped slow my margarita consumption.

"I gotta say, I'm really happy to have Fun London back." Harley rests her head on my shoulder and hugs my arm. Her blond bob tickles my skin.

She looks like a little pixie, especially when she's sitting beside me, since I'm a good head taller than she is.

"I'm always fun," I say indignantly.

Even as her phone buzzes with another message, Avery sets it facedown on the table.

She and Harley exchange a look before Avery turns her gaze on me. "Every time you get into a relationship you turn into 'Serious London.'" She makes air quotes around the unpleasant nickname.

"That's ridiculous. I do not."

Harley nods her agreement. "Sorry to break it to you, but you totally do."

I glance from one to the other, and have to wonder if they're both drunk. "Have you two been talking about this? I mean, you must have if you've picked nicknames like Fun London and Serious London." At least they're not calling me something worse.

"We don't mean it in a bad way," Harley assures me.

"I don't know that saying I become an 'unfun' person when I'm in a relationship can be taken in any other way but bad." I have no idea where they're coming up with this.

Harley hugs my arm again. "We literally just noticed it before we came out this evening. You've been on the fence about Daniel for weeks now, and the second you broke things off, it was like a switch flipped. All of a sudden Serious London went on holiday and Fun London came out to play." She taps my empty margarita glass. "Over the past eight months, I can count on one hand how many times you've come out with us for drinks and had more than one margarita. Daniel was a wet blanket, and he was weighing you down with his 'poor me, it's so hard to be a professional photographer blah blah blah' complaining." She hiccups loudly.

I was already aware that neither of my sisters had warm feelings for Daniel.

"I'm surprised it lasted as long as it did, to be honest," Avery says from behind the rim of her pint glass.

"Well, his travel schedule was partly responsible for that." I tried to make it work about four months longer than I should have, and struggled to convince myself that I was more into him than I was. I really did want him to be "the one." On paper, he seemed like the perfect boyfriend. But as with all of my failed relationship attempts, we fizzled out. Like a fire made with wet wood, I could never find that spark people talked about. Ironic, given my last name is literally Spark.

I finally found the lady balls to break it off three days ago. And managed not to chew my nails to stubs before I had the dreaded conversation with Daniel, which is a feat on its own. My relief at it coming to an end was a pretty decent indicator that I had done the right thing. Of course, I felt bad about it since Daniel believed everything was going great. I'd had to give him the whole "it's not you, it's me" spiel. It was mostly true, and a lot better than telling him that kissing him was about as stimulating as an empty room with white walls. So I embellished a bit, saying I wasn't looking for something serious at the moment.

Post-breakup, I did what I always do—I shifted my focus back into work, both at Spark House and my online Etsy store. Except tonight, Harley suggested we celebrate my freedom, and apparently the return of Fun London with drinks, so here we are.

"He was too needy," Avery says.

"And kind of pretentious." Harley wrinkles her nose.

I shrug. They're not wrong. He was both of those things. "And also fairly uninspiring in bed."

The server returns with our drinks, and we toast to cutting free pretentious, needy men.

Avery's phone pings for the seven millionth time this evening.

"Speaking of needy, is that Declan?" My lips are a little loose, thanks to the drinks. And I think my jealousy is probably showing. Not that I want to be in a relationship where I'm attached at the hip. It's more that Avery and Declan are ridiculously in love with each other. When they're together, you can practically cut the sexual tension with a knife.

Avery gives me her unimpressed face. "He's trying on suits and asking about the difference between periwinkle and sky blue."

"Why doesn't he just google it?" Harley pops the cherry from her drink into her mouth.

"I have no idea. Honestly, *I* don't even know the difference between periwinkle and sky blue. Or if they're the same color. I just said let's go with our rec team colors. All he has to do is show them our old jerseys, and they can go from there."

"I love you, but I will not be wearing a bridesmaid dress in team colors, especially when those colors are blue and maroon," I tell my sister. "Lines need to be drawn somewhere."

"I thought it would be way cool if we had a whole soccer-themed wedding. It could be super casual."

This doesn't surprise me. Avery is an athlete and an adventurer through and through, so I couldn't imagine her wedding not incorporating what she loves. She and Declan met in college and became best friends as they bonded over sports. It was an interesting turn of events last year when they got together after she was in a serious car accident. Declan became her caregiver while she was healing, and they realized what everyone else already knew—they'd been in love with each other for years but hadn't been willing to face it. And now they're getting married. I'm happy that they're so in love, but at the same time, it shines a light on how *not* in love I was with Daniel. I want to find my person, but I don't have a male best friend to fall for.

"You just don't want to wear heels." I take another sip of my margarita, licking the salt from my lips.

A glint of light grabs my attention, and I glance at the table kitty-corner to us. A man wearing a watch lifts his beer to his lips. My gaze meets his briefly before I turn back to my sisters.

Harley leans in closer. Even though her drink is light on alcohol and high on sugar, she's tipsy. She has an even lower tolerance than I do. "That guy over there is totally checking you out." She tips her chin in his direction.

I slap her thigh under the table. "He is not. He's probably checking *you* out. Or the game that's on the TV behind us."

"The TVs are on the other side of the bar. And he's definitely not looking at me. He's looking at you. His buddy keeps snapping his fingers at him like he's trying to get his attention and failing."

Avery starts to turn around, so I kick her under the table. "Don't you dare look over there."

"Ow! That was totally unnecessary. I just wanted to take a peek. Geez. Chill out." She slides along the bench seat.

"What are you doing?" As if I need my sisters drawing attention to us, especially with Harley being halfway to drunk. She gets loud when she has more than one drink. Sometimes it's embarrassing for more than just her.

"Going to the bathroom. I'm two beers in, and I need to break the seal." Avery wags her brows and points at Harley. "Don't worry, I'll be super discreet about checking him out, unlike this one."

"I wasn't obvious!" Harley defends herself. Loudly.

I elbow her in the side, causing her drink to slosh and a small puddle of liquid to spread under my pile of stars. "Can you use your inside voice?"

"It's not like I'm shouting through a megaphone. Besides, there's music, and sports, and conversations going on all around us. It's not as if that guy can hear us talking about him." Harley chases her straw around her drink until she finally manages to snag it with her lips.

Avery does a terrible job of being sneaky while taking a peek at the guy, who happens to be looking our way when she passes his table.

"He's doing it again. I bet you a million dollars he's working up the nerve to come talk to you," Harley murmurs. "And he's kinda hot."

I snort indelicately. "I sincerely doubt that. No one actually comes up to someone in bars anymore. Besides, I'm with my girl gang, which is doubly off-putting. Also, if you had a million dollars to throw around on bets, I guarantee you would not be running social media for Spark House."

She shrugs. "It's not a bad gig."

"It would be great if Avery would let us hire someone to help out this year." I swipe at the rim of my drink and suck the salt off my finger.

"You know how she feels about hiring nonfamily members." She swirls her straw in her glass.

"Maybe we can adopt an extra sister," I suggest, and Harley giggles.

I glance over at the guy, unable to stop myself from looking, and meet his gaze. He lifts his beer and his eyes crinkle with his smile. I give him a quick smile back, which I'm sure looks more like a constipated grimace, and pick up my own drink, trying to hide behind it.

He's not just kinda hot, he's Bunsen-burner-blue-flame hot. He has a beard, which usually I'm not a huge fan of. But it's not one of those "alpha male, I'm using facial hair as a reason not to engage in personal grooming" beards. Even with the facial hair, I can tell that he has high cheekbones and a square jaw. His hair is chestnut brown and a little unruly at the sides, as though he's overdue for a haircut.

He's dressed in jeans and a T-shirt with the word RECYCLE on the front in faded capital letters. Despite his casual attire, there's something about the way he carries himself. When he raises his hand to stop the server passing by, she grows visibly flustered. As though having his attention on her is too much for her to handle.

The watch is another thing that piques my curiosity especially since it seems a bit of a contradiction to his jeans and T-shirt ensemble. It's not a sports watch, but an older one, maybe an antique. He looks to be in his thirties, and not many people in this generation choose to wear anything but a Smartwatch, favoring the ease of a cell phone when they need to know what time it is.

Avery returns, and we finish our drinks, flagging down the server for the bill, to which she gives us an awkward smile.

"So, um, your bill has already been paid." She inclines her head marginally in the direction of the table with the hot guy. "He picked up the tab."

"Oh wow. Okay. Well, that was nice." Especially since we racked up quite the bill with our drinks.

"What about the tip?" Harley asks, digging into her purse.

Our server holds up her hand. "Oh no, he was more than generous."

"You're sure?"

"Absolutely." She nods.

Avery and Harley exchange another one of those knowing looks. My stomach does a flip-flop as our server moves on to another table and the hot guy slides across the bench seat and rises. He's tall, must be over six feet, and lean. Broad shoulders that taper down to a narrow waist. I glance at his feet and notice his scuffed running shoes.

He rolls his shoulders back and crosses over to our table. He nods to my sisters but doesn't really look at them, his eyes on me. Now that he's right in front of me, I notice they're a deep mossy-green color, reminding me of a Colorado forest. "Hi." A slow smile forms as his gaze moves over my face.

I feel it like a gentle caress and heat travels through my veins. It's an unexpected reaction, so my own "hi" comes out rather breathily. "Thank you for the drinks and the food. You really didn't need to do that."

His grin widens, showing off perfectly straight, white teeth. "Well, I wanted to make a good impression, and have an excuse to come over and talk to you."

Harley squeezes my leg under the table. I don't risk looking at her because I'm sure she's smiling like a loon.

"You certainly did that. Make a good impression, I mean." Why am I so awkward right now? And why does it feel like this man is sucking all the oxygen out of the room and turning my brain cells into mush?

That gets me another smile. "I wanted to apologize if it seemed like I was staring. I hope I haven't made you uncomfortable."

I touch my fingers to my lips and resist the urge to play with my hair, but just barely. Why does this man make me feel like a starry-eyed high school girl? "You haven't made me uncomfortable."

"Good. That's very good." His tongue drags across his bottom lip. "I just needed to tell you that from across the room, you were beyond stunning, but up close." He lets out a low whistle. "You are an absolute work of art."

I fight with my eyebrows not to rise. This guy has all the lines. "Oh really?" I lace my fingers together and set my chin on them. "The kind of art you might hang in your living room?"

"Bedroom, actually."

I laugh. I can't decide if this guy is too smooth for his own good. Or mine. I have to wonder how many times he's dropped these lines on other women and they've ended up in his bed as a result.

"That sound is music to my ears," he says, his white-toothed smile still in place. "I knew I'd be kicking myself if I didn't come over here and at least say hello." He slides a small piece of paper across the table, roughly the size of a business card. "I'm going to leave my number, and maybe if you're interested, I can take you out for a drink, or dinner, or a hot air balloon ride."

I can see exactly where this will go if I take that card from him. And while getting into bed with a random, attractive man might be fun, I know it's not the right thing for me. Before I can really consider what I'm doing, or fully absorb the last part, I put a hand out to stop him. "I'm very flattered, but I have to be honest with you. I won't call you. I have a boyfriend." The lie tastes sour on my tongue. Although, had it been three days earlier, it would have been the truth.

Avery does some kind of cough-choke thing, and I kick her under the table and get Harley on the back swing.

His smile falters for a moment, but he doesn't break eye contact. "That's disappointing, but unsurprising. I didn't see a ring, so I'd hoped maybe luck was on my side." He tips his head to the side. "Is it serious?"

"Pardon me?"

"You and this boyfriend, are you two serious?"

This guy is unbelievable. "And if we are?"

"Hmm." He withdraws his hand and tucks the paper in his pocket. "I'd hate for karma to pass judgment on me and get in the way of our future together, so I'm just going to hope I run into you again when you're single. Have a lovely night, ladies." He nods to my sisters and gives me one final lingering glance before he winks. "Thank you for existing."

And then he walks away.

Our table sits in silence, and Avery cranes her neck to watch him leave.

"Oh my God. Did that just happen?" Harley whisper-yells.

Avery smacks my arm. "Why did you tell him you had a boyfriend?"

I deflate. "Because I just got out of a relationship and the last thing I'm looking for is a rebound. Plus those lines were unreal. I'm sure he does this on a weekly basis, and some poor unsuspecting woman ends up in his bed and then never sees him again."

"You could have at least taken his number, though!" Avery says. "What would have been the harm in that?"

"What if he was *the one*?" Harley glances out the window, maybe checking to see if he's still in the parking lot. Harley is a real believer in fate and karma and everything happening for a reason.

"If he was *the one*, there would have been a sign, don't you think?" Like a meteor shower. Or *the zing*. Or a shooting star.

Avery shrugs it off, as is her way. "Well, I guess now we'll never know, will we?"

When we leave the bar, I tip my head up. The sky is clear, stars sparkling above our heads. And of course, one shoots across the night sky. I roll my eyes. It's just a coincidence. Not a sign. Taking that guy's number would have been a mistake. One I saved myself from making with a little white lie.

2

JUGGLE ALL THE THINGS

LONDON

THREE MONTHS LATER

I arrive at Spark House an hour early on Monday morning. The hotel is an old converted house on a huge piece of land, allowing us to set up unique events and provide an intimate, eclectic space for guests. It is sort of like a cross between a bed-and-breakfast and a small boutique hotel. It's been in our family for three generations, and Avery, Harley, and I took it over when our grandmother decided to retire a couple of years ago.

While I love working with my sisters, some parts of this job aren't particularly easy for me, so I like giving myself extra time to prepare when no one else is here and I don't have an audience.

Today I have to touch base with one of our prospective clients who asked for a call first thing this morning. They emailed late last night with a list of questions. I don't want to lose out on this opportunity, so I figured it would be a good idea to come in early and rehearse my answers. I have a million other things to do today, such as making prototypes for this weekend's centerpieces, but this is my first priority.

We could definitely use this particular client's business, especially since we're looking at expanding our kitchen facilities so we can host larger events. That kind of renovation comes with a pretty hefty price tag, though.

After the call, I can shift my focus to something a bit more enjoyable.

I drop my bag beside my desk and fire up my computer. I spend a few minutes drafting my responses and tweaking the language before I read it aloud. I fuss over word choice and inflection, going back and changing the wording a few times. My goal is to be able to sell them on hosting their event here.

"Why is this so freaking hard?" I grumble.

"Why is what so freaking hard?" Harley asks, startling me.

"Why are you here so early?" I feel my face turning red with embarrassment. Normally when I rehearse calls, I do it in private, and sometimes in front of a mirror.

"I'm not. It's almost nine. Avery and I just got here."

"Oh. Where's Avery?" I glance at the clock on my screen. It is indeed almost nine, which means I've been trying to compose a conversation for more than an hour, and I have less than twenty minutes left to prepare for this call.

"In the backyard, trying to decide where she wants to set up the outdoor component for this weekend's event." She tips her head to the side. "Is everything okay?"

"Yeah." I rub the back of my neck, feeling the tightness there.

"I should have done this last night." I hit print on the file, so I have all of my responses in front of me. "Can you read this over and tell me if I'm missing anything?"

"Sure, of course." Harley grabs the sheets and drops into the chair across from me, scanning them. "What is this for?"

"The Kendalls. I had a call with them last week about a potential event in the fall. It's a really great initiative. They host a holiday-themed event for terminal kids. I have a follow-up call in a few minutes." I hate the nervous flutter in my stomach, like it's full of butterflies, and not the nice kind. I haven't eaten yet and won't until after I speak with them.

She stops reading for a second to glance at me, a slight furrow in her brow. "Is this why you came in early?"

"I wanted to get it out of the way, so I didn't have to worry about it all morning." Worrying is something I excel at, unlike preparing for a phone call.

"It looks good to me. I don't think you have anything to be anxious about." Her gaze shifts to my star jar as I toss another puffy one in with the rest. It was empty this morning, and now it's already half full.

"I just don't want to mess this up. If we get their event, and we do a good job, they might let us host it every year. And I think it's a really great cause."

"You've got this, London. You're going to be fine."

"Okay, thanks." I take a deep breath. "Can you hang out, though, until after the call, so I have backup in case I need it?"

"Sure."

"Thanks."

I take a few deep breaths before I make the call to the Kendalls. I'm on edge at first, and I can hear the anxiety in my own voice.

Harley gives me the thumbs-up and then the calm down signal, mouthing, *You've got this.* It turns out all my worrying and fretting this morning was for nothing, because fifteen minutes later I'm cracking jokes and setting up a meeting for them to come in next week to sign paperwork and put down a deposit.

"See, I told you! You had it in the bag before you even made the call."

"This stuff is always so stressful for me," I admit as I deflate in my chair.

Her smile drops, and she rolls one of my stars between her fingers. "Always? As in every time you call a new client?"

"Basically, yes."

"Oh wow. I had no idea. I thought this kind of thing was totally in your wheelhouse."

I put on a good show, even for my sisters, but the truth is, I got stuck in the role as the person who handles the business and financial side. I think it's because I'm organized and am good with numbers, so I just fell into this position.

"Not even a little bit in my wheelhouse." I give her a wry smile. "I have a decent game face, but this call was unexpected, and I didn't want to screw it up because they have all these great sponsors that they work with. I thought it would be good for Spark House to have that kind of connection, especially with what they're doing for those kids."

"Maybe Avery should field those calls?"

"She already manages all the event coordination stuff once things are set up. It wouldn't be fair to put more on her." I dump my star jar into the tote bin under my desk. I use the stars for centerpieces and decorations for events, so they're not completely without a purpose.

"Yeah, but if stuff like this is taking up hours of your day, how effective is that?"

"It's not usually this bad," I backtrack. "Besides, Avery's already a ball of stress, and having her take on more stuff around here isn't going to make that better."

"We really need to hire someone to help out, even part-time would be better than nothing," Harley says.

"You know I'm on board; it's Avery we need to convince. With her already being worried about the wedding, and now the whole proposal for expanding the kitchen, I can't see her jumping at even more change."

"Don't I know it. I wish she weren't so hardheaded about this." Harley shakes her head. "Sometimes I feel like we need to revisit this unanimous decision making and go with majority rules. We'd get a lot further that way."

"Yeah, but then Avery would be miserable, and she'd accuse us of conspiring against her," I point out.

"Maybe after the wedding it'll be easier."

"We can only hope."

Harley and I tried to broach the subject a few weeks ago, and Avery nearly bit our heads off going on about how this is our legacy and blah blah blah. We gave up when she started in on the importance of keeping it a family business. "Heads up, she's going to be asking about flowers for her wedding. For someone who is usually awesome at planning events, her wedding seems to be a hot mess."

"That's because it doesn't have anything to do with sports. They should just get married in a stadium, during a soccer game at halftime or something." I open the box of photos that were left for me for the upcoming wedding anniversary event.

Harley's eyes flare and dart around, possibly to make sure we're alone. "Don't you dare say that in front of Avery!"

"Because she'll think it's a great idea?"

Harley picks up one of the wedding photos. "For sure she would. As it is, she's been tossing around the idea of having a soccer net as the archway. They should probably just say 'I scored' instead of 'I do.'"

I laugh. "I can actually see this all happening in my head."

"Me too. Let's never mention it again. It's not as if Avery needs more ideas. She's trying to incorporate everything she loves into one day. It's either going to be awesome or a shitshow."

"Let's be real, it's probably going to be both. You know she'll try to organize the entire thing and be the bride at the same time."

"Yup. If either of us gets married, can we just agree to hire wedding planners, so we don't do this to ourselves?"

"Absolutely." I hold out my pinkie and Harley links hers with mine.

Harley will definitely settle down eventually, but I'm not so sure wedding bells are in my future. Harley has been destined for motherhood her entire life, always the caretaker. I stepped into that role after our parents passed away, or at least I tried to. Avery had been in college and I'd been a freshman in high school. Harley was in middle school, and their loss rocked us all. I don't know if it's possible to ever truly recover from losing your parents in such a devastating way, but the days keep passing, and we keep on going.

I continue flipping through the box of photographs that chronicle the Wilsons' life together. Their daughter has done a great job pulling images that tell a story and organizing them from first date, to their wedding, pregnancies, births, children's weddings, and grandbabies and great-grandbabies.

I stop at a picture of the Wilsons' thirtieth wedding anniversary and a lump forms in my throat.

Harley gives me a sad smile. "Mom and Dad's anniversary is next month."

I nod. Every year on our parents' anniversary, the three of us celebrate together. It's always bittersweet, in part because their wedding anniversary is also the anniversary of their death. They'd gone on a trip, just the two of them, a little weekend getaway, but there had been a huge storm and an even bigger accident on the highway. They'd never come home, and our lives had been changed forever.

If they were still here, so much would be different. My job, my life, our family.

"What do you want to do this year? Should we book a table somewhere? Or just watch a movie and order in?" Harley asks.

Our parents' first date was dinner and a movie. "We should order in and watch *When Harry Met Sally*."

Harley nods. "That sounds perfect."

"I think so too. We'll order all their favorite foods and celebrate their love together."

We shift away from the topic of our parents. I still find it hard to talk about them. No matter how long they've been gone, that wound always feels fresh. I worry that part of my problem with relationships is that I'm afraid to get too close to anyone other than my sisters because partners can walk away so easily, but family is different. At least ours is. I know what it feels like to lose someone essential to my life, and the possibility that I could give my heart to someone who will discard it is terrifying. So I don't.

Harley and I go over the plans for the weekend, her schedule of posts leading up to the event, and the other things she handles around Spark House. While her main role is social media director, she often manages random tasks when things get overwhelming or we're juggling preparations for multiple events. Which is basically all the time now.

Last year when Avery was in the car accident, both Harley and I had to take on a lot of tasks that weren't in our previous job descriptions. While we made it work, there's a reason Avery is the face of Spark House, and Harley and I function more in the background. Sure, I make connections with other businesses, but Avery is the one who builds relationships with clients and comes up with ideas for the events. She's the real heart and soul of Spark House.

Harley and I work together on the fiftieth wedding anniversary collage, arranging the photos so we have a visual progression of the Wilsons' relationship. At one point, I have to excuse myself to the bathroom so I can collect myself. If there's one thing I can't stand, it's tears. Other people's are fine, but I thoroughly dislike shedding them. It makes me feel weak. And like I don't have control over my emotions. I try to stay in check most of the time, otherwise I get anxious, and then I'm liable to spiral, which isn't something I want. It used to happen often after my parents passed. The panic was hard to manage sometimes, but I've found ways to cope.

We're just putting the finishing touches on the collages—there were enough photos to make ten—when the phone rings. Harley and I both glance at the name on the screen.

"Holt Media? Why does that sound familiar?"

Harley shrugs. "You answer. I'll look them up and feed you details if you need them."

"That's a smart plan." I give her a thumbs-up while she speedily types on her phone. If I were alone, I'd search on my desktop, but Harley is accustomed to doing almost everything on a six-inch screen.

I clear my throat, roll my shoulders back, and answer the call. "Hello, Spark House, London speaking, how may I help you?"

"Hello, London, I'm Mitchell, the personal assistant to CEO Jackson Holt, of Holt Media and Consulting. I was wondering if you had a moment to speak."

That's a mouthful of a title, and the CEO part puts me on alert. "Of course, how can I help you?"

Harley's eyes go wide, and she turns her phone around so I can see what she does as she mouths, *Holy shit.* I put my hand over the receiver and peer at the screen. The Instagram account shows that Holt Media and Consulting has over three million followers. And I thought Spark House was doing great with a hundred thousand.

Who are these people? I mouth at my sister.

"I have no idea, but you need to talk to them," she whispers.

I tune back in just in time to hear: ". . . new initiative. Our social media relations manager has had a conversation with one of your business liaison partners, who suggested we meet with you. We'd like to hear more about your hotel to see if you'd be a welcomed addition to our network. Our company helps connect other companies who are working toward the same goals. Your green campaigns are something the CEO here is particularly passionate about, and we like your mission statement. We're seeking out more family-run companies like Spark House. I see you're based in Colorado Springs, and we're currently in Colorado hosting an event in Denver. Would you or someone from your staff be interested in meeting with myself and our account manager to see if you'd be the right fit for Holt Media?"

Wow. This is exactly what we've been looking for to take us to the next level. And maybe make the projected kitchen renovations possible sooner than we thought. Avery is going to freak out.

"Yes. We would. Absolutely be interested. In a meeting, that is." And I better be able to string a full sentence together during that meeting.

"Excellent. We have an opening tomorrow at eleven a.m. I'm aware it's very short notice, and we understand if it's not adequate time to fit us into your schedule. If it's not possible, we can revisit in a month or so."

I flip to our calendar, and I see that Avery has the morning blocked off for her own wedding planning and Harley is scheduled to take a bunch of promo shots for our new brochure. I have a morning meeting, but it can be moved around, which means that I'll be the one to take the meeting. The nerves start, but I urge myself not to let it get to me until after I end the call. "Eleven a.m. tomorrow morning sounds perfect. I'll be there."

"That's fantastic. Thank you for your flexibility, Miss Spark. Our event is at the Concord. Do you know where that is?"

"It's downtown. That's a Mills Hotel, correct?" I can picture it in my head. It's a gorgeous hotel that boasts stunning views.

"Yes, exactly. We'll email you with the details and directions."

I give him my email address and scribble down the name of the hotel, while Harley looks it up. I thank Mitchell, probably more times than is reasonable, and tell him I look forward to meeting him in person tomorrow. I end the call with shaking hands and turn to Harley.

We both check to make sure the red light is off on the phone before we jump out of our chairs, grab each other by the shoulders, and shriek in unison. "Holy crap! I'm meeting with Holt Media tomorrow!"

"I know! This is crazy awesome!" She starts jumping up and down so I join her, but stop abruptly.

"I don't know anything about this company. Oh my God, Harley. I don't even really know what the heck this meeting is about. He said something about connecting companies and adding us to their network."

"We definitely need to do some research," Harley says.

"Avery should be the one taking this meeting. You know how she is with presentations; she lives for talking about how great Spark House is." She's a natural and I'm not.

"But you'll be awesome. It'll be just like the phone call this morning."

Which I spent an hour preparing for. "What if I screw it up? This is a big deal, Harley. Do you think Avery can move around her thing tomorrow?"

She shakes her head. "She has to meet with the caterers or else everyone is going to eat hamburgers and hot dogs at the wedding. And remember, they called us on a recommendation, so they're already invested. You've got this."

"I've got this," I repeat.

And just like that, I have an entirely new to-do list.

3

PRESENTATE, DON'T HESITATE

LONDON

Harley, Avery, and I have taken over the living room in Avery's apartment, laptops perched on couch cushions, take-out boxes littering the coffee table. We're doing Holt Media research and trying to figure out what all I'll need to focus on when I meet with them tomorrow.

"Okay, let's review what we know so far about Holt Media. Then, if you want, you can run through the presentation you usually give to new prospective clients, although you're nailing it, so I'm not sure you really need the extra practice." Harley pops a mint into her mouth.

"I still think it would be helpful if you fired some questions at me on my next run-through. The kind you think they're going to ask based on what we know about this initiative." I wish I'd asked more questions when I was on the phone with Mitchell this morning. Normally I'm so much more composed, but then

I don't typically have a massive multimillion-dollar media company asking for a meeting.

They sent along a packet of information, which was helpful in the general sense, but it was only a three-page overview. Had I had the opportunity to read it over before they called, I would have had a list of questions prepared. As it is, I have two solid pages of notes on the overview of Teamology—the new initiative that pairs green companies with prospective sponsors—including a full page of questions.

"I can definitely fire questions at you, but you've presented our business plan and our mission statement so many times, you basically know it by heart." Avery pops a chocolate-covered peanut in her mouth.

I added a bunch of new slides this afternoon. Typically, I revamp it every month or two just to keep it fresh and update the featured events, tailoring it to whoever I'm presenting to. It had been almost two months, and since this is a very green, very influential company, I made sure to highlight those events in which we were strongly green-focused.

"Right. Okay." I nod a few times and take a deep breath. I don't think I'm going to sleep very well tonight.

"Who is the CEO of Holt Media and Consulting, and how long has he been the CEO?" Harley asks.

"This one is easy. Jackson Holt. He's the founder of Holt Media, and he started it up about eight years ago. When he was only twenty-seven years old. Prior to Holt Media, he made his fortune as an app developer. He's most well-known for Pic Please, an image-and-video-based social media app and also Break into Love, which is a dating app with ridiculously high rates of positive matches thanks to the Q-and-A feature used before people even go on their first in-person, face-to-face date. And"—I raise a finger because I know Harley is about to move on to the next question—"his least successful app was Keep It Clean, which partnered green companies in similar regions, but there were limitations for its use, and he wasn't able to properly vet the green companies, which is how Holt Media and Consulting was born." I fold my hands around my mug. "As a side note, one of the major issues they had was due to the fact that people kept confusing it with a dating app geared toward individuals who were waiting until marriage before they consummated their relationships."

Declan, who's been mostly quiet sitting at the kitchen table with his laptop propped in front of him, pops out an earbud. "Did I hear that right? There's a dating app for people who want to remain virgins until they're married?"

"It's more common than you'd think."

"It also seems like it would be a prime target for douchebags looking to pop cherries," Harley says.

"Hence the reason both of those apps are no longer available," I say. "Aside from that, how on target am I?"

"So good, it's almost like you've googled him all day long," Avery says while flipping through the website on her laptop. "Oh yeah, wow. That app tanked hard. Doesn't look like this guy is hurting as a result, though." She stops chewing on her straw, eyebrows lifting as she lets out a low whistle. "This guy has an absurd amount of money. His net worth is close to a billion dollars. What the hell does a thirty-five-year-old with that much money do all day long?"

"Run a media and consulting company and watch his investments make him more money." I mean, it's pretty obvious. "One of the things they're probably going to ask is how we can keep the

costs down for our clients and remain committed to green initia-
tives since they can be cost prohibitive for smaller businesses, but
I don't know how to answer that."

"Well, that's the whole point of their initiative, isn't it?" Declan laces his hands behind his head and leans back in his chair.
"They have the resources and the ability to pair smaller, family-
run businesses like Spark House with bigger sponsors to help
reduce those costs. Your job is to make the client happy within
their budget, and it seems like it's Holt's job to help facilitate that
in an eco-friendly way and effectively grow your business. The
point is that it's symbiotic on all levels, for all parties."

I type furiously as he speaks, trying to get down the gist of
his response. I'm once again reminded of how this job does not
come naturally to me. But for Declan, on the other hand, this is
the kind of thing he loves. "Maybe you should be the one meeting with them," I grumble.

"If Avery and I didn't have to meet with the caterers, I'd be
happy to tag along." He gives me an encouraging smile. "Besides,
your sisters are right, you have it. It was one question, and I live
and breathe numbers."

"Such a math nerd." Avery rolls her eyes.

"You love my math nerdiness." Declan winks at her, and she
blows him a kiss, then turns her attention back to us. "Uh, have
either of you seen what the CEO looks like?"

"Who cares what he looks like? He's probably balding and
has those hair implant things." I'm aware this is untrue. I've seen
the pictures of him. I know exactly what he looks like. Refined,
classy, and more attractive than any man with that much money
has a right to be. He *should* be balding with implants, and about
twenty years older than he is, but it's clear genetics dealt him a

royal flush in the looks department, and his business savvy has carried him a long way.

"You mean plugs?" Harley picks up her phone and taps a bunch of buttons, then scrolls at lightning speed with her face about three inches away from the screen. It's amazing that she doesn't have a hunchback or terrible eyesight. "Hold on, I think I found him. Some huge social media influencer has tagged him in a bunch of photos. I've heard of her before too. Selene Angelis. Her following is unreal."

I would like to stay on task here. And since I'm already aware of Jackson Holt's extreme attractiveness, I'd also like to move on from this topic. Plus, it's closing in on ten thirty, and I'm hoping to get to bed before midnight. Not that I think it's going to make a difference regarding the quality of my sleep, but a girl can hope.

"Holy mother. Wow. If this guy has plugs, they're pretty incredible." She turns her phone around so we can see what she sees.

On the tiny screen is the same man I stumbled upon in my Holt Media research. There's something familiar about him, but then, he is a media mogul and a tycoon, so I'm sure I've seen his face before. He has dark hair that's styled with some kind of product, full lips, high cheekbones, and an aura that commands attention. And that's just a picture. I can't imagine what he must be like in person.

Avery snatches the phone out of Harley's hand and whistles softly. "Wow. He looks like a superhero-businessman mash-up."

"What does that even mean?"

"Look at that jaw and those eyes. That can't be his real eye color. They're like emeralds. I wonder if he can laser things with his eyes. It's not normal to be that good-looking."

"It's probably photoshopped. Can we focus? It's not as though the CEO is going to be sitting in on this meeting anyway. It seems below his pay grade and something he'd pass on to any one of his hundreds of employees while he's busy doing whatever CEOs do." Apart from watching his money grow, or making snow angels in a pile of hundred-dollar bills. It's probably something I'd do. Naked. Well, maybe not naked, but in a bikini.

"How do you know? Maybe it's his baby, and he wants to be involved in every aspect of it." Avery tosses Harley her phone.

"I highly doubt that, but if I run into him, I'll tell him you think he's hot. How about that?" I offer.

"There is literally zero chance you would ever even consider doing that. Remember the time you were standing in line behind the lead singer of the Lumineers? They're your absolute favorite band, and you didn't even try to get his autograph."

"He was getting a coffee. And he was clearly in disguise."

"He was wearing a ball cap and sunglasses inside the coffee shop. That's not really incognito when you're famous." Harley sweeps the pile of puffy stars sitting on the coffee table into a ziplock bag and sets it aside. "Anyway, it's getting late. Should we think about heading home?"

"One more run-through and then we can go?" I ask.

"For sure." Avery picks up a rogue star, tosses it in the air, and bats it toward Declan. It beans him on the head. She grins and turns back to me and Harley. "Let's take it from the top."

4

COMPOSURE, DON'T YOU DESERT ME

LONDON

I don't take any chances with my sleep and pop a melatonin before bed. It does the trick, and I fall into a mostly solid sleep. The best and worst part about melatonin is that it gives me strange, vivid dreams. In the dream, I'm trying to flip through my slideshow, but the button is stuck and it won't go to the next slide. I'm getting frustrated, and suddenly, instead of my presentation, there's an old video of me and my sisters dancing to "Lady Marmalade." I wake up sweaty and embarrassed. It's barely five in the morning, but there's no way I can go back to bed.

I get up and check my presentation—there is no "Lady Marmalade" video.

I shake off the dream and try not to read too much into it. While I take a long, hot shower, I practice my presentation.

I get dressed, blow-dry my hair, and apply makeup, all while quietly reciting the facts I know about Holt Media.

Harley's standing in the middle of the kitchen, pouring herself a coffee when I come out of my bedroom, looking for outfit advice. "How's this? Would a pantsuit be better? Maybe that would be a more professional option." I'm currently wearing a gray cap-sleeved dress with a black jacket and black heels. It's not very exciting as far as outfits go, but I prefer to be understated in these situations.

"I think you look great."

"I'm going to try on a pantsuit and then we can decide." I leave her standing in the kitchen and go back to my bedroom to change.

Three outfits later, Harley puts her foot down. "They all look fantastic. I say go with the pantsuit though, since that's the one you keep coming back to."

"Okay." I run my hands over my hips. "I just feel like I need to really bring it today. This is a huge opportunity."

Harley takes me by the shoulders. "Look at me, London."

I drag my gaze away from my reflection. I know I need to take the stress-panicking down a few notches.

"They called us, not the other way around. They need to sell *us* on *them*. I'm sorry I can't go with you, but if anyone can do this, you can. Once you get started, you can sell a space heater to a desert dweller." Harley has always been great at pep talks.

"Their connections are a big draw."

Harley smiles. "Which is something they already know. They have a name. And maybe we don't have a huge one, but we have a solid client base, and we're growing exponentially. Which they're aware of if they did any research at all."

"This is super true." I exhale what I'm assuming is a coffee-scented breath in my sister's face. To her credit, she doesn't even flinch. "If we get this, it could open so many new doors for us."

"You're absolutely right, it could."

I don't want to get my hopes up, but so much could change if we can secure this exposure and these connections.

"We'd be able to hire more employees, and Avery couldn't stonewall us anymore. We'd have to if we end up with more events and clients." I try to tamp down my excitement over the thought. "I could spend more time on the centerpieces and that kind of thing. And my Etsy side business could actually grow." As of right now, I'm fighting to keep up with the limited orders I'm currently able to fulfill.

"Avery will want to buy yurts."

"She's obsessed with the freaking yurts. I think she honestly just likes saying the word *yurt*."

"It's gratifying, almost like dropping an f-bomb," Harley agrees. "I could maybe take on a side nanny gig again." Harley's eyes light up like she's a kid in a candy store.

"You need to find a guy in his thirties who's looking to settle down and have a family, like stat." I snap my fingers.

Harley loves babies the same way every human with a heart loves puppies. She's destined to be a mom. In fact, she used to be a full-time nanny until she started working with me and Avery at Spark House.

She waves a hand around in the air. "It'll happen one day."

"I really hope we win them over." The more I talk about it, the more I want it.

Her smile is soft and maternal. My baby sister is wise beyond her twenty-five years. "If it's meant to be, it'll be. They already think we'd be a good fit, now we just have to make sure they're the right fit for *us*."

My meeting isn't until eleven, but I leave at nine thirty so I can get a lay of the land and one more practice round with my presentation. I move to the back seat of the SUV, so I'm behind the cover of tinted windows, pop my earbuds in, and go over the entire thing from start to finish before I head inside.

The Concord is an opulent hotel in downtown Denver. Vaulted ceilings, state-of-the-art architectural designs, sleek lines and beautiful curves with dark trim, and luxurious furnishings make it the perfect combination of contemporary and classic.

I looked up what it costs to stay a night here, since it's good to know what the going rate is. Even the most economical room would be considered a splurge. Mills Hotels are some of the most renowned in the world, and they're basically everywhere. Because they are so different than Spark House, I'm not concerned about the rumors of them expanding into Colorado with more properties. The people who can afford to stay here generally aren't the type of people looking to book an event at Spark House.

I make my way to the conference center and sign in with the receptionist stationed outside. I take a seat in the makeshift waiting room, which is empty apart from me. Even with all the research we did last night on Holt Media, I feel woefully uninformed about what exactly it is that they want to discuss with me. Apart from a few Instagram posts by that Selene woman regarding the Teamology initiative Holt Media is planning to roll out, there isn't much available online about it.

While I wait, I review my list of questions. I wish I could do something constructive with my hands, but making origami stars in a waiting room doesn't exactly send out a chill, polished vibe. So instead, I clasp my hands and settle them in my lap.

At ten fifty-eight, a man appears at the doorway. He's wearing a charcoal-gray tailored suit and polished black shoes, and he's holding a tablet. His dark blond hair is cut short and neatly styled. In fact, every single person I've seen come through here is incredibly poised and put together. He adjusts the frames of his glasses and glances at his tablet. "London Spark?"

"I'm London." I shoulder my bag and stand, running my hands down the front of my pants to smooth them out, but also to absorb any dampness on my palms.

He gives me a warm smile and extends his hand. "I'm Mitchell. We spoke on the phone yesterday."

"It's a pleasure to meet you, Mitchell." I give him a firm handshake.

"And you as well, Miss Spark. Thank you for making the time to come out and meet with us today. I'm aware you have a very busy schedule. You're hosting a fiftieth wedding anniversary this weekend, is that correct?"

I nearly stumble over my response, surprised that he knows this. "We are. It's been such a joy to organize. It's amazing to see all of these people come together and celebrate love that has lasted generations."

"It certainly seems that way based on your social media posts."

Of course he would check out our social. "Ah yes, my sister Harley manages that side of things. She's great at promoting the companies and businesses we work with to make our events special."

"That's an important part of the event process." He nods his agreement. "My parents celebrated their thirty-fifth recently, and we had a big party to celebrate. Fifty years is quite the accomplishment."

"Especially if they're not hiding each other's hearing aids so they can't override the other's decisions on what the color theme should be."

He chuckles. "Sounds like maybe you've had some experience with that in the past."

"You would be correct." I smile, already more at ease. Harley's right; they wanted this meeting with me. And I'm better at this than I give myself credit for.

"Aren't you hosting the championship dinner for the University of Colorado's college soccer team the following weekend? It must be quite the shift."

I appreciate that they've done their homework on Spark House. "It is. Take down and turn around can be quick at times. Some events require extensive setup—like the soccer dinner, for example."

"I imagine. You're quite unique in your approach to the events you host." He opens the door to a conference room and ushers me in ahead of him.

A woman sits on the side of the table facing the door. She glances up from her tablet, eyes moving over me, taking me in. I roll my shoulders back and stand a little taller. I remind myself that I'm here because they called me, not the other way around.

"London Spark, this is Tish Malvern, the senior account manager for Holt Media."

She rises and reaches across the table, holding out her hand. Her smile is stiff and a little on the frosty side. I assume they've hosted a lot of these meetings.

"It's wonderful to meet you. Thank you so much for having me."

"You're very welcome, London, I'm sure." She motions to the table, which is meant to hold at least a dozen people, not just three. "Why don't you have a seat and we can tell you a little bit more about the Teamology initiative at Holt Media."

"That sounds perfect." I slide into the chair across from her, and Mitchell rounds the table to take the seat beside her.

Tish sits ramrod straight, nothing but a tablet, a folder, and a glass of still water in front of her. Mitchell, on the other hand, flips open his tablet and sets it up so the cover is facing me. It reads KEEP CALM AND DRINK DECAF. He also has a travel mug set up beside him with a red circle and a line through the word DECAF. Clearly he's the one with personality here.

"As Mitchell explained yesterday, Holt Media is starting a new initiative. New to Colorado, anyway. Our hub is in New York, and we've rolled out something similar with great success. We pair companies open to sponsorships or sponsored ads with companies who have similar goals and beliefs. Specifically, we're looking to help companies who prioritize the environment and going green to connect and cross promote. The goal is to stream-line revenue and provide opportunities for smaller companies to flourish. What's different this time is that we're working with Selene Angelis, who is heading the social media marketing plan. We think with the combination of company-driven social media outreach and social media influencers, like Selene, we'll have even more success than our first initiative. We were referred to you by Go Green, who said that despite some early hiccups, they've been very pleased working with Spark House."

"The Go Green team has been incredible. It's absolutely an honor to be considered."

"We're glad you could make it. Would you like to tell us about Spark House and how you feel your model supports our green focus?"

"Absolutely. Are you amenable to a multimedia approach?"

"Of course."

Tish leans back in her chair, and I rise and move quickly to the front of the room. It only takes a minute to connect my tablet and bring it up on the screen, but a minute of silence can feel like an eternity, so I fill it with light, but purposeful conversation.

"Spark House is different from other family-run hotels in that while we host events such as wedding anniversaries, we also provide the opportunity for dynamic events meant for team building. Mitchell and I were discussing the unique premise of Spark House. Our focus has always been on community and bringing people together. Which is why we go above and beyond at every step. Something I'll touch on more a little later."

I pull up the slideshow, starting with our mission statement and launch into my presentation—the one I usually give to new potential clients or business partners—pausing to answer their questions and explain how over the past several years, we've shifted from a typical event hotel to a more dynamic, unique, and interactive model that has resulted in a significant uptick in our business. "As opportunities to increase efficiency have become more widely available, we've adopted new processes to facilitate a greener experience."

I click onto the next slide as a man walks by the open door and then backtracks, stepping into the conference room. I pause and glance uncertainly at Mitchell and Tish.

When all they do is stare at the man who has entered the room, their faces reflecting low-level panic, I decide my best bet is to address the elephant in the room. Or in this case, a rogue man in a suit. "Hi there, I'm London Spark, of Spark House Event Hotel. Would you like to join us? I've just gotten started." I motion to the slideshow and give him what I hope is a welcoming smile.

A bead of sweat trickles down my spine.

His gaze moves over me with a familiarity that's startling. It takes me less than half a second to place him. He's the CEO of Holt Media. He crosses the room and extends a hand, forest-green eyes locked on mine. It's unnerving, and even worse, oddly stimulating in all the wrong places.

"Jackson Holt, CEO of Holt Media. It's a pleasure to meet you again, Ms. Spark."

Again?

"It's an honor to meet you, sir. Thank you so much for the opportunity to present." I'm grateful that it doesn't come out all pitchy, thanks to my current state of shock. I know very little about this man, apart from what I read about his business accomplishments, but it's enough to make me feel like I'm meeting a celebrity.

I slip my hand into his, and my entire body breaks out in a wave of goose bumps. I fight not to succumb to a full-body shudder. As it is, other parts of my body respond with an inappropriate level of excitement.

His gaze lowers briefly to our clasped hands before it meets mine again, and his smile widens. My heart nearly stops before it shifts into a full-on gallop.

In pictures, Jackson Holt is stunning. In person, he's a force.

His hair is styled, but a tad too long at the sides, giving it a slightly unruly appearance. His eyes are a vibrant shade of green reminiscent of evergreens; his lashes are thick and dark and long. His jaw is glass-cuttingly defined with high cheekbones. Charisma drapes him like an aura.

He's hardly said a thing and I have the urge to give him my online banking password. Not that I have a whole lot of funds for him to get excited about. But still.

"My apologies for interrupting." He finally releases my hand and drops into the chair closest to the front of the room, and consequently less than three feet from where I'm presenting.

"Mitchell, may I see the file for Spark House, please?" Jackson gives him a tight-lipped smile.

"Of course, sir." He passes him a package of information containing the handout I brought with me and a thick file.

Mitchell and Tish exchange a questioning look as Jackson quickly flips through my proposal. It gives me a brief opportunity to inspect Jackson a little closer and figure out why he looks so familiar, and not just because I spent a ridiculous amount of time staring at his picture yesterday.

And then it hits me like a sledgehammer. Three months ago when I was at the bar with my sisters, he was the guy who bought our drinks and asked me out. And here he is. The CEO of a massive company, a self-made almost billionaire. Who wanted to go on a date with *me*. Which would explain why he said it was nice to meet me *again*. And I turned him down. Crap. I hope he's not going to try and sabotage this meeting. Or embarrass me. Is he? Where are Harley and her pep talks when I need them?

How I'm going to maintain my composure for the remainder of this meeting is beyond me.

Before I can launch back into my presentation, another man steps into the conference room. "I'm so sorry to interrupt," he directs the comment at me and then turns his attention to Jackson, tapping his wrist. "We have a meeting."

Jackson motions toward me without even looking at the man. "As you can see, I'm in a meeting right now."

The man in the doorway looks to Mitchell and Tish, who both shrug. "I definitely see that, but we're scheduled to meet with Lincoln Moorehead in ten minutes." He leans against the doorframe, one brow arched.

"I trust that you can handle it on your own, and send my apologies. I'm needed here. Close the door on your way out, and make sure the *Meeting in Progress* sign is up so there aren't any more interruptions while Ms. Spark is speaking."

The man stands there for a few more seconds, looking annoyed and maybe slightly amused. I have no idea what's happening. "You got it, boss." Eventually the door closes with a quiet click.

"Once again, I apologize, Ms. Spark. That's the last of the interruptions. Don't feel as though you need to start from the beginning. But I'd love a brief history of Spark House." He flips through a couple of pages. "It says here that this is a family-run business?"

"That's correct. The original owner had been planning to sell to developers, but my great-grandmother saw the opportunity, and she and my great-grandfather purchased the property."

"Real estate is always a wise investment," Jackson says.

"She thought so, and I have to agree. The property has been passed down through the generations, and we've been fortunate in that we've been able to secure grants to help make it a more energy-efficient, green-friendly hotel and event facility. My parents were one of the first to secure a grant for a solar farm, which helps reduce our carbon footprint and provides energy not only to Spark House, but to the surrounding community members. Our neighbors are farmers, so in exchange for energy, we receive locally sourced produce and eggs."

"That's a very symbiotic relationship you've formed."

"Absolutely. We like to cultivate and foster relationships with local companies."

"Is that wise for your bottom line?" Jackson taps his pen on the table and crosses his legs.

"Trading resources? You said yourself, it's symbiotic."

"But is it the most fiscally responsible way to practice business? Small companies often have to charge a premium in order to turn a profit," he states. "Which in turn means you'd have to pass that on to your clients. That would deter some business ventures, would it not?"

Oh hell no, this guy isn't going to ruin my chances of being considered for this initiative because he's butthurt over me turning him down. "It's quite possible. But I would argue that paying slightly more while knowing you're investing in the reduction of your carbon footprint and supporting a small and community-focused business can be a draw for the right kind of client. We don't necessarily want to entice customers who are just looking for something cheap and easy. We're about providing superior service with a unique spin."

"And you think that's enough to grow your client base?"

"Maybe I'm not understanding the purpose of this venture correctly, but isn't that the entire point of the Teamology initiative? To help facilitate that growth in a fiscally responsible way?"

His expression remains remote for several long seconds, and the only part of him that moves is his finger when it taps twice on the table. "We're looking to partner with strong, green-friendly businesses who are also aware of the importance of the bottom line."

"Which isn't always about the cheapest option," I argue. "We've seen a twenty-five percent increase in new bookings over the past three years. And last year, we secured our first sponsorship, which allowed us to nearly double profits and invest in more local businesses." I flip to the slide showing our business growth over the past few years and the way we've been able to invest in more opportunities as a result. "Sometimes it can be slightly more expensive than outsourcing, but the positive side is that we're supporting inside the community and it tends to balance out in the end. We're looking ahead, to the long-term benefit for our community and the longevity of our business."

"You had a few hiccups with Go Green at the beginning. How can I be sure that won't happen again? As you're aware, the social media side of this venture is integral to its success." He steeples his hands, exposing the vintage watch on his left wrist. His chin rests briefly on his pointer fingers.

It irks the hell out of me that he seems to be deriving great enjoyment from putting me on the spot like this. "We've learned from our mistakes, and we don't plan on repeating them. Over the past six months, we've developed a great working relationship with Go Green, who is a major sponsor of ours, adjusting many of our practices to line up with their mission. We've omitted all nonrecyclable plastics and have shifted to paper products whenever possible. We've also started using linen companies who have adopted environmentally responsible cleaning practices."

"And you feel that's enough to make up for your earlier oversights?"

I struggle not to talk with my hands, I'm getting so agitated. "Look, you invited me here and asked me for this meeting. Last minute, I might add. I rearranged my schedule to accommodate you, not the other way around. If you don't think Spark House is a good fit for this initiative, then please just say so and I'll be on my way. We have an event this weekend, and I'd prefer not to waste any more of my time or yours."

A smile flirts at his lips for a moment before he nods. "My intention isn't to waste your time, Ms. Spark, just to ascertain whether our goals align. Your role at Spark House is what exactly?"

I feel like I'm getting whiplash from this conversation. I don't know what's up or down at this point. "My sisters and I own it, and while we split up most of the work, I handle the business relationships. This includes managing contracts, accounts payable, and finances. In addition, I liaise with other green companies who can provide services, depending on our events. I also work on securing sponsorships with green-focused companies, so we're able to provide excellent services to our clients, among other duties." I'm fairly certain he doesn't want to hear about my trips to estate sales and my researching used goods to repurpose. Or my origami addiction.

"And it's just you and your sisters who run this operation? That seems like quite the endeavor." His gaze lifts. "What about the rest of your family?"

"My parents passed, so my sisters and my grandmother are all the family I have." I swallow down the lump in my throat.

His expression softens. It's the first hint of anything other than a powerful businessman that I've seen. "I'm sorry."

"Thank you. So am I. I think they'd be proud of what my sisters and I have accomplished, though."

"I'm sure they would be." He leans back in his chair, staring at me, and flips a pen between his fingers. There's a slight pause, short enough not to be completely awkward, but long enough to make me self-conscious.

"I think you would be a perfect fit for the Teamology initiative. Spark House sounds amazing and like somewhere I'd love to visit." He turns to Mitchell and Tish, who I've actually forgotten are still in the room with us since Jackson took over the meeting. "Can you look at my calendar and come up with a few dates that might work for an event at Spark House? I'm thinking about the charity auction that's coming up."

"Isn't that supposed to be in New York?"

He waves the comment away. "We'll host another one. There can never be enough charity auctions as far as I'm concerned. Wouldn't you agree, Ms. Spark?"

"Absolutely." I'd pretty much agree to anything at this point, in part because I'd like my anxiety level to come down from a ten to something more reasonable, like a five, but also because hosting a Holt Media event seems like a great idea.

I don't know what to make of what's just happened, considering I didn't even get halfway through my presentation. And I'm thinking neither do Mitchell and Tish, based on their slack-jawed expressions.

"Wonderful." Jackson gathers up the folder of information, tapping the pages on the table, straightening them out. "Ms. Spark, would you happen to have a few minutes to spare?"

"Of course." I'm still reeling from this entire thing, and I'm a little bit afraid I've just gotten in bed with a lion.

"Excellent." He rolls his chair back and pushes to a stand. "Why don't you come to my office and we can talk there." His gaze is still fixed on me when he says, "Mitchell, please forward all of Ms. Spark's contact information. And I'd like three to six prospective dates for the charity auction. Ms. Spark, do you happen to have a calendar of available dates that you'd be able to share with Mitchell to help facilitate that?"

"Absolutely. I'll share the link to our online calendar right now." I quickly pull it up on my tablet and send it to Mitchell.

"Perfect. I'd like those dates in the next twenty minutes so we can get this underway."

Mitchell pushes to a stand. "Sir, should we discuss—"

"We'll have time to talk on the flight back to New York this evening."

Jackson steps in to help me pack up my things. I say a quick thank-you to both Tish and Mitchell, who still look bewildered, and follow Jackson out of the conference room, feeling very much the same way.

5

HOW PERFECTLY PERFECT

JACKSON

I'm fairly certain my team thinks I've lost my mind. It's understandable. I don't generally blow off meetings with CEOs of multimillion-dollar companies to sit in on ones for sponsorship liaising. But when I realized who was presenting, I couldn't pass up the opportunity.

I saw the moment recognition registered. A look of sheer panic crossed her face, but she recovered quickly. And she certainly held her own in an unprecedented situation. So while I'm sure my team is wondering what the hell I'm doing—and in some ways, so am I—I definitely think Spark House is a good fit. I need to give whoever it was who sourced them out a raise or a bonus of some kind.

London is quiet on the walk down the hall to my temporary office.

"We're in the process of securing office space in Colorado, which is why we're set up here for the time being," I tell her.

"Are you relocating from New York?"

"We're expanding, and Colorado is very green-focused." I open the door to the makeshift office I've been using for the past several days and usher her inside. "We're striving to have our space be as efficient as possible, so there are some necessary modifications before we can move in."

"But your home base is New York, correct?"

"That's right. For now." As much as I enjoy the city, I do love the mountains and I've found myself wanting to escape the fast pace and trade it in for something less hectic. "Although we have several offices set up around the United States."

"Chicago, Seattle, Atlanta, Los Angeles, Las Vegas are a few of the biggest ones. You employ more than twenty thousand people across the country," London says.

"You've done your research."

"It's impressive how much you've accomplished at such a young age."

"I'm thirty-five. I'm not that young."

"Most thirty-five-year-olds aren't usually running massive corporations that they've built from the ground up. It's certainly something to be proud of."

"What if I just got lucky?" I pull out a chair and motion for her to take a seat.

She arches one of her perfect eyebrows. "You don't get where you are because of luck. Good timing maybe, smart business practices and a charismatic personality, yes. But definitely not luck."

I nod, taking in her slightly stiff posture. I'm about to address the elephant in the room, but she does it before I can.

"You look so different without the beard. And the suit. You

look different." London motions to my attire, eyes following the same circuit as her flailing hand, which she quickly clasps with the other one and settles them firmly on top of the table, leaning in. "Are you seriously planning to give Spark House this opportunity or is your plan to dangle the carrot in front of me and then pull it away for turning you down?"

"Pardon?" I'm more than a little taken aback by her directness, and the question itself.

"This whole meeting, you showing up out of nowhere, am I supposed to believe it's all a coincidence?"

I take a seat so we're eye to eye. "Despite how it may appear, Spark House being chosen was entirely coincidental. As for dangling carrots, that's not how I operate."

Her fingers press together, the knuckles turning white. "So you being a jerk in that meeting had nothing to do with a bruised ego?"

"A jerk?" I feel my eyebrows lift. I should not find the way she's schooling me attractive right now.

"With the way you put me on the spot. Or is that how you are all the time?"

I don't know how to respond. I consider my line of questioning in the meeting. It seemed appropriate at the time, something I'd ask anyone who was making a presentation. However, now that I'm viewing it through her lens, I realize that given the circumstances, I could see how she's misconstruing my thoroughness as being purposefully hard on her. "In this particular case, my behavior was inadvertent."

"So you're often inadvertently intimidating?"

I lean back in my chair, hoping to appear casual and less . . . intimidating. "In business affairs, I tend to be a straight shooter. Which may come across as harsh at times."

London purses her lips and regards me shrewdly. She sucks her bottom lip between her teeth for a second before setting it free. "You seem to be a pretty straight shooter outside of business affairs too. You really look very different than when I first met you." It almost sounds like an accusation.

I rub my chin. It's mostly smooth, only a hint of shadow. "Ah yes, well, I'd just returned from a camping trip."

London's eyes narrow suspiciously. "Camping? In a tent?"

I laugh, appreciating how perceptive she is. I realize what she's getting right now is contradictory to the version of me she met a few months ago.

"No, not in a tent. In a trailer." I leave out the fact that it's more of a luxury mobile home, set on a remote lake between Boulder and Colorado Springs. As much as I love the escape, it hadn't been a particularly pleasurable trip. I'd needed a reset after spending a few weeks in Peru, helping oversee the cleanup of a chemical spill. Mostly I drank scotch, ate whatever food was brought to me by delivery persons every few days, and pondered my existence.

I knew I'd reached my time-out limit when my best friend, Trent, flew in from New York to get me. And we'd ended up at the pub. After a shower and a change of clothes, of course. I wasn't a complete barbarian. The liquid courage was a strong force that night. So was the knowledge that I wasn't getting any younger, and that every single relationship I'd had ended the same way: I worked too much and I wasn't emotionally available.

It wasn't untrue. I was highly aware that I kept everyone—apart from a very select few—at arm's length.

Except that night.

There had been three women at the table, but if asked, London would be the only one I could describe. Long blond hair the color of butter that fell in waves past her shoulders. Warm green eyes, wide and expressive. Perfect regal nose and lips that were made for kissing.

She'd been so alive, her laugh musical, and her easy conversation with the women she was with told me they were a unit. The best of friends.

I watched her pull strips of paper out of her purse and turn them into what looked like little balls. But when I'd approached her table, I realized they were stars. Tiny puffy stars. I'd taken one, sure she wasn't going to miss it.

I approached her like everything in my life, head-on, take the reins. I'd probably come on too strong, considering the way it had blown up in my face. But here she is again.

Just as beautiful as I remembered. And now I have an excuse to get to know her. But I realize I've boxed myself into a corner. I've just committed to a business deal with her. Which means I have to remain professional.

Dammit. Why the hell did I get involved? I couldn't help myself. It was as if my mind acted on its own accord, and my mouth just said things without allowing my brain to think them through.

And now she's asked me something and I've been so busy living up in my head that I've missed it completely. "I'm sorry, can you repeat that?"

"What kind of trailer?"

"Are you familiar with trailers?" She doesn't give off a high-maintenance vibe, but she's polished, so I would be surprised if she knows much about RVs.

She gives me a sly look and props her delicate chin on her equally delicate hand. "Are you dodging the question?"

I fight a grin. "Why would you think that?"

She leans back in her chair, relaxing a little, and I get a glimpse of the woman I saw at the bar all those months ago. That's who I want to get to know. The woman who smirks at me. "Come on, Jackson." She lines up the pen so it's perfectly parallel with her phone. "I can't imagine you're used to roughing it in an old school pop-up from the seventies. I'm sure it's all tricked out. Energy efficient. Requiring little to no propane or electricity to function."

"What if it *was* an old pop-up trailer from the seventies?"

"I'd want some photographic evidence."

This time, I can't hold back the laugh. "It's actually an old Airstream trailer. From the seventies. I had it gutted and made some modifications, so it is, in fact, energy efficient. It's probably not quite as flashy as one might expect from me, but I'm the only one who ever uses it, so it just needs to be functional."

"I bet it's very peaceful."

"Incredibly so. Have you ever gone camping, London?"

"I used to be a Girl Scout, and my parents always sent us to camp for a week. Although, I'll be honest, my older sister Avery is the outdoor adventurer. I liked it better when we had the little cabins instead of the tents." She stops fiddling with the pen and clasps her hands again.

"That's fair. I was a Boy Scout as a kid, too, and those tents were always full of daddy longlegs."

"Always! Although they're harmless. Despite being the most venomous spider out there."

"But their mouths are too small to bite," I supply.

London tips her head, smiling. "Such a random fact."

"Mmm." I nod my agreement.

London bites her lip. "Can I ask you a question?"

"Absolutely."

"You honestly didn't know about my meeting today?"

"Not until I walked by the conference room and saw you standing there."

She nods once and looks away. "I need to tell you something."

"Go ahead." I'm curious as to what it is based on her expression.

"I lied when I told you I was in a relationship. When we met at the bar, I mean." Her eyes go wide, and the pink in her cheeks deepens to red and travels to her ears.

I'm taken aback by the sudden shift in topics, unsure why she feels she needs to admit this. Also, that bit of news stings, but I force an amused smile. "You lied about having a boyfriend?"

"Yes. No. It wasn't really a lie. Oh God." She runs a hand down her face. "I don't even know why I said anything. And I'm making it sound worse than it is. I'd literally just gotten out of a relationship. We'd broken up three days earlier, and it seemed easier to say I was still involved than try to explain that I wasn't in a place emotionally to handle going on a date. And I honestly had no idea when I'd be in a place to date again. I had a lot of self-doubt. It's kind of my thing."

Her expression is priceless, and while I could let her off the hook, I enjoy seeing this much less composed version of her. So different than the woman I met at the bar and the one who put me in my place in the conference room. "Lying about being in a relationship is your thing?"

"No. That's really the only time I've done that. Lied about my relationship status. The breakup was just so fresh. And honestly, I was a bit shocked."

"Shocked by what?"

"That you approached me in a bar. Especially since I was with my sisters. In a world of right swipes and dating apps, that took some serious courage. I felt awful about lying. But going on a date with you was the last thing I should have been considering. It wouldn't have been fair to either of us."

"That makes perfect sense to me. I appreciate your candor." I mean it. Most women would have just taken the number and never called.

Her gaze dips down and back up again. "I'm still sorry I lied. I feel like I've just gone to confession."

"It's fine, London. I appreciate you being honest with me, even if it is several months after the fact." I absolve her of any further awkwardness by shifting the topic away from her personal life. "Can I offer you something to drink? Would you like tea or coffee? Or water? We have sparkling and still. Whatever you'd prefer. I'll have my assistant place an order, and you can tell me about Spark House events so I can get a better idea of what might work for my team."

While I'd like to know more about her relationship status, I realize it's not appropriate, or professional.

Her thumbs circle each other. "I can absolutely do that."

I pick up my phone and dial Mitchell. "What would you like to drink?"

"Just water is fine, thank you." She presses one thumb down with the other, presumably to stop them from twiddling.

"Still or sparkling?"

"Sparkling would be lovely."

"Perfect."

Mitchell appears in the doorway, glancing from London, sitting primly in her chair, to me. "Sir?"

"Can you have the kitchen send up a bottle of sparkling water? And I'd like a coffee. Milk and sugar on the side, please. London, are you sure you wouldn't like a coffee as well?"

"I'm sure, thank you."

"Of course, sir. I would like to remind you that you have a flight scheduled at four this afternoon to New York."

"I'm aware. If we need to move the flight, we can."

"If you have somewhere you need to be, we can always schedule a call at a later date," London offers.

"That's unnecessary. The jet is mine, so it won't be an issue if we need to leave a little later than planned. I don't have another meeting until tomorrow morning. Are you hungry? I haven't had lunch. Mitchell, can you also have them send up a charcuterie board?"

"Of course, I'll order it right away."

Mitchell disappears, and I turn back to London, who appears shell-shocked.

I give her what I hope is a friendly smile. "Is everything okay?"

"Oh yes. I'm fine. This is all just a bit more than I expected today."

"Would you care to elaborate?" It's a bit more than I expected too, but I'm not sure it's for the same reasons.

"Well, first there was the phone call yesterday from Mitchell, which was a surprise all on its own. And then my sisters and I did some research and realized how amazing of an opportunity this could be, and now here I am. I thought you were a regular guy."

"I am a regular guy."

London's right brow arches. "Regular guys do not have private jets and don't blow off meetings and flights so they can have sparkling water and share a charcuterie board with someone whose hotel he's booked a charity event at, despite not really knowing what that event will entail, or much about the hotel."

"Mmm, you have a point. And that makes me sound like a brat. And uninformed."

"Are you a brat?" Her eyes flare again, and her teeth sink into her bottom lip.

I want to tell her to stop doing that, not because I'm particularly worried about her lips, but because it continues to draw attention to them in a way that's distracting.

"If I see an opportunity, I usually take it. If that makes me seem a little bratty, well, I guess I am. Why don't you tell me about Spark House's setup, and we can set the parameters for the charity event. And nail down some dates." The sooner the better for the auction.

An hour and a nearly empty charcuterie board later, we have three prospective dates for the auction, a preliminary list of essential items, possible dinner menu options, an outline of room costs for guests who would like to take advantage of the quaint hotel, and a phone call arranged for next week.

I walk London out of the hotel and find myself whistling in the elevator on the way back up to the office.

Trent is sitting in my chair when I return to my office.

"You want to tell me what the hell that was all about?" He motions to the mostly naked charcuterie board and the glasses sitting on the table.

"I'm taking a vested interest in the Teamology initiative."

Trent is my best friend. Has been since we were kids. He's one of the very few people in this world that I trust, so it doesn't make a lot of sense to give him evasive answers.

He crosses his arms and pokes at his cheek with his tongue. "You mean you're taking a vested interest in that Spark House blonde. Dude. You have never blown off a meeting, especially not one with Linc fucking Moorehead, who, by the way is directly connected to the sponsorship thing. What in the fuck, bro?"

I drop down in the chair across from him. "You and Linc have a great working relationship. I'm sure I wasn't even missed."

"He said you better not stand him up next week."

"What's next week?"

"His wife's birthday. You're obviously invited, and so am I. It's on a Saturday, and since all you do is work, I'm pretty sure your schedule is clear. Now back to the blonde. What's the deal?"

"You remember when you forced me to leave my trailer a few months back?"

"Yeah. Of course. You smelled like rotten hot dogs before you showered away two weeks of lake-water stink."

"Do you remember the three women who were at the table across from us?"

His brows pull together before they shoot up. "Are you talking about the woman who shot you down?"

It's not often that I get turned down for dates. Although, I also usually don't look like a derelict lumberjack either.

"She was the blonde from the bar."

"No shit," Trent says in amusement. "So did she turn you down again?"

"She'd just gotten out of a relationship."

"Or so she says." Trent still derives a great deal of enjoyment from that whole situation.

"Anyway, I thought it was the perfect opportunity to talk to her again. Except I screwed myself, because now I've committed to a charity event at her hotel, and we're going to include her business in the Teamology initiative. Which means dating her is off the table." I flip a pen between my fingers. "And I couldn't even ask her if she was still single because how inappropriate is that when you're already involved in a business venture?"

"Can you back out of the charity event?"

"Then I'm an asshole, and she definitely won't be interested in a date." I tap my lips, trying to figure out a way around this.

"Is dating her even a good idea?"

"Well, I can't date her, at least not right now."

"Maybe that's not the worst thing in the world. This way, you can take things slower and get to know her first. Make sure your instincts are right on this one, and she's interested in you for the right reasons," he says.

"I guess working with her will give me a better sense of whether or not that's the case." In the past, I've dated women who have been interested in me for my connections. And the potential for a cushy, pampered life. I don't know London well enough to be sure either way.

"If you really want to date her, I can handle the charity event. That way you're not working with her directly?"

I consider that for a moment. Trent handling all the phone calls, possibly having meetings with London. Nope. Not going to happen.

"It's okay. I'll deal with the charity event. I'll just have to keep it strictly professional until it's over. How was the meeting with Linc?"

"Good. He's interested in the Teamology initiative. He and

his sister have worked hard over the past few years to move Moore-head in a different direction, and he'd like to be part of this."

"I think they'd be a good fit. I'll give him a call later. Anything else I missed?"

"We need to start building relationships with the smaller media companies here in Colorado."

"So they don't think we're coming in to buy them all out." I'm not in the business of steamrolling smaller media outlets. I'd rather partner in whatever way I can and help them grow. "I've got a shortlist. We can get moving on that."

Mitchell knocks on the door. He has my carry-on bag. The suits and casual clothes I brought with me on this trip will stay in Colorado.

"Excuse me, sir, but the car is waiting to take you to the air-field. If you leave within the next ten minutes, we'll make the four o'clock departure. Otherwise, there isn't a takeoff time until five fifteen."

Trent grabs his things, and I make sure I have everything I need before I leave the office.

Mitchell falls into step beside me as we head for the elevator.

"Can we look at my schedule for next Friday?"

He brings up my calendar on his tablet, the same one I'm looking at. "You have a phone call with Spark House at noon and then a meeting with your financial planner at two in the afternoon."

"I'd like to move the meeting with my financial planner. And don't schedule anything for the rest of the afternoon. I'll make up for it with longer hours on Monday. Also, I think we need to expedite preparing an adequate office space in Colorado, and I'd prefer Colorado Springs. And I'd like to secure an apartment."

"A rental, sir? Do you have a timeframe for which you'd like to lease a space?"

"No lease. I'd like to own. I think I'll be spending more time here in Colorado, and I'd like to prepare for that."

6

AREN'T WE CHATTY

LONDON

my sisters come rushing out of Spark House to greet me with matching expectant expressions as soon as I pull into the driveway.

Avery opens the driver's side door before I put the car in park. "So? How'd it go?"

"We got it. They want to work with us. And they want to host a charity event here!"

"Ahhh! Yay! That's so awesome!" Harley practically tackles me with a hug. Avery throws her arms around both of us, and I absorb their joy and approval like a sponge.

This is one of the reasons I love working with my sisters. All the presenting might trigger my anxiety, but when things like this happen, it gives me the satisfaction and peace of mind I need. Working with Holt Media and their influencers could give us more stability, and that helps keep us together. My sisters are all I have, and as much as working at Spark House isn't necessarily my dream, I don't want to give up the closeness it affords us.

"You need to tell us all about it. We ordered Thai takeout and it just got here," Harley says as she pulls me toward the employee entrance.

They usher me inside, and we get comfortable in our office. I'm not all that hungry thanks to the charcuterie board Jackson ordered. I likely wouldn't have eaten any of it, but he kept slathering crackers with different cheeses and chutneys and jams and fruit combinations, insisting I try them. I didn't want to say no and offend him, so of course I ate every bite. It wasn't much of a chore since everything was delicious, but I'm still full.

I shake my head when Avery tries to pass me a spring roll. "Seriously? These are your favorite, and you've been gone all day. That must have been some meeting."

While they eat, I pull out paper strips and start folding them into stars. I'd wanted to do that all throughout my meeting with Jackson. "So remember how I said the CEO definitely wouldn't be sitting in on the meeting?"

Harley stops with a forkful of green curry chicken halfway to her mouth. "Did you meet Jackson Holt? Is he as hot in person as he in pictures?"

"I did, and he's hotter."

"Holy shit. What was he like? I want all the freaking details!" Harley is pretty much bouncing in her seat.

I explain what happened, how he just appeared out of nowhere and decided to stay for the meeting and asked that we plan a charity event for Holt Media.

"No way! That's beyond awesome." Now it's Avery's turn to be excited. "The whole influencer campaign is fantastic, especially if it helps us gain more clients and sponsors, but this is beyond. They have that social media guru woman on retainer, so you know that charity event is going to get serious press. This could really put us on the map."

"It's pretty amazing, isn't it?" I don't think the reality of the whole thing has truly hit me until right now. My stomach churns with a mixture of nerves and excitement.

"If this goes well, we could look at expanding in the next couple of years," Avery muses, eyes glinting. "And we could get started on the kitchen expansion as soon as my wedding is over!"

She's right, we could do those things, but I wish I shared her enthusiasm over growing even more. While I love Spark House and the way it keeps us connected, expanding means my limited spare time will likely dwindle further. "We'll have to hire someone or more than one someone if that happens. We're barely managing as it is with the three of us."

"Once my wedding is over, it'll be fine. I know I've had a lot of stuff going on outside of Spark House the past few months, but I'll be back to business as usual."

Harley and I glance at each other. "It hasn't been business as usual since before you got engaged, though," Harley says.

"And we're not getting any less busy," I add.

"Well, I think we have things under control right now, and I don't have much left to manage for the wedding. Besides, I don't think we need to yet, so the subject is closed."

I decide it's not worth getting into a fight over right now. We have no idea how this whole thing with Holt Media is going to work out yet, and I'm hoping that we'll reach a point where Avery doesn't have a choice but to concede. Hopefully one of us doesn't have to have a nervous breakdown for that to happen.

Harley clearly wants to alleviate the tension, so she changes the subject. "Back to Jackson Holt. I want to hear more about him."

I toss another star on the table to join the small constellation I've created. "Do you remember that guy who asked me out at the bar a few months back?"

Harley frowns, and Avery taps her lip with her spring roll before she says, "Oh! Do you mean the bearded dude who paid for our drinks?"

"That's the one."

"Sure, but what does that have to do with Jackson?" Harley seems annoyed by my apparent topic change.

"They're the same person."

Harley's fork clatters to her plate and green curry splatters her chin. She wipes her face with her napkin. "Come again?"

"Jackson Holt and the man who asked me out are the same person."

"No. No way." Harley grabs her phone and quickly pulls up Jackson Holt's social media profile, squinting at the picture on the screen.

I wait for her to come to the same conclusion I did. That they are in fact the same person, one Instagram ready, the other post-two-week stint in an Airstream camper in the Colorado wilderness.

"I can't believe it's the same guy. I mean, the eyes are really the thing that stand out, aren't they? He was so beardy and here he's so . . . refined. This is awesome! Did you tell him you're still single?" Harley asks.

"What? No, of course not." I dump out my star jar because it's almost full already.

"Why not?"

"Because we're hosting an event for his company, and they've just asked us to be a part of the Teamology initiative."

"Did he ask if you're still single?" Harley looks so hopeful.

"No, of course not! But I might have told him I lied about being in a relationship."

"What?" both my sisters shout at the same time.

I throw my hands in the air, and a star goes flying across the room. "I didn't mean to tell him. He's so charismatic, he compelled the information out of me. And he seemed to appreciate my belated honesty."

Harley waves the explanation away. "When are you seeing him again?"

"We have a call scheduled for next Friday. I need to have a preliminary plan for the charity event ready by then."

"It's just a call?" Harley tips her chin up and arches a brow.

"Yes. It's just a call. He's based in New York. Whatever you're thinking is probably way off base. He doesn't even live in Colorado, and we're doing business with him. He'd just spent two weeks alone in the Colorado wilderness when he asked me out. He probably would have hit on a grandma."

"Uh-huh." Avery crosses her arms.

"He didn't ask me out again." But we spent nearly two hours in his office after the meeting talking about the charity event—which is to raise money for cancer research—and it wasn't until his assistant popped his head in to remind him that he still had a flight to catch back to New York that he realized how late it had gotten.

Harley leans back in her chair. "Check your email."

"Why?"

"Just humor me and do it."

I roll my eyes but flip open my laptop and pull up my email. I have at least thirty new ones that I need to manage, which instantly gives me anxiety over all the work I have to catch up on just from being away for an afternoon, but at the top is one that stands out from the rest.

"He's already emailed you, hasn't he? I can tell by the look on your face." Harley grabs the laptop and clicks on the message.

London,

It was a pleasure meeting you again today. I look forward to our call next Friday. Please don't hesitate to reach out to me directly if you have any questions, or if there's anything you wish to discuss prior to our call. I have the greatest confidence that the charity event will be a resounding success, and I'm pleased that you're coming on board as part of our new Teamology initiative.

Regards,
Jackson
CEO Holt Media

You can also reach me by phone: 555-242-0310

"That email was sent at three forty-two in the afternoon," Avery points out. "How much do you want to bet he sent that minutes after you left?"

"He walked me out, and it was probably more like half an hour later," I mutter.

"He might not have asked you on a date, but all signs point to him still being interested."

"We're hosting an event for his company. It makes sense that he would email me about it to confirm the call for next week. And he seems a lot like the kind of guy who would follow up on things right away."

"He could've had his personal assistant email you. He also added his phone number at the bottom, and I bet you an entire batch of snickerdoodle bars that it's his personal line." Harley starts typing away.

"What are you doing?"

"I'm replying for you."

"What? No! Don't do that!"

"I'm just thanking him, not telling him you think he's the hottest man to walk the face of the earth and that he makes you moist."

Avery and I make matching gagging sounds.

"Don't worry, I'll read it to you before I send it." Her fingers fly across the keyboard.

I would try to steal my laptop back, but it's pointless. Harley is small and quick, and Avery is agile and athletic. She's also not afraid to put me in a headlock. "Please don't put anything in there that will embarrass me."

Harley purses her lips. "It will be one hundred percent professional. I promise. But you need to respond because self-made near-billionaires don't like to be kept waiting, and it speaks volumes about him that he blew off a meeting to sit in on yours and then spent two hours shooting the shit with you, even if it was about the charity event, and he's emailing you directly." How she can type and talk at the same time is beyond me. "I'm just thanking him for the opportunity and telling him I also look forward to the call on Friday." She hits one final key. "And sent."

"I thought you were going to read it to me before you sent it!"

"Oh. Right. Oops." She's grinning, though, which tells me she did it on purpose. She passes me back the laptop. I read over the email she just sent. She wasn't lying about the content, but she failed to leave out the fact that she also gave him my cell number.

The first thing I do when I wake up the next morning is check my email. My stomach flutters when I notice I have two from Jackson.

London,
Good morning. I hope you're doing well today.
Based on your website, Spark House has hotel accommodations for a maximum of fifty guests, but there's a note about alternative options. I'd like to add that to the list of things to discuss next Friday.
Best,
Jackson

The next email reads:

My apologies for the back-to-back messages. I've created a list of topics for our meeting next week and am attaching a link to the file. Feel free to review it at your leisure and make any additions you believe are necessary.
Best,
Jackson

Suddenly my phone buzzes with a message from an unknown number. I pull up the contact and find that I have two messages, one new one and one sent half an hour earlier. My phone is always on Do Not Disturb until five in the morning so my sleep isn't interrupted.

> Is hobbyhorsing really a thing?
> Best,
> Jackson

The most recent one, sent two minutes ago reads:

> Never mind. I now have the answer to that question. I'll
> have you know that I spent a good half an hour falling
> down a rabbit hole in which I watched an inordinate
> number of videos of GROWN MEN riding around on
> brooms with horse heads. The world is a strange place.
> You'll find several questions regarding your hobbyhorse
> event on my list of things to discuss.
> Best,
> Jackson

I think it's hilarious that he signs his messages like they're emails. I wait until I've had my coffee before I compose a response.

> Good morning. It seems you've been busy researching.
> ☺ I'll review the list of questions and make sure to
> prepare accordingly. Hobbyhorse enthusiasts are
> particularly passionate about their sport. We're hosting
> them again this year. I'm sure I can get you a guest
> invitation should you decide you'd like to attend. I

should warn you that they're highly competitive. Last
year they created quite a ruckus.

When I get to Spark House, I have another new message.

A ruckus you say? I'm intrigued. I'll add that to my list of
questions, which is growing quickly.
Best,
Jackson

I can't help myself, as soon as I tackle voicemails and make
the necessary calls, I hop on email and open the Google Doc
Jackson has set up. It's ridiculous the way my stomach flip-flops
over a freaking list of questions.

It's a very organized list, broken down into sections with bulleted points and questions. There's even a section not related
to the charity event titled: NON-EVENT-RELATED QUES-
TIONS.

I laugh when I see questions pertaining to hobbyhorses and
all the mascot conventions we've hosted. As I scroll, I notice a typo,
so I fix it with track changes on and continue reading through
the questions. I start color-coding each section, separating them
into accommodations, food, and event themes, adjusting his lists
and breaking them down.

A chat bubble pops up on the right side of the screen.

London?

My hand goes to my hair, and I look around, as if he's going to magically appear. I roll my eyes at myself and click on the flashing bubble.

Hello. What can I do for you?

Just like on my phone, dots appear and inchworm until a new message appears:

What are you doing to my list?

I bite my lip, unable to read his tone.

Organizing it for you, unless you'd prefer I refrain.

He responds right away:

Do you find my organizational skills lacking?

I type back:

Not at all. But as the event manager, it's often my job to create task lists and color-coding helps me keep track. If you'd prefer certain colors, please do let me know.

I scroll down to the bottom of the list and create a new category titled JACKSON HOLT. I color-code it green—to match his eyes—and start a new bulleted list.

- Takes coffee with sugar and milk

- Enjoys the outdoors (specifically camping in trailers)
- Sensitive about lists

A new message appears:

I'm not sensitive about lists.

He starts typing in the document, adding *NOT* in bold green letters in front of "Sensitive about lists."

I grin. Jackson Holt has a sense of humor.

I have a meeting in five minutes, but don't think I won't be back to check on this list later.

I wait until his user icon disappears from the screen before I use the strikeout function to cross out *NOT* and replace it with *VERY*.

Over the course of the week that follows, Jackson and I communicate almost daily through the Google Doc. Usually it's first thing in the morning, before meetings take over for him and event preparation takes over for me. It's always about Spark House. And an update on the things he's added to the list. He doesn't need to do this, as each time the document is updated, I receive an email alert, but I find I look forward to those daily messages.

They've become the first thing I check in the morning and the last thing I look at before bed.

7

PICNIC PLEASE

LONDON

The following Friday morning I'm up at an ungodly hour. Usually I get up a few minutes before my alarm goes off at 5:07, but today my eyes pop open at four thirty and I can't go back to sleep.

Jackson scheduled a Zoom meeting, but I'm uncertain whether this will be a video call or an audio call, so I err on the side of caution and take extra care getting ready for my day. I pick out a dress—it's supposed to be warm and balmy today. And the peach chiffon over the white underlay is a particular favorite. Maybe after our call, I'll spend some time getting the field ready for the weekend. Avery is in charge of the major setup, and I always focus on the small details, the things that make it personal like color coordinating the benches and seating to go with the team jerseys when we're hosting a sports-related event and dinner.

After I arrive at Spark House I spend the next hour preparing centerpieces for upcoming events. This weekend we're hosting a soccer awards banquet for my sister's college alumni, so everything is color coordinated to work with the team uniform in black and silver with gold accents. I found some cool round bowls and octagonal gold decals. Each bowl will be decorated with the stickers to resemble a soccer ball, then filled with white sand and a circle of fake turf with a miniature soccer net and players.

If I could, this would be the part of the job I'd spend most of my time on. Unfortunately, it's a small part of a much bigger picture, so I focus my energy on putting together the first one of everything and leave it to the part-time staff to make the rest.

Once that's done, I head back to the office, tackle any new emails, and review Jackson's agenda and questions. I have to admit, he's incredibly thorough. It's hard to concentrate on any one thing, and I find myself wishing I'd scheduled this call for earlier in the day so I can get it out of the way.

Harley comes barreling into the office and skids to a stop in front of my desk, very nearly knocking over the centerpiece I was working on earlier.

"You have a visitor."

"A visitor?" I glance at the time on my computer screen. It's eleven thirty-two. My conference call with Jackson is in less than half an hour. I've been counting down the seconds since I sat at my desk thirty-nine minutes ago. "But I'm not expecting anyone."

"I think you'll be happy about this one." Her smile is almost maniacal.

"But I have a call soon."

"With Jackson. I know. He's early."

"What are you talking about?"

Avery appears in the doorway, wearing the same ridiculous smile as Harley. "She's right here." Avery sweeps a hand out like she's Vanna White preparing to turn letters.

Jackson steps around the corner, and my mouth instantly goes dry and my palms dampen. I don't understand how anyone can get anything done when he's around. He fills up the entire room with his presence and seems to suck the air right out of it.

He's dressed in a crisp gray suit with a pale peach tie, in the same shade as my dress. It's as if we color coordinated today, like we're going to a school dance. I drink in the sight of him, from his polished shoes to the gorgeous smile, dark hair tamed with product, and vibrant eyes that I want to drown in.

What the hell is wrong with me? I'm supposed to be working with him, not eyeing him like a chocolate bar and bag of chips during Shark Week.

I roll my chair back and rise on slightly unsteady legs. "Hi, Jackson. I didn't realize you were in Colorado. I thought this was supposed to be a Zoom call." My voice is pitchy, as though I'm suddenly channeling a teenage boy.

"You're right, but this morning I decided I wanted to come out and see the place, get a real feel for it. And almost all of my meetings this week have been Zoom calls, so I figured I'd change it up. Get some fresh air."

"Right. Okay. Well, this is a pleasant surprise." At least my lady bits are pleasantly surprised. The rest of me is a little unprepared to deal with Jackson in three dimensions.

I introduce Jackson to Avery and Harley, who both thank him for the opportunity.

"Selene has an amazing following," Harley says. "I think it's great that you're partnering with her for this initiative. It's wonderful to see a company like Holt Media working with influencers to help promote businesses in an organic way."

"That was exactly the thinking behind it," Jackson says. "And Selene is very savvy when it comes to this side of things, so bringing her on board was definitely something we can all benefit from."

A ding comes from the front of the hotel, signaling another arrival, and Avery excuses herself to find out who it is. Harley makes small talk with Jackson while I get all my notes together and my tablet. I hadn't planned on pulling my sisters into the meeting this time around apart from introductions. I wanted to be able to share the proposal for the charity event first, then bring them in. Now everything is upside down.

Avery returns carrying a basket. A picnic basket. Complete with a red-and-white-checkered blanket. The kind you see in movies. "There was a delivery for you, Mr. Holt."

"For me?" He eyes the basket suspiciously and takes it from Avery.

"Would you like to set it down?" I clear a spot on my desk.

"Thank you." He plucks the white card tucked under the blanket and flips it over, his brow furrowing for a moment before one eyebrow lifts. "Ah, it appears my assistant has sent along lunch."

"Oh, well that was thoughtful," I say.

"That it is." I can't quite read Jackson's expression.

"I have to run to the store to pick up some supplies. *Heavy ones.* So I'll need your help, Avery," Harley declares in a very obvious way.

"Yeah. For sure. I'm with you on the heavy supply shopping. You two enjoy your lunch meeting. We'll be back in an hour or so."

"Or a little longer." Harley backs up a step, still grinning.

"But shouldn't you be here to discuss the event?" I don't know that it's a good idea for my sisters to leave me alone with Jackson. On a business level, I can hold my own; on a personal level, I'm a little overwhelmed by his sudden arrival.

Mentally I recognize that he's here because we're planning a charity event for his company, but the rest of my body seems ridiculously unaware of that and on very high alert.

"We'll be back in plenty of time to discuss the finer details once you've gone over the proposal." Harley grabs her purse. "It's great to meet you, Jackson. Again. Thanks so much for the drinks last time."

I want to poke her in the ribs and tell her to shut it.

"You're more than welcome. I guess it was in the stars for us to meet again."

"And this time London is super single," Avery says.

"Didn't you say you both had to go somewhere?" I shoot a glare in their direction, wishing I could mute them.

"Right. Yes. Enjoy lunch. We'll be back in a bit." Harley winks at me and flounces across the office, shooting a grin at Jackson on her way out.

I clasp my hands in front of me. "I'm sorry about that. My sisters can be a lot to handle."

Jackson smiles. "I like them."

"Me too, most of the time." I motion to the picnic basket. "Should that be refrigerated?"

"It appears to be insulated. I can leave it here, unless there's a better spot for it?"

"Leave it here. There's a picnic table out back. We could eat out there since it's such a nice day?" It's framed as a question rather than a statement.

"That's perfect." He motions for me to lead the way.

I grab my tablet, so I can make notes and refer to his endless questions.

I lead Jackson through the office, pointing out Harley's and Avery's desks. Avery's is a standing desk, but she also sits on an exercise ball about fifty percent of the time. Harley's desk is neat and very organized, like a kindergarten teacher's desk. Mine is mostly organized, apart from a few random pieces of paper and a few puffy stars that haven't made it into the jar yet.

"Would you like a tour of the grounds first, or the hotel?" Since I didn't expect an in-person meeting, I can't be sure exactly how organized things are. With an event this weekend, the barn will likely be a little chaotic, but the rest of the hotel should be clean and ready.

"The grounds first, if that's okay with you."

"Absolutely." I lead him through the hallway that spans the back of the house. It's a sprawling estate with gorgeous gardens that bloom all year long.

"This is quite serene, isn't it?" Jackson falls into step beside me as we stroll down the cobblestone path.

"My grandmother was particularly enamored with the gardens here and spent a lot of time planting them so they would be full of color all year long. We even have flowers that bloom in the winter, so there's always color."

"It must be quite picturesque in the winter," Jackson observes.

"It definitely is. During the summer months, we'll often hold weddings out here. And couples love the gazebo for engagement photographs." I motion to the structure at the end of the path. It's covered in blooming vines, making it the perfect romantic backdrop.

Beyond the gazebo is the fountain; wildflowers decorate the perimeter.

"Does this still run?" Jackson asks.

"Not at the moment, but we have plans to restore it, hopefully sooner rather than later."

"It would be great for photos," Jackson muses.

"Oh yes, absolutely."

We pass through an archway, lilac bushes framing either side. Beyond the gardens is a massive expanse of green space, where we host the athletic component of some of our events.

On the right is the pool house, and to the left, a short distance away, is the barn. And far off in the distance are the mountains, the tips white with snow even though it's June. It's the most beautiful, peaceful view.

"This is an incredible property. Do you live here?"

"Not on site but we spent a lot of time here when we were growing up. It's like a second home for us. When we took over the hotel for our grandmother, we considered living in the pool house, but felt it would be better to live off property, otherwise it would be hard to find a work-life balance. Harley and I have an apartment about twenty minutes away, close to the downtown area. It's kind of like being between two different worlds. I get the serenity I love being here, but the separation I need from my work by living downtown."

"I can understand not wanting to live where you work. It can be a challenge to separate the two."

"It can. I try to leave work at work, but it's not always easy. And when we have back-to-back events, it's nearly impossible. What about you? Your home base is New York, but here you are in Colorado again. It can't be easy to live out of a suitcase and a hotel room all the time."

"I'm actually looking into buying a house in Colorado since we're expanding and setting up an office here."

"You're planning to be here more often?" The possibility makes my insides all fluttery.

"I am. I like to oversee the setup of our new office, and I enjoy Colorado."

"It really is beautiful."

"It is." He nods his agreement, eyes shifting away from me to the view of the mountains.

I show him around the rest of the property, stopping frequently to talk about the upcoming events we're hosting and show him the props and pieces we're assembling for one of Avery's famous obstacle courses.

"This reminds me of a more user-friendly *Survivor* challenge," Jackson says.

"In a lot of ways, it is. Avery loves that show more than is reasonable. She's watched every single season."

"Oh wow. Even the ones where things went downhill, and it became more of a model competition than a social experiment?" Jackson asks.

"Even those." I chuckle. "She used to make us watch them with her. At least until she moved in with her fiancé. Now he gets to deal with it."

"It's not your favorite show, then?" Jackson asks.

"I don't mind it. I even like some of the seasons, but I've watched them so many times, so often, I could definitely not watch it again for a while and be totally fine with that."

Jackson laughs. "Fair. If *Survivor* isn't your speed, what is?"

I shrug. "I don't have a lot of time for TV, but when I do, I like craft and DIY videos. Usually, I watch instructional stuff on YouTube. I have a few channels I subscribe to."

"Are you the creative one out of your sisters, then?" Jackson asks.

"I think we're all creative in different ways. Avery's excellent at organizing and coming up with cool ideas for events. She basically runs the show in that respect. I like the setup and design part and liaising with local companies who supply us with our event needs. Harley, our younger sister, is great with a camera and social media."

"It seems like you've got it all covered. Are you in the middle of your sisters, then?"

I nod. "I am."

"Does that make you the peacekeeper?"

"That's more Harley's role. I just try to find the balance between the two of them. I pick up the slack where I see it's needed. What about you? Do you have any siblings?" In all my research about Jackson Holt, I didn't find much about his family, apart from the fact that he lost his parents when he was in his early twenties due to illness.

He shakes his head, his smile suddenly a little stiff. "Nope. I'm an only child, but I have a very close friend named Trent who's pretty much like a brother. We grew up together and he works with me now."

"That must be a very special friendship, then." I can't imagine that it would be easy to lose your parents as an only child. All that stability suddenly gone. At least I had Harley and Avery to rely on, and my grandmother.

"It is. We grew up next door to each other when we lived in Lewiston."

"And you stayed close all this time?" I remember reading an article about that. There had been issues with soil contamination in the house he spent his early childhood in. It's strange to know so much about this man already, through tabloids and articles, but it makes me feel like a bit of a voyeur into his life. I don't know how much I should or shouldn't say.

"We did. I grew up in a very blue-collar area. It turns out the land they built the subdivision I lived in was contaminated by a chemical spill, and the company had tried to cover it up. We were only there for a few years, but it was enough. I lost both of my parents to cancer that we believe was caused by the chemical contamination. Trent's family and my family were very close growing up, and when my parents were sick, they would often step in and care for me, so we were very much like brothers."

I reach out and put my hand on his forearm. "I'm so glad you had his family for support. Are Trent's parents okay?"

Jackson nods once, his gaze fixed on my hand. I drop it quickly, realizing the prolonged contact meant to console might have the opposite effect. When I lost my parents, I was the one who did the hugging, rather than the one seeking the hugs. It was easier to provide comfort than it was to accept it. I could control my emotions better that way.

"Trent's mother had cancer a few years back, but they were able to catch it early enough."

"That's good. So she's okay?"

"She is. She's in remission now and that's what's important. The last thing I wanted was for the people who had been there with me through all of this to end up like my parents."

"It's a hard place to be in mentally, though, I'm sure. Wanting to save someone else from the same fate as your parents."

"If I'd been a few years earlier on the app development frontier, I might have been able to help my own parents the same way, or at least extended their lives." He blows out a breath. "You said you lost your parents too." His eyes are heavy with sadness.

There's something about shared grief. The way it binds two people through common suffering. It's a painful but also comforting point of connection. "When I was fourteen. They died in a car accident."

"I'm so sorry. I don't know what's worse, sudden death or knowing that it's coming and not being able to do anything to stop it."

"They both have their challenges, I think."

"How long have they been gone?"

"It'll be thirteen years on the fifteenth."

"That's soon. Next week."

I nod. I didn't realize we were so close to the anniversary of their death. "My sisters and I always do something special to celebrate them."

"It's good that you have them to lean on."

"It is. I'm lucky that we're as close as we are, and that we have this place to keep us that way. I guess it's similar to the way you and your friend Trent get to work together."

"I'm sure in a lot of ways it is. Did you start working for Spark House as a way to stay close to them?" he asks, seeming genuinely interested.

"I wanted to make sure I could be there for my younger sister. Harley really struggled with the loss after our parents passed, which isn't surprising since she was twelve. And while our grandmother is wonderful, Harley needed a different kind of stability. I stepped in and tried to be her safe place during those years. We're very close as a result. We live together, we work together."

"Do you drive each other crazy?" He smiles, his expression mirthful.

"Surprisingly, no. She's easy to get along with, and she really tends to go with the flow. But in taking on that role, I spent very little time fostering friendships outside of my family after high school. I didn't go away for college like my older sister, Avery, did because I didn't want to leave Harley behind, and I worried it would feel like another loss."

"That's a selfless thing to do."

The friendships I'd formed in college had faded. I just didn't have the time required to maintain them—or didn't make them enough of a priority. "Anyway, it's not much of a sacrifice when this is where I get to be." I shift gears, realizing I've been going on about my family instead of talking business like I'm supposed to. "Do you want to see the barn? It's probably a bit of a mess."

His brow arches. "Do you have livestock?"

I chuckle. "Not for a long time. It's been converted so we use it mostly for storage and preparing for the next event."

"Oh, well then, I definitely want to see what's inside. This behind-the-scenes kind of stuff always interests me."

I push open the door and flick on the lights. "Over the years we insulated the space against the elements and added lighting."

In the center of the room is a series of eight-foot tables arranged in a square. The centerpieces I've been working on for various upcoming events line the table closest to us, and there are three different stations, each one filled with the supplies necessary to mass produce the centerpieces.

"What is all this?" Jackson crosses over to the soccer centerpiece.

While I was managing emails this morning, two of our part-time staff had been working on replicating my design. There are now twenty soccer-inspired centerpieces lining the table.

"Just the centerpieces for our upcoming event."

"And they're made in-house?"

"Oh yes. I source all the items from either recycle warehouses or estate sales. The estate sales are my favorite, if I'm going to be honest."

"You design all of these?" Jackson picks up the centerpiece and turns it around, inspecting it closely.

"I do. I put together the first one and then we have a team who recreates the rest. Often it's high school kids looking for volunteer opportunities, or sometimes interns." I clasp my hands behind my back so I don't fiddle with the ones sitting on the table.

"You're quite talented, aren't you?"

I shrug. "It's the fun part of the job. Anyway, should we head back to the main house? I can show you the rooms and additional accommodation options, or would you prefer to go over the questions you have first?"

"Why don't we review the questions and have a bite to eat? We'll save the accommodations for the end." He checks his watch, the one he was wearing the first time I met him in the bar. "If we have time."

"Sure."

We head back to the house, so Jackson can pick up the picnic basket.

We cross the yard to the picnic table set up under the apple tree. We'll move the table later in the season, once the blossoms start to fall, but for now, it's the perfect mix of shade and pretty scenery.

The scent of the blossoming flowers is heady and sweet, and

the scene is classically romantic. I remind myself that while un-conventional, this is still a business meeting.

I take a seat across from Jackson, and we unpack the basket, which contains all the makings for a charcuterie board filled with cheeses, meats, fruit, and sweet and savory treats. We spend the next hour nibbling away at the food, reviewing his questions and my proposal for the event.

"Do you think it's best to have the auction items set up in a different room? Wouldn't it be better if guests were able to browse the items the entire time?"

"The ballroom and the dining hall are connected. We can keep the doors open, so guests are able to move between the rooms. My fear is that if it's all in the same room, we won't be able to showcase the auction items properly and the dining hall will be too crowded."

Jackson taps on the edge of the table. "Ideally we want guests to be in the same room as the auction items for most of the evening to inspire bidding."

"Yes, of course. We can arrange for the cocktail hour to be held in the auction room, and the dining room can remain closed until it's time for dinner. They'll have a view of all of the items from where they're dining, and if you think it makes sense, we can have a few of the more standout items inside the dining area."

"That's a good idea. Has Mitchell sent you a list of the do-nated items yet?"

"Just yesterday. It's a very impressive list. And a great way to bring attention to such an important charity." It's a foundation that provides financial and respite support to families with termi-nally ill parents, so they don't have to go through it all on their own. They provide meals, among other services and support for youth who are in the same position Jackson once was. "I've actually already set up a preliminary layout for the auction room. Would you like to see?"

"Already? You work fast."

"I was inspired." I pull up the room blueprint on my tablet, and Jackson goes through the layout. "We felt it would be a good idea to feature each item and the business that donated it on social media leading up to the auction. That way we can show our appreciation for each business that has made a contribution."

"Harley will handle that?"

"Yes, but I can have Mitchell vet each post, and we can create a schedule for those."

"I'll actually have our team coordinate with Selene so everything rolls out smoothly."

"Okay, whatever works best. I don't want to step on any toes."

Jackson nods and flips his pen between his fingers. "Also, any kind of video feeds that you plan on putting up need to be vetted by my team."

"You mean for this event?"

"Specifically yes, but once we've matched you with sponsors, we'll also need to have approval."

"Where the sponsors are concerned or are you talking on a broader level?"

"We don't want anything going up that could negatively affect our strategic roll out of Teamology, and you've had a couple of instances in the past where things that probably shouldn't have made it online, have, so we'll want to make sure that doesn't happen again."

I cringe internally thinking of Avery's turtle rant on Instagram.

She'd been healing from her injuries in the car accident last year, and her friends had come over with snacks. Some of which happened to be pot brownies. She ate all of them and went off about the lack of bendy straws in her life and how the turtles were responsible for her strife. It hadn't been up for long, but the damage it did was enough.

"We're very careful about what gets posted, and having to run everything we post through someone outside of Spark House isn't conducive for easy social media management. I don't think we can agree to that." While I understand his concern, we don't need someone coming in and telling us what we can and cannot post.

Jackson studies me for a moment, perhaps weighing how serious I am. He must realize that I'm being earnest because he gives a stiff nod. "Selene can be very particular about that kind of thing, but I'll talk to her." His expression softens and he rests his forearms on the picnic table, leaning in. "Now, I really need you to tell me about this hobbyhorse conference. I had no idea this was a thing, or that it incited such violence."

The abrupt shift in topic throws me, and I stumble over my response. "Oh, uh, yes, well, I don't think it usually is a violent sport. At least not that I've witnessed, apart from that one incident." I tell him about the event, and the fight that broke out with the jousting hobbyhorsers, and how one of the men seemed interested in Avery.

"No offense meant to your sister, but I would hazard a guess that any woman who would give them a shred of attention was probably a viable dating option, no?"

The squirrels who have been busy doing their squirrel thing seem to have gotten wise to our picnic, and now they've started barking at us from the tree, sending petals from the blossoms floating down around us.

"They're definitely a different breed, but they're really great guys. Some of them are married with families who support their very unusual hobby. There are a few who would probably benefit from your dating app. Break into Love is very successful. One of the most well-reviewed dating apps out there with a very high level of match success."

"Have you used it?" He picks the fallen petals off the charcuterie board.

Something in his tone makes my stomach flip, so I avoid answering directly. "Harley and I set our sister Avery up with a profile. Although that was before she and her best friend realized they were in love with each other."

I have his undivided attention again. "Did she go on a date before she discovered that?"

I nod, thinking back to how adamant we'd been that she go on that date. It set in motion a series of events that none of us could have predicted. "She did. His name was Brock, and we nicknamed him Brock the Rock. It was probably one of her worst dates, but in defense of your app, she didn't spend much time filling out the questions, which I believe impacted the results."

He gives me a wry grin. "Are you trying to make me feel better about the fact that my app failed her?"

"Not at all. The app failed her because she was already in love with someone else and gave half-assed answers to all the questions. I'm pretty sure I still have it on my phone." I pull it out of my bag and scroll through my apps. I log into Avery's profile, having been the one to set the password. All three of us have access to it, but I think Avery deleted the app from her phone once she and Declan became a thing.

I show Jackson my sister's profile; half of the initial questions are completed with one-word answers and "sports" seems to be her favorite response. "What about you? Have you used your own app?"

"I have actually. When I first created it." He looks away, toward the mountains in the distance.

"And? What were your personal results?" I try not to sound too eager for that information.

"I travel a lot for work. It makes relationships very challenging."

It's a closed-off answer, and it makes me want to ask more questions. I find it interesting that the same man who developed an app meant to connect people, and a highly successful one at that, doesn't use it.

"But you're not opposed to relationships or dating. Otherwise, you wouldn't have asked me out all those months ago," I point out.

He smiles wryly. "No, I'm not opposed."

I bite the inside of my cheek, considering my options, and decide to be bold for once. I like him and I like spending time with him. It's my turn to put myself out there like he did last time. "Maybe next time you're in Colorado, we could go out for dinner."

He freezes for a moment. "For dinner?" he echoes.

Here goes nothing. "On a date."

His expression shutters, and he's silent for a moment. All the confidence I had a second ago drains out of me. "I don't think that would be a good idea." His phone pings, and he glances at the screen, a slight furrow in his brow. "I didn't realize the time. I need to head out so I can make my flight on time."

"Right. Of course." I'm so mortified, I wish there was a pool of lava for me to jump into.

Everything is suddenly awkward as I help him pack up the lunch and walk him back to his car. I don't know what to do with my hands, or what I should say, but apparently we're ignoring the fact that I just embarrassed the hell out of myself by asking him out.

"One of my staff will be in touch next week with a preliminary guest list." One hand is in his pocket, the other flipping his keys around his index finger.

I try not to sound like a prepubescent teen when I respond. "I'll keep an eye out for that. And I'll be in touch soon with preliminary figures for the event."

"Perfect. I'm sure we'll speak soon. Thank you for showing me around and letting me monopolize your afternoon." He turns and gets into his car.

The windows are tinted so dark, I can only make out his shadow.

I wait until after the car disappears down the driveway before I let my shoulders sag. I can't believe that just happened. How the heck am I going to avoid bursting into flames of mortification every time I talk to him after this?

8

IT'S JUST BUSINESS

LONDON

It's five forty-five on the anniversary of my parents' death, and I've already been awake for an hour. I don't need to be up at all, since this is one of the rare days we take off without fail every single year. That, and our birthdays if they're not on a weekend. If they are, we schedule a day midweek to celebrate.

I'm up this early because I have Etsy orders that have been piling up over the past week, and I need to tackle them before I get more behind than I already am. It doesn't feel at all like work, though. I'm surrounded by pieces of paper. Pages out of books, to be precise. Not new ones, but the old ones that are so dog-eared, the library is getting rid of them, or ones that have been picked up from thrift stores. I start by dying the edges with watercolor paints, and then I turn them into flowers that become either decorative wall art or a wreath. They're perfect gifts for book lovers and combine some of my favorite mediums to work with.

It takes me about half an hour to get into my groove, and then

I can usually kick out a project every twenty minutes, allowing me to make quick work of all the backed-up orders. I need to thin out my selection in my store since I'm running low on stock for some items, and I just can't see having the time to replenish my supply with it being the busy season at Spark House. Not that we have much of a slow season anymore.

By nine thirty I've managed to complete all but two orders, which just appeared in the past half hour. I package them all up and have them ready to be picked up by Verna, our postal lady, who's here so often, we're on a first-name basis.

"Whoa, what time did you get up this morning? Or should I be asking if you even went to bed?" Harley is standing in the middle of the living room in her rumpled jammies, sleep lines etched into the right side of her face. Her hair sticks out all over the place because she's a middle-of-the-night thrasher.

"Around four thirty. I had some projects to take care of."

"I would have helped you with those if I'd known. I didn't realize you were behind on your Etsy stuff."

"It was just from last week."

"This is from last week? Wow. Things are really picking up in your store." Harley arches an eyebrow at the pile of boxes at the front door.

"They're just big boxes."

"A lot of big boxes."

"I got a little behind because we're juggling a few extra things, and I've been spending more time on the charity event for Holt Media." Every time I mention anything that has to do with Jackson and Holt Media, the embarrassment I felt that day returns in full force.

Harley gives me a sympathetic smile. "I'm sorry things are so awkward there. Are you sure you don't want me to try to manage the calls and emails again?"

I told Harley and Avery what happened when I, in an effort to be bold, asked Jackson out. Since then, I've mostly been dealing with Mitchell, but whenever I add to or check on the Google Doc, I get all nervous and sweaty, worried he's going to be in there at the same time as me. I tried to pull Harley in to take over communication, but Jackson refused to take the bait, so I'm stuck in this awkward position. And unlike him, I don't have three months to get over the sting of rejection.

"It'll just take a little time to shake off the awkwardness." I print out the two new orders and the shipping labels to go with them.

"I still can't believe he said no. He was there for three hours. We came back while you two were having lunch, and you were so engrossed in whatever you were talking about, you didn't even notice us. So we went out for lunch and then picked up a few more things because we didn't want to interrupt."

"You should have come out, you might have saved me the humiliation." I keep playing it over in my mind. It was just so abrupt. One second we were talking about dating apps and the next he was running for his car.

So mortifying.

"You were deep in conversation. All signs pointed to go. Or at least that's how it seemed." She flops down on the couch.

"I guess we all read it wrong." Me included.

"When do you have to meet with him again?"

"I don't know. Hopefully not too soon. I need some time to get over the rebuff. Although with their new office opening in Denver, I imagine he'll have to come back sooner than later. He said he was buying a place here." Not that I'll need to be aware or involved.

"Denver's pretty close to Colorado Springs. Maybe he'll change his mind about the date," she offers.

I laugh and shake my head. "There's zero chance I'm going to put myself out there again after that. He couldn't get out of here fast enough. I should have thought it through before I said anything. Now I'm locked into working with him until the charity event is over."

Harley sighs and makes a face. "I don't get it. He doesn't have to be involved in any way in this charity thing. I bet if you asked his team, they'd all tell you it's the first charity project he's been this heavily involved in."

"That's untrue. Earlier this year, he was in Peru helping clean up a community that was devastated by a chemical spill. He was right in there, helping build a holding facility for all the displaced people, and he helped fund a relief hospital as well."

"And how do you know all of this?"

"Jackson and I talked about it."

"Exactly my point." Harley picks up one of my finished flowers and helps curl the edges.

"What's exactly your point? I think that proves *my* point." That he gets involved in things he's passionate about, regardless of potential awkwardness.

"Usually business associates don't talk about personal stuff. Or show up for what was supposed to be a phone call with a picnic basket. It just doesn't make sense that he said no to the date."

"His assistant sent the picnic basket. Maybe he's in a relationship. I didn't even think to ask." The thought makes me cringe again.

"Maybe. Things just don't add up." She drops the finished flower on the coffee table and flounces off to the kitchen.

"Can you pour me a coffee?" I call after her.

All talk of Jackson ceases when Avery shows up fifteen minutes later with cinnamon buns from Sweet Sensations. It's part of our yearly tradition and how we celebrate the memory of our parents. It's always a bittersweet day, full of comfort food, a little sadness, and a whole lot of special memories.

Like every other year, we pull out the photo albums our mother made when we were growing up. She was big into holding onto our memories. And it's something the three of us have continued. Harley always takes amazing pictures, and I pick out a bunch for her to print, and then we spend part of the day working on a new album while we watch our parents' favorite movies. It was something we started with our grandmother, and we've carried on the tradition.

Last year she was away in Italy. She came back for a few months, but she met someone during her travels, and now she has a boyfriend. They decided to head back to Europe this spring and who knows how long they'll be gone this time. I'm happy that she's found someone. She deserves happiness after all she's lost.

Around two in the afternoon, the door to our apartment buzzes with a delivery. "Did one of you order takeout or something?" I ask my sisters, who are busy shoving popcorn in their faces and laughing at *When Harry Met Sally* playing on the screen.

"Nope. Maybe you ordered something for one of your projects and you forgot about it?" Harley motions to the coffee table, which is now filled with my Etsy creations.

"That's always a possibility."

We're barely into summer, and I'm already thinking about the holidays because I like to plan ahead. And I have boxes and boxes of puffy stars hanging around. I use them often for centerpieces, but I have so many extra stars that I've decided to fill those clear Christmas globe ornaments with them and sell them in sets of six. I've also started shellacking the bigger ones so I can use them as decorations on refinished photo frames. It's like adding a finish coat of nail polish so they stay in their shape and won't disintegrate when they're wiped down.

I buzz the delivery person in and wait by the door until they show up in case I need to sign for something.

Instead of being one of my orders that I've forgotten, it's a giant bouquet of white flowers. I sign for them, my heart skipping around in my chest as I carry them into the kitchen and set them on the counter.

I find the card attached to the flowers.

Neat, careful handwriting fills the small note card.

London,
I know days like these can be tough. Thinking of you and
your sisters and hoping that you're sharing memories and
taking comfort in each other.
With deepest understanding and empathy,
Jackson

I'm confused. I remind myself that he's just being thoughtful. That we share a similar kind of loss, one he's only too familiar with.

"Please tell me it's not more of your star strips!" Avery calls from the living room.

I carry the bouquet into the living room. "It's not star strips."

"Oh wow! Who sent those?" Harley asks as I set them on the mantle.

"Jackson."

"Jackson sent you flowers?" Avery parrots.

They exchange a look.

"He's aware we lost our parents today. We were talking about it last Friday. He lost his parents too. Not the same way, but he understands what it's like. He was being thoughtful. He sent it to all of us."

"Really? All three of us? Was there a card?" Avery asks.

Harley hops up from her seat and rushes back to the kitchen and reappears a moment later. "The card is not in fact addressed to all three of us. It's addressed *only* to London."

"He mentions both of you, though," I mutter.

"Not by name."

"He's probably being extra nice because he turned me down and feels bad or something." I cross my arms. "I bet he had his assistant send them."

Avery grabs my hand and pulls me onto the couch beside her and Harley takes the other side. The springs in the center are starting to go, so both of them slide toward me. "He wrote that card himself."

"You don't know that for sure and neither do I because I've never seen his writing." I toss a puffy star on the table. "I'm working on a project with him, and he made it clear that he does *not* want to date me."

"Or maybe he realized he made a mistake and this is his way of smoothing things over. The guy flew from New York to Colorado for a freaking meeting and then turned around and went home," Harley says. "Maybe you caught him off guard when you asked him out."

"He's opening an office here. And who knows when he flew in? Him having his assistant send us flowers on the anniversary of our parents' death does not mean he regrets saying no. He runs a multimillion-dollar company. He can afford to be exceedingly thoughtful."

"Okay. It's just him being thoughtful and having his assistant send you a really stunning bouquet of flowers because he knows that today is the anniversary of our parents' death." Harley does that thing where she repeats what I've just said back to me.

I struggle back to my feet. "I should probably send him a message to thank him." Even as I think it, butterflies start flitting around in my stomach. Not the nice kind, the anxiety-inspired kind. I leave my sisters in the living room and nab my phone from the kitchen counter, where it's been sitting all day.

He must be one of those people who pays very close attention to detail. Which makes sense considering how successful he is. But his thoughtfulness today makes me emotional in a way I don't know how to deal with. I'm used to my sisters being there for me, but I've never known someone else who has suffered the same kind of loss. The absence of a parent's love is something that isn't explainable. Even with the support of our grandmother, an integral part of who we are was taken from us. We had such loving and wonderful parents. They were involved in every facet of our lives. They were always present, always aware, always there. Until they weren't anymore.

I take a deep breath and start to compose a message, but decide a call is probably better. It's the middle of the afternoon. I'm sure he's in a meeting. I can just leave a quick thank-you message. It's the considerate thing to do. And I need to get over my embarrassment eventually. This is a good start.

I pull up his contact and have to take a few deep, calming breaths before I hit the call button. I fully expect it to go to voicemail, so I'm unprepared as the low, deep baritone of Jackson's voice fills my ear.

"Hello, Jackson Holt speaking."

Just those words make my knees suddenly weak. Or maybe it's the fact that he unexpectedly answered the call. I drag a chair away from the kitchen island and it makes a horrible screeching sound. "Hi. Hey. Hello. Sorry about that."

I drop into the chair and squeeze my eyes shut, wishing I could rewind about thirty seconds.

"London, hello. How are you?" Genuine concern laces his words with soft comfort.

"I'm good. The flowers were very thoughtful. Thank you." It comes out choppy and awkward.

"I'm glad to hear that. I know you mentioned that you take today off and spend it with your sisters. I wasn't sure what that would look like, but I wanted to send you all something."

That he remembers seems significant, but at the same time, he's lost his parents too. So he knows exactly what it's like to be where I am today. "It was very kind of you. The flowers are stunning."

"It was nothing, really. I know these days can be difficult."

"They can, but thoughtful gifts like these make it better." I bite my tongue, trying to swallow down the apology for asking him out last week and making things tense. It doesn't work, though. "About last week, I'm so sorry I made things awkward."

"You don't need to apologize, London. With us working on

the charity event together, I feel it's important to keep things strictly business, otherwise it can get complicated."

"Of course. I totally understand." I close my eyes, glad he can't see my red face.

"I have a meeting I have to be in, but I'll be in contact again soon. I hope you and your sisters are able to enjoy the day with each other."

I thank him again and end the call.

I have no idea how to take his response. Does that mean he wanted to say yes, or is that him being nice again?

All I know is that I'm more confused than I was before.

9

JUST ANOTHER SMALL ADVENTURE

LONDON

Over the course of the week, I email back and forth with Mitchell about the event, and I continue to update the shared Google Doc. Occasionally Jackson and I are both in the doc at the same time. I always wait for him to initiate a chat, which most times he does, and I can't get a read on him. Sometimes it is strictly business and other times he's asking me about how my week has been going.

It's Saturday, and I'm awake at five a.m. It really doesn't matter what day of the week it is, because I rarely, if ever sleep in. Instead, I'm in bed working, not so casually checking our Google Doc to see if Jackson is also up.

Two hours later, my phone rings. I nab it off my nightstand and answer without checking the caller ID. "Hello?"

"Good morning, London." The deep, low timbre is unexpected.

I pull the phone away from my ear and check the screen. Yup, I'm not imagining things. "Hi, Jackson. Is everything okay?"

I can't think of many reasons for him to call me on a Saturday morning.

"Everything is fine. I realize it's early, but I saw that you were in the Google Doc not long ago and figured I would chance giving you a call."

"Ah. Okay. Is it about the event?"

"Yes and no. I, uh . . . I'm in Colorado Springs and I wondered if you were available this morning."

"Available? For what?" My stomach flips.

"There's an estate sale outside of Woodland Park, and I noticed that you had it marked on the calendar you shared with Mitchell. If we left in the next hour, I could have you back to Spark House by noon, one at the very latest. Would that work for you?"

It takes me a few moments to process everything he's just thrown at me. "You want to take me to an estate sale?" I shut down the part of my brain that wants to call this a date.

"I felt it would be a good opportunity to discuss the event and do something you enjoy at the same time. I appreciate everything you've been doing for Holt Media."

I pull up my calendar. "I thought the estate sale wasn't until tomorrow."

"It isn't, but I made a call and was able to procure early access. That's if you'd like to go."

Our event isn't until this evening, and we finished most of the setup last night. I could definitely make this work as long as I'm back around lunchtime. "I would like to go."

"Excellent. Now my next question is, how soon can you be ready?"

I roll out of bed and check my reflection in my dresser mirror, cringing at the state of my hair. "Uh." I flick on the bedroom light so I can get a better look. I washed my hair yesterday, so it should be fine until tomorrow. "It shouldn't take me too long. Do you want to meet me at Spark House?" It's a little closer to Woodland Park.

Jackson clears his throat. "Well, that would be unnecessary since I'm very close to your building."

"Close to my building?" Great. I'm parroting him again.

"Just down the street, actually."

"From where I live?" I have so many questions, like what in the world is he doing down the street from my apartment at seven on a Saturday morning.

"That's correct."

"Do you want to come up, then?" The words are out before I can fully consider what I'm offering. Which is a glimpse of me looking far less polished than usual.

"I don't want to impose. I realize I've sprung this on you with no warning."

"You're not imposing." Confusing, yes. Imposing, not really. "Just send me a message when you're parked and I'll buzz you up."

"I'm already parked." This time he sounds halfway between chagrined and amused.

"Oh, well then. Buzz away."

"I'll just be a moment." I hear his car door closing, and the hum of traffic at street level. I rush down the hall as the buzzer goes off. I let him in and end the call with a hasty "I'll see you in a minute." I stand there for a second. I think I'm in shock. And then I realize I'm standing in the middle of my apartment, wearing only a nightshirt, and my hair looks like it's gone a round with a tornado.

There's no time to get changed, so I hurry back to my room and shrug into my bathrobe. My next stop is the bathroom, where I yank a brush through my tangled hair, ripping out several chunks in the process. I throw it up in a messy bun because it's the better option. There's nothing I can do about my lack of makeup. I do a quick rinse with mouthwash and spit as the doorbell chimes.

"Oh my God, London. He is here. At your apartment." I tell my reflection. As if it needed stating out loud. I think I'm losing my damn mind.

Harley appears in the doorway of her bedroom, looking a sleepy mess. "Is someone here?"

"I got it! You can go back to bed!" I call over my shoulder as I rush down the hall.

I don't even have time for deep breaths. Instead, I throw open the door and adopt what I hope is a bright, fresh smile and not completely maniacal. My breath leaves me in a *whoosh* as I take in the sight in my doorway. I suck in some much-needed oxygen and release it with the word: "Hey."

I've seen Jackson in two different states of dress: ultra-casual in a pair of jeans and a T-shirt that looked like it had seen better days, and a suit. So I'm highly unprepared for business casual on Jackson. Business Casual Jackson, just like Slightly Unkempt Jackson and Suit Jackson, is utterly scrumptious. He's wearing a short-sleeved black polo and a pair of gray khakis. He's paired them with black-and-white brogues.

I am fully prepared to admit my love for his shoe choice.

His gaze moves over me in a slow, easy sweep, and by the time his eyes reach my face, I'm sure it's on fire. Way to nail the lid on the ever-having-a-chance-with-him coffin. He tips his head fractionally, and a warm smile makes his eyes crinkle at the corners. "Did I wake you when I called?"

I glance down at my robe, making sure it's closed and not showing off my *Sleep Like It's Your Job* nightshirt. "I was awake. I was checking emails and looking at the doc while I was in bed. It's a bad habit."

"I do the same thing." His smile widens.

I don't even want to know what shade of red my face is as I step back and sweep a hand out. "Would you like to come in for a minute? Please excuse the mess."

He glances around the kitchen. There are two glasses on the counter and a single popcorn bowl, but otherwise it's tidy. "Are you sure you have time to entertain this today?"

"Absolutely. Make yourself comfortable. I'll just be a few minutes."

"Take your time. I'm happy to wait."

I lead him to the living room, which is definitely not as tidy as the kitchen. I sweep a handful of stars off the coffee table and dump them in a bowl, which I take with me to the kitchen. I rush back to my bedroom, debate whether I can forgo a shower and decide I can't. I grab an outfit and hightail it into the bathroom to take the fastest shower in the history of humanity. I should honestly win a Guinness World Record for how quickly I'm able to shower, dress, put on makeup, and fix my hair. Eight minutes and seventeen seconds has never felt like such an incredible accomplishment.

Harley meets me in the hallway, her eyes the size of saucers. "Jackson Holt is sitting in our living room," she whispers.

"I know."

"I almost walked in there wearing this!" She motions to her

pajamas. They're Disney-themed. She's had them since she was nineteen. They were a gift from one of the families she used to be a nanny for. They're not particularly revealing, but they are more suitable for someone ten or under. Still, they're cute, and I'm assuming they're comfortable.

"Sorry. I should have said something."

"What is he doing here? Are you going somewhere with him? Did he change his mind about the date?" Her voice rises with each question.

I flick her shoulder. "Shh! Keep it down. He just got here—" I check the time on my phone. "Eleven minutes ago. There's an estate sale. He secured early access, so we're going this morning. I'll be at Spark House by one at the latest. And everything is pretty much ready for the event tonight. I can make phone calls and answer any last emails on the way to the estate sale. Is that okay?" I bite the inside of my lip. I don't usually dump work on Harley since she and I are often picking up the slack for Avery these days.

She waves me off. "It's fine. Better than fine, actually. Have fun on your estate sale shopping date."

"It's not a date. It's a meeting with an estate sale thrown in."

"Okay. Whatever you say." She smiles brightly and brushes past me. "Enjoy your not-date."

I find Jackson sitting right where I left him, on the living room couch. He's flipping one of my origami stars between his fingers.

"All set! Sorry to keep you waiting." I adjust the strap of my purse.

His gaze lifts, and I feel it sweep over me like a lover's caress. *This is business, not a date.*

"No apology necessary, London, considering I just high-jacked your entire morning." He pushes to a stand. "Shall we?"

I'm not prepared for the experience of being willingly trapped inside an elevator with Jackson. Everywhere I look, there he is, reflected back at me in the mirrored glass surrounding us. It's one thing to be near him, but this is very, very different. Even standing on the opposite side of the elevator feels too close. The scent of his cologne is stronger and more potent in here. I use the mirrored walls to surreptitiously check him out.

I swallow repeatedly and grip the handrail, searching for something banal to discuss as we descend to the lobby. I've never understood why people have felt the urge to get it on in an elevator. Until now. Especially with all the mirrors, which would give me an amazing view of Jackson from all sides, if I were to say, climb him like a tree.

Stop it, London. I have no idea how I'm going to manage in a car with him for the half-hour drive to Woodland Park.

"Everything okay?" Jackson tips his head the tiniest bit and his tongue peeks out to wet his bottom lip.

"Oh yeah. Everything's fine." I'm holding the handrail so tightly, my knuckles are turning white. "This was just a bit of a surprise. Especially after last time." I bite my tongue to prevent more idiotic things from leaving my mouth.

"How do you mean?" I can practically feel his eyes on me as he slips his phone back in his pocket.

I force myself to meet his gaze. In a normal setting, under normal circumstances, this would be fine.

I flail a hand between us, and because we're in a small el-evator, I almost touch him. "Oh, you know, because I—" The elevator doors slide open, and I breathe a sigh of relief that I don't have to finish that statement.

I bolt from the elevator toward the front entrance and burst out onto the street, practically gulping down fresh air like I've been holding my breath under water for two minutes. Which incidentally is about four times as long as I can reasonably hold my breath.

I at least have the wherewithal to hold the door open for Jackson.

I plaster on a smile and glance beyond him to my reflection in the mirrored glass, toning it down so it looks less anxiety-stricken and closer to normal. "Should we stop and grab coffees for the trip?" I point to the café next to my building. "They have the best pastries."

"Sure, that's a great idea." An amused smile plays on his luscious lips.

Between my soaring body temperature and the inappropriate tingles below the waist, and how difficult I'm finding it not to stare, this morning is going to present a challenge in personal restraint.

"Do you have any suggestions, London?" Jackson asks when we approach the cashier and the case full of pastries.

"The chocolate croissants are to die for and the cinnamon buns are the best in the universe. They also have a cinnamon latte that is heaven in your mouth," I tell him.

"Is that what you're having, then?"

"Yes, please."

He turns to the young woman standing behind the counter. "I have it on good authority that the cinnamon latte and the cinnamon buns are to die for. Would that be accurate?"

She blinks a few times and reaches up to touch her hairnet. "They are to die for. We usually run out of both by ten in the morning."

"Well then, it's fortunate for us that we're early risers. We'll take two of each." He holds up a pair of fingers, smiling widely.

I try to pay, but Jackson insists on getting it. Once we have our order, we leave the shop and step back out onto the street. The lazy Saturday morning traffic buzzes around us, dogs walking their owners passing by, their tongues lolling as they trot happily along.

Once we're both standing on the sidewalk, my hand shoots out. "Let me take one of those for you!" He's holding both of the coffees and the bag of pastries.

He graces me with another amused smile. "That's okay. I have it. I'm just over here." He inclines his head to a sleek gray Tesla. Which, of course, makes sense since he's all about being green.

"I didn't know you could rent Teslas." Obviously I'm poking fun.

Jackson arches a brow. "You can't."

"Doesn't it take a year to get one of these?" At least that's the impression I had.

"For most people, yes."

"But not for you." It's more statement than anything. It's really starting to set in how big a deal it is that Jackson has taken Spark House under his wing. And that he's allocating so much time to our event. It's a good reminder to keep things professional.

"No. Not for me." His smile is wry as he sets the coffees and paper bag on the roof, opens the door, and extends a hand.

I don't want to be rude and not take the offer of assistance, but I remember exactly how it felt to shake his hand and the lasting impact on my body. And this time I'll be trapped in a car with him for at least thirty minutes. *Trapped* is probably the wrong word. It's not as though I'm *not* going to enjoy being in the car with him. The problem is how much I enjoy his proximity.

I suck in a quick breath and slip my fingers into his palm.

Nope.

I did not imagine my previous reaction. Just like last time, my entire body breaks out in a wave of goose bumps. It starts at my arm, travels all the way down to my toes, and sends a skittery feeling along my scalp. I fight a shudder and lose the battle. My fingers flex around Jackson's, and I swallow past the lump that's suddenly clogging my throat.

It makes me think of those romance books my gran used to read. Sometimes I'd scoop one up and flip to the sections with the dog-eared pages. Those seemed to be Gran's favorite and also the steamiest sections.

I'd always been fascinated by the descriptions. The way these women reacted to the hero—the butterflies, the tingles. It had never happened to me. Until now. And here I am, about to be locked inside a space that feels claustrophobically small, especially with all the things currently happening in my head and my body.

Just stay cool, London. I force a smile and drag my gaze away from our clasped hands. Up to the open V of his collared shirt, along the closely shaven expanse of his neck. His Adam's apple bobs, and when I reach his mouth, his tongue peeks out and skims his bottom lip. It feels like a thousand years have passed by the time my eyes finally lock on his. What I see reflected back at me makes all the blood that's currently residing in my face redirect itself toward the center of my body, and every muscle south of my navel clenches in tandem. I've never had someone look at me the way Jackson is right now.

It makes this that much more confusing, because he looks like he wants to pounce on me. I don't understand what's happening.

"In you go." His voice is a gentle hand sweeping down my spine.

I cannot be imagining that there's something between us. I climb into the passenger side and can't decide if I want to cry with despair or relief when he releases my hand.

One of the coffees appears in front of my face. I'm very careful to take it from him without making contact with any of his fingers. "Thank you," I squeak.

"Always my pleasure, London." His smile is wry, and I don't think I'm imagining the amused glint in his eye.

He rounds the hood and drops into the driver's seat. Without his coffee or the bag.

"Jackson?" My voice is still higher than it should be, but at least it's down from a helium-level squeal.

"Yes?" He touches his finger to the ignition and the engine purrs to life, as his gaze shifts my way.

I point to the roof. "Your coffee."

His eyes flare. "Shit."

I'm stunned motionless for a moment because I've never heard him swear before. He's always incredibly proper and composed, but right now he's not, and it makes me feel the teensiest bit better. And still very discombobulated about this whole thing.

He reaches for the door handle, but I'm quicker. "I've got it." I grab his coffee and the bag from the roof, gulping in fresh air—well, as fresh as it can be for a downtown street—and drop back into the passenger seat. I take one last haul of non-Jackson-scented air before I pull my door closed again, locking me inside with his charisma and the delectable smell of his cologne.

"Here you go." His fingers brush mine as I transfer the coffee to his waiting hand, sending a small shiver through me.

I crack the window and clutch my own coffee with both hands. "This is a really nice car." *Awesome, London. Way to keep the conversation rolling with stupid observations.*

"Thanks. It gets me from A to B and is as gentle on the environment as a car can be, so I like it too." He gives me another sidelong glance.

"Harley and I have a hybrid. And we share a car. Mostly because it's more economical than both of us owning one, and we live together so it makes sense." If I can just keep talking about nothing, I'll be able to survive today without adding another item to the list of humiliating things I say to Jackson.

"That's smart and responsible."

"And better financially." I take a sip of my coffee and let my eyes slide his way. Thankfully his focus is on the road and not me. I should have picked something I could guzzle, since my mouth is dry, but buying a plastic bottle of water in Jackson's presence seemed similar to taking God's name in vain in front of a nun.

I'm currently too nervous to even consider putting more than coffee into my stomach. I dive into work-talk mode and spend the entire drive reviewing the plan for the upcoming event, going over the items up for auction. "Oh! If you have a little time when you drop me off at Spark House, we can visit the room where the silent auction will be held since you didn't get to see the space last time." I remind myself not to say anything about the way he bolted.

"That would be a good idea." He taps his fingers on the steering wheel. He's been driving with his hands at ten and two the entire time apart from when he takes a sip of coffee. "I don't have another engagement until this evening."

"Oh? What kind of engagement?" I blurt without thinking, like I have a right to know his personal schedule. I have the strangest uncomfortable feeling in my stomach.

"I'm looking at a couple of properties in Denver before I head back to New York."

"That's exciting. I thought maybe you had a date or something. I probably should have asked that before. If you were in a relationship. I guess I just sort of assumed you weren't. And you know what they say about assumptions making an ass out of me." I bite the end of my tongue. There I go again. "I'm so sorry. I should stop."

He smiles. "I haven't been on a date in quite some time."

I dab at the edge of my coffee cup with a napkin, soaking up the drip of tan liquid. My blouse is pale, and I don't want to risk a stain. "How long is quite some time?" I cringe. "Sorry. Again. I don't know why I asked that."

"It's been several months. Since before that camping trip I went on."

"I'm the last person you asked out?"

"You are."

"Oh. Well. That's . . . I'm sorry I said no." Did he say no to me because he's not attracted to me anymore? Maybe he's not interested now that he knows me better. Why did I not consider that before now? Well, I might as well ask. I don't have much to lose. My dignity was left behind long ago. "When you said you didn't think it was a good idea for us to go on a date because it could complicate things, was that just you letting me down easy?" I consider unbuckling my seat belt and throwing the door open, but that would leave Harley on her own to deal with Avery.

"That wasn't my intention at all, London. I realized after you joined the Teamology initiative and with the event that you're hosting for me, that I'd put us in a difficult position. That's all."

I entertain shoving the entire cinnamon roll I still haven't touched into my mouth to stop myself from asking what other positions he'd like to put us in. Instead, I say the next thing that I think.

"Why aren't you in a relationship? I mean, you're successful and you"—I gesture to him—"look like this." I can't read his expression, but it seems as though he's fighting a smile.

He shrugs. "Relationships are successful for people who want them to be."

"Does that mean you don't want a relationship?"

"I've been burned before, and that's made it a challenge for me to invest in a relationship." He cringes. "That sounds transactional. What I mean is that I'm not sure it's fair to my prospective partner if I'm not all in and they are."

I nod, settling into my seat, intrigued by the turn in this conversation. I can't decide if this is a warning to change the topic or an invitation to ask more questions. But if I can keep him talking, it means I won't stick my foot in my mouth. "That was why I ended my last relationship. I realized he was far more invested. He'd started talking about moving in together and asking how I felt about a family and kids, and I realized that we were in two very different headspaces."

"So you ended it before he could get in any deeper?"

And before he got locked into a life that would never make him happy, but I keep that to myself. I don't want to end up alone, but I also don't want to settle. "I did. I felt horrible."

"How long were you two together?"

"Um . . . maybe a little less than a year?" We'd been approaching the one-year anniversary, and I knew I had to end it before that milestone.

"What was your longest relationship?" Jackson reaches for his coffee, gaze shifting briefly to my hands clasped in my lap before returning to the road.

"I had a boyfriend in college for almost two years, but he went to med school out of state and I stayed here. Harley was just starting college, and I was finishing up, and I didn't want to leave her. What about you? What's your longest relationship?"

He taps on the steering wheel. "I had a girlfriend in college. And a friend with benefits thing over the years."

"Were either of them serious?"

"I proposed once." His smile holds strain.

"What happened?" These are the pieces of Jackson I want to know. The parts of him that he gives me little glimpses of. Layers of humanity and humility under the refined businessman who seems unstoppable and unflappable most of the time.

"She said no."

"Well, clearly she's an idiot. What the hell is wrong with her?" I slap a palm over my mouth. "I'm sorry, that was so rude."

Jackson barks out a laugh. "I appreciate your vote of confidence, but she was right to say no. Especially since we weren't even dating at the time."

"What?" I don't even understand how that would happen.

His expression shifts to chagrin. "Well, in my defense, my parents had only passed six months earlier, and I'd been asking for all the wrong reasons. Marrying someone for stability is not the same as marrying someone for love. She saved us a world of grief."

"Oh, that must have been so hard."

"It was more embarrassing than anything." He glances at me. "Why do I always find myself baring my soul to you, London?"

"We're just talking about life, and it seems we've both had curveballs thrown at us. Like recognizes like sometimes, I think."

"Hmm, I suppose that's true. You're very easy to talk to."

"So are you, when you're not busy being intimidating and all business." Or decimating my ego with rejection.

He chuckles again. "I'm sure you would be unsurprised to hear that you're not the first person to say that about me."

The car GPS dings, signaling that we need to turn off the winding country road and down a long, equally winding driveway.

"Holy wow, this is unbelievable," I murmur when the sprawling mansion comes into view. It's rustic, yet elegant, with thick wood beams, smooth stone, and floor-to-ceiling windows that provide a stunning view of the front yard. Cobblestone paths snake through the gardens, all in full, lush bloom. Archways covered in flowering vines and a water feature make it feel like a magical wonderland. I half expect to see a deer drinking at a babbling brook or Snow White and Cinderella to sashay past us, singing to the birds and cooing to the mice.

Set back away from the road with the mountains as the backdrop, it has an elegant, yet cottagelike feel, but on a much larger scale. Peaked roofs and floor-to-ceiling windows highlight the warm glow coming from the interior. It's an interesting mix of modern and classic styles. I've never seen anything like it.

"An entire village could live here. It actually probably takes that many people to maintain this place. Do you know why they're having an estate sale? It didn't say in the advertisement. I hope it's not because they have to." I reach for my coffee, even though it's basically empty. If I don't have something to keep my hands busy, I'll start biting at my nails. I have star strips in my purse, but I didn't think pulling them out while we're in the car seemed like a good idea.

"They're renovating a wing, and they're aware that not everything can be kept for all eternity."

"Oh well, that's a good reason to get rid of things. And also true. Sometimes you have to part with treasures. We've renovated a few of the bedrooms in Spark House over the years. They each have a different theme partly because they all came from different estates. It's a bit eclectic, but that's what gives it personality."

"That's smart."

"We thought so. Moving them was a challenge, but Avery's fiancé and all of her friends were great about helping out, and young enough that a case of beer and some pizza was more than enough payment."

"You've worked hard to get where you are, haven't you?"

I lift a shoulder and let it fall. "Spark House is Avery's baby. She loves organizing events and coming up with ideas on how to make them really stand apart from anyone else's. And I love my sisters, and I didn't want to lose the connection we have, so I stepped up to the plate when my grandmother retired."

"Is this what you always wanted to do?" He parks the car.

"Go to estate sales?" I unfasten my seat belt and grab my purse from the floor.

He grins. "Run Spark House."

"I figured eventually I would take my place in the family business, but I thought I wouldn't have to do it until later. After I'd had a bit of time to pursue my own passions. Or at least I thought I'd have the time to do both. Spark House keeps growing, and there's only the three of us to run things."

"You have other staff, though?"

"We do, but the management side of things is just me and my sisters, and it's not entirely natural for me. It's not that I don't enjoy it. It's just that there isn't a whole lot of time left over for me to do other things."

"What about all the centerpieces? Do you enjoy making those, or is that a chore?"

"Oh, I love making those." We both open our doors.

Somehow, he manages to make it around the front of the car and is at my side, offering me a hand before I even have one foot on the ground. I brace myself for the jolt, and this time, I manage not to make any weird noises. I'm still covered in goose bumps, but that's preferable to any of the possible alternatives.

Jackson's fingertips rest at the small of my back as we make our way up the front steps. I feel those tiny points of connection like a current running through my body. Combined with my excitement over the estate sale, and I feel a lot like I've consumed an entire pot of coffee and snorted a pound of sugar.

"I need to warn you about something, Jackson," I blurt when we reach the massive front doors. They must be twelve feet high, a stunning pattern carved into the black stained wood.

"I'm listening."

I tip my head up and find him staring down at me intently. His cinnamon-y breath breaks across my cheek. He's so close, I can see the flecks of gold in his eyes. "I really love estate sales."

He grins, and if my lady parts could, they would sigh. "I already knew that."

"No, I mean, I *really, really* love estate sales. My gran and I used to go all the time when I was a kid. I get a little giddy. Sometimes too giddy. So I'm going to apologize in advance if I do or say anything embarrassing."

"I don't know that a preemptive apology is necessary, but I suppose the warning is appreciated. How giddy are we talking? Like kid-in-a-candy-store level giddiness? Or more like first time at Disney World?"

He's smiling again, and I get lost in the warmth of it for a moment before I respond. "More like first time at Disney after having eaten six bags of cotton candy."

Jackson's eyes flare. "Ah, that's a fairly high level of giddiness. I look forward to witnessing this."

I don't have a chance to say anything else because the front doors swing open. I half expect a butler or even two, but instead, an older man wearing a bright smile and in a gray tweed suit is standing in the opulent foyer. "Jackson, it's wonderful to see you again." Instead of extending a hand, he pulls Jackson in for a brief, very real hug.

"I'm sorry it's been so long, Harmon. It's been a busy year."

"No apologies necessary. I heard about your time in Peru. Very noble. Your parents would be proud." He turns his attention to me, his eyes alight with curiosity. "And you must be London Spark. Jackson has told me wonderful things about you."

I swallow down my surprise and confusion and extend my hand. "It's lovely to meet you, sir."

"London, this is Harmon East. He owns Enviro Enterprise, one of the leaders in green paper product manufacturing. You're already affiliated with a number of the smaller local businesses that he has partnerships with," Jackson explains.

I fight to maintain my composure, subtly clearing my throat. "It's an honor. Enviro Enterprise has been such a pioneer in green products. My eleventh-grade geography independent study project was all about the impact your company had on the way we manage paper product recycling."

For a moment, I want to sink into the ground. I can't believe I'm talking about a high school project with this man; he must think I'm such an idiot. But then Harmon's smile widens. "I hope you got a good grade on that project."

"Ninety-four percent."

"Ah, clever and forward thinking. I see why Jackson was so adamant I meet you. I've been told you have a family-run event hotel. Why don't you tell me a little about it, and I'll show you around the estate?" I spend the next twenty minutes fielding questions from Harmon, explaining what we do at Spark House, how it started, and how my grandmother was always looking for the best and cleanest ways to run a hotel, researching the companies we did business with. By the time my sisters and I took over, we had a clear plan and were moving toward a green-friendly approach on all levels.

"I need to visit Spark House."

"We're hosting a charity auction next month to raise money in support of respite care, specifically for families with a terminal parent and younger children, if you're interested in attending," Jackson offers.

"Absolutely. You'll send me the details?"

"Of course. I'll have Mitchell forward everything to Colleen."

"Perfect. I'll leave you to browse the wing. Everything in the bedrooms is available, and we have several sets of mismatched china and a dining room that we're looking to liquidate. If there's anything you see that you'd like, you can flag it and we can set it aside for you." He turns to me. "London, it was a pleasure to meet you."

"You as well. I hope I see you next month."

I wait until Jackson and I are alone before I whisper, "I can't believe you did that!"

"Did what?" Jackson's hands are clasped behind his back, his expression giving nothing away.

"I didn't realize this was going to be an introduction to someone like him."

"Estates are often owned by influential people. I thought it was a great way to feed two birds with one scone. Don't you agree?"

"Don't you mean kill two birds with one stone? And yes I agree, but some advance warning would have been nice!" I realize I'm admonishing him and probably shouldn't be.

"My phrasing is less violent, and I'd apologize, but it's clear that Harmon is completely enamored with you." He arches a brow in challenge. "And you'll get to meet him again in just a few weeks."

"If he comes to the event."

"I have a feeling he will. And if all goes well, you'll have your first sponsorship under your belt, and that's before the actual initiative rolls out." Jackson grins, clearly very pleased with himself.

I tip my head up so I can meet his stunning, amused gaze. "This was all part of your plan, wasn't it?"

"It wasn't a bad plan."

"Why are you doing this for me?" I can't figure him out, and it's driving me mad. I love what he's doing for Spark House, but I also want to get naked with him. And I have no idea where he stands on that because his answers are always vague. He's the king of mixed signals. None of it makes sense.

"Because I believe in you, London. We all come from modest beginnings at some point. I see the greatness in what you're doing and the potential for growth. The way you approach this is authentic and real, and I want more people to see that."

My heart stutters at his earnest expression and his warm tone. "Thank you." I step forward and wrap my arms around his waist without thinking.

And suddenly our bodies are flush. My cheek makes contact with the soft cotton of his polo. I can hear the strong, steady beat of his heart. And I realize, with horror, that I've spontaneously hugged him. At least I've managed not to do a hip roll.

I'm about to release him and apologize for making things awkward yet again, when his arms circle me in return. He pats my back, sort of like I'm a kid who needs consoling. "No thanks necessary," he murmurs. "It's a joy to see you shine."

He drops his arms, and I take a huge step back so I'm no longer in his personal space. "We should look around!" I'm back to sounding like I've huffed helium, and I'm eleven million percent sure that my face is literally on fire.

For the first time since we entered the wing, I take stock of my surroundings. We're in the middle of the dining hall. The table is set with china. It's immaculate and amazing, and I can't imagine how much time and energy must go into making sure everything is dust-free. "Oh!" I clap my hands once, then lace my fingers together so I don't look like an excited seal. "This is incredible."

I leave Jackson standing at the edge of the room and flit around, taking inventory of all the items up for sale. There are so many treasures. Although most of it is far too expensive to even consider purchasing. But there's a set of teacups with missing saucers that would be perfect for a Tea Social we're hosting later in the summer.

I move through the rooms, Jackson at my side, chuckling quietly when I get excited over something I find particularly interesting. I'm nattering on about all the fun things I can make and how I need to come up with something fall-themed for my Etsy store when I realize we've ended up in one of the bedrooms.

"This is like something right out of a fairy tale," I murmur, coming to a stop in the center of the room, under the chandelier. It's made of pink teardrop crystals that refract a million rainbows when the sun shines through a gap in the curtains. The bed is a four-poster king-size masterpiece draped with white gauzy fabric. The comforter is a pale icy blue, the ceiling a darker shade of the same color, like a midnight sky speckled with the Milky Way. The floors are white marble threaded through with gold. Everything about this room screams fantasy.

I cross over to the bed and find the gap in the curtains, running my fingertips gently over the satin sheets, touching rainbows as I go. "When I was a little girl, I wanted to be Cinderella so badly."

"You wanted an evil stepmother and glass slippers?" Jackson asks with a hint of teasing in his tone.

I chuckle. "Not that part. It was the magic of it all, the fairy godmother, the transformation from ordinary to extraordinary."

"There's nothing ordinary about you, London."

"Quirky and extraordinary aren't the same thing." I skim the curtains and round the end of the bed. "Once, our class went to a radio station for some kind of field trip. It was around the holidays, and I think I was maybe six or seven. My teacher's name was Ms. Barrie. She was lovely. Anyway, I had this friend named Candy. She was adorable. All blond curls and blue eyes with this name that fit the holidays, and I was standing beside her when they asked her name, so when they asked me mine, I lied and told them it was Cinderella."

Jackson laughs. "Why did you lie? London is a beautiful name."

"Not when you're a kid. I see London, I see France, I see London's underpants was very popular and annoying when I was growing up."

"Ah yes, I can see that."

"Anyway, Candy outed me and I was mortified. But that year for Christmas, all my presents were Cinderella-themed."

"It sounds like a good Christmas."

"It was. One of the best, really." My parents had found the whole thing hilarious. And despite my embarrassment and how irritated I'd been that my supposed friend had tattled on me on live radio, I grew to love that memory, and the memory of that Christmas, which was distinctly tinged in a Disneyesque light. They'd even gone as far as finding a Cinderella-style dress and my mom gave me a Cinderella makeover. It didn't matter that my hair wasn't the right shade of blond—that was Harley, and she always kept it cropped in a short bob, much to my dismay.

I'm pulled out of my mental musings when my phone buzzes in my purse. It must be hitting something metal or plastic because it's loud and jarring. I rummage around and manage to find it at the bottom of my bag, but it's already gone to voicemail by the time I check the screen. I've missed several messages from Avery and now a phone call. It's already quarter to twelve.

"That's my sister. I'll need to call her back."

"Of course, I'll give you a minute."

Jackson leaves me alone in the bedroom while I dial Avery.

"Why are you in Woodland Park?"

"I'm at an estate sale."

"When are you going to be here? We have an event to set up for, and we're three centerpieces short, and no one can find the linens for the tables! The guests are supposed to start arriving at four-thirty, and the dining room isn't even close to ready!"

Avery isn't usually one to panic, even when we're on a tight timeline. "I'm heading back now. The linens should be in the laundry room. I wanted to freshen them up because it had been a few weeks since we used those ones. They're all pressed and laid out on the table. You'll want the silver and black napkins, alternating. Those are already prepped in the baskets next to the linens."

"A freaking email or a note with all of this information would have been awesome, London. And maybe a little warning that you were taking the morning off to go to an estate sale. Especially on an event day. Harley is almost in tears."

"I'm sorry. I didn't realize how late it was. I'll be there as soon as I can. We're leaving right now."

"We?"

"I'm with Jackson. He knows the family holding the estate sale, so he was able to get us an early appointment. And an introduction to the owner."

"Well, that's just great. I hope your morning of shopping for things we probably don't need is worth it." And with that, she hangs up.

I blow out a breath. Avery's hostility is a frustration I don't need right now.

Especially since she's been MIA lately because she's taking the business of planning her own wedding on like it's a second full-time job.

Which I understand. She wants it to be awesome, and we don't have a mother who can help with any of those things, and Declan's mom is pretty useless.

I step out of the bedroom and into the hallway. Jackson is leaning against the wall, thumbs flying across his phone screen. His gaze flicks up to me. "Everything okay?"

"I didn't realize how late it was. I need to head back so I can help prepare for the event tonight."

"Of course. I should've kept better track of the time."

The only thing I have time to purchase from the estate sale are the teacups. It seems like a bit of a waste, especially since there were other things I would have liked to have laid claim to, but I've already been gone all morning. And we need to stick to a strict budget if we're going to manage the kitchen expansion this fall, which isn't going to be cheap.

I thank Harmon for the opportunity and tell him I hope I'll see him at the Spark House event. Jackson has a brief conversation in low tones that make it impossible to hear what he's saying, and then we're off, heading back to Spark House.

I fire off a message to Harley to make sure she's okay.

I'm fine. Pretty sure it's [shark emoji] week for A tho
[eyeroll]

I frown and send one back that reads:

She said you were in tears?

I get the laughing emoji in response and then suddenly my
phone is ringing. "I'm so sorry, I need to take this."

"Go right ahead. I'm aware I've monopolized more of your
time than I should have on an event day." He smiles, but there's
strain in it and maybe a hint of concern.

I answer the call from Harley. "Any tears I may have shed
were a result of Avery dropping a chair on my freaking foot. She's
a gong show today. And if you tell her I said that, I'll deny it with
vehemence. I think Declan's mom is causing problems with the
wedding, and there was some kind of blowout last night."

"Between her and Declan?" My fingers are at my lips. I drop
my hand to my lap so I don't start biting my nails.

"No, just his mom getting all involved and insisting that if his
dad comes, he's not allowed to bring wife number five or seven
or whatever number he's on. Which means Declan is stressed,
and that in turn stresses Avery out. You know how it is. Especially
with their history and his dad trading in the last wife or whatever.
It's kind of like its own soap opera. I think Ave is low on sleep
and high on stress, and I also think Declan may have suggested
eloping again."

"Oh no."

"Oh yes. Everything is under control here. It's just Avery who isn't at the moment. She's having a day."

"That seems to be more and more frequent lately."

"I know. We need to find a way to convince her that it can't be the three of us running things forever. Mom and Dad may have done it themselves, but Spark House wasn't anything near what it is today. And we can't wait until we have adult kids to help out before that happens. Unless we want to adopt a bunch of sixteen-year-olds with an interest in event hotel management."

I can almost see Harley rubbing the space between her eyes. "Are you okay?"

"Yeah, just venting. It's Avery, and you know how she gets."

"I'm sorry I'm not there to help you run interference." And I truly am. Harley is good at being a level head, but neither of us is particularly experienced with a flustered Avery.

"Eh, it's fine. I gotta go, though, I'll see you soon."

"See you soon." I end the call with a sigh.

"Have I gotten you into trouble by taking you away for the morning?" Jackson's brows pull together.

I don't know how he manages to look even more attractive with a furrow, but he does. I want to run my thumb along the bridge of his nose to smooth it back out and watch it happen all over again.

"It's fine. Everything is under control." It's a lie, but the last thing I need is Jackson realizing that Spark House isn't a perfect utopia.

"It doesn't sound like everything is fine. Is there anything I can do to smooth things over with your sisters?"

"Avery, my older sister, is getting married and she's determined to plan the entire thing herself."

"Is that a bad thing?"

"Typically, no. She's a great event planner. It's honestly her calling in life. However, trying to plan every aspect of your own wedding while running all of these other events at the same time isn't exactly reasonable, and she's in denial about us needing to hire more people to help with the administrative stuff."

"Ah, that can't be easy."

I shake my head. "It's really not. And usually you have a mom to help out, but we don't, and I think that adds an extra layer of conflicted feelings for Avery."

"She has you and your sister, though."

"She does, but it's really not the same. Moms come with life experience and perspective. We've hosted at least fifty weddings over the past few years and seen so many different family dynamics, all the way from the best to the worst. I want her to have this, and I want to be supportive, but I also want to have a life and some breathing room, and I don't feel like I have any of those things right now."

"Is there any way you can make her see how hard this is on you and Harley?"

"I don't know. The only person she listens to other than me and Harley is Declan, her fiancé. But he knows her, probably better than we do. He wouldn't tell her to give up control of Spark House."

"But isn't that what a partner should do? Call you on things that no one else can?"

"Normally, he does. He's really good for her. They're good for each other. Relationship goals and all that. They both love hard."

"And what about you? Do you love hard?"

"I'd do anything for my sisters."

"I don't mean your sisters. I mean in relationships."

When he asks questions like this, it makes me question why he cares. Another mixed signal. "Honestly? I don't think I've ever truly been in love. Not the way they love each other, anyway. That all-consuming, soulful kind of love that has the power to turn your entire world upside down. They broke up for a while, and I'd never seen Avery so devastated. And I've seen her experience enough of life's disappointments to know that he's her penguin."

"Her penguin?"

"Her soulmate. They were meant to be together. I've never been that upset by the ending of a relationship. Sure, I've been sad and looked to Ben & Jerry's and margaritas for comfort, but it wasn't the kind of heartbreak that took months to recover from. Take that guy I was going out with earlier this year—Daniel. The part I was dreading wasn't being alone, it was hurting his feelings. I kept putting it off, thinking maybe something would change and that spark would suddenly happen, but it never did."

"Ah. I see. So, if you'd broken up with him sooner, you might have taken my phone number." I can't tell if he's serious or poking fun at me.

"And then you would have found out firsthand just what a relationship train wreck I am."

"Or maybe we would still be here, and going to this estate sale under different circumstances."

I laugh, but it's high and a little reedy. "Do you want to know what my sisters call me when I'm not in a relationship?"

"What's that?"

"Fun London."

"And what do they call you when you're in a relationship?" He glances at me out of the corner of his eye.

"Serious London."

"And what are the key differences between Fun and Serious London, apart from the obvious?"

"I don't know, but apparently when I'm in a relationship, I'm a real drag."

"Hmm." His tongue peeks out and his lip curls up in a half smile. "Well, you've been pretty fun to be around as far as I'm concerned."

"That's because I'm not in a relationship." I cross my arms, feeling like I've just proven my point.

"I suppose as long as you don't go out with any random guys, you'll remain Fun London."

"Works for me, since I have no intention of dating anyone." I roll my head on my shoulders, trying to figure why everything feels suddenly tight.

"I'm in the same boat, so this should work out well. Especially since I very much enjoy Fun London, and Serious London sounds like she wouldn't be up for surprise estate sales."

"Now you're making fun of me."

"Not at all. I just wonder if it's not necessarily you who is the issue, but the guys you're dating. It's possible that this Fun London is authentically you, and that this serious version is a result of poor matches, but that's a topic for another day." He pulls down the Spark House driveway. "I have a business associate that I'd like to introduce you to next week if you have availability, say on Wednesday? It would be a dinner meeting, and they are very big on networking and conversation, so it would be preferable that you don't have engagements first thing in the morning on Thursday. Do you think that would be something you could manage?"

"Next weekend we have a birthday party on Saturday night, so midweek works perfectly for me."

"Excellent. I'll have Mitchell set everything up and let you know what time on Wednesday."

"That's great. Thank you again for a fun morning."

"Thank you for indulging me." We exit the car, and Jackson retrieves my box of teacups and walks me to the door. "Please extend my apologies to your sisters for keeping you so long. I'd wish you good luck for tonight, but I don't think you need it. I'll see you next week, Fun London."

10

SNEAKY SNEAKY

LONDON

Are you sure you're okay with me going to this dinner meeting and coming in a little on the later side to-morrow?" I ask for what must be the hundredth time. The question is directed at Avery. I already know Harley is more than fine with it.

"We're sure," Harley replies.

I stop leafing through the stack of papers on my desk and glance at my sisters, focusing on Avery.

"I'm sorry I freaked out last weekend. It won't happen again, and I'm one hundred percent sure that I'm okay with this whole thing." Avery has the decency to look chagrined. "Including you not being here first thing tomorrow morning."

We had a bit of a blowout when I got back to Spark House after my morning with Jackson at the estate sale. Avery was angry that I'd gone at all, and I reminded her that she's been taking off plenty of time for emergency wedding stuff. My meeting with

Jackson was meant to help our event hotel and make things easier for us, not more of a challenge. I once again suggested that we need more help on the admin side of things, which, as expected, did not go over well.

We had to put a pin in the argument because of the event that was starting, and I got the cold shoulder for the rest of the night. We haven't come back to it since then, but we'll have to eventually. Part of me hopes that while I'm at this dinner, something happens to make her see what Harley and I already know—we're getting too big for just the three of us to manage.

"I've left a list of the things that need to be tackled this afternoon, but you can message or call if you need anything or if anyone has questions." I slide a folder to the edge of my desk with all the files on our weekend event.

"We've got it handled," Avery replies. She's determined to prove we don't need extra help.

"Yup. We're good to go here." Harley gives me the thumbs-up while grinning at Avery.

"What's this about?" I motion to their faces. They've been acting strangely all morning. "Why are you being all weird about this?"

Harley drops her arms to her sides. "We're being supportive, not weird. You've pretty much taken care of everything, so Avery and I are going to look at bridesmaid dresses that aren't in team colors."

Avery rolls her eyes. "Blue and maroon aren't a bad combination."

"On a jersey," Harley and I say at the same time.

"The flowers could be in team colors," I suggest. "And the centerpieces. I can mock something up for you tonight when I'm back from the meeting," I offer.

"You probably won't have time for that tonight," Avery says.

She has a point. I'll be at a dinner meeting this evening, and I'll be missing this afternoon to prepare for the meeting and go over some paperwork, so there will be emails to tackle later. "Tomorrow night, then." I slide the folder into my bag, along with my laptop and tablet, then I glance at the time. I should be leaving for Denver shortly.

"How do I look?" I smooth my hands over my hips. I'm wearing a simple, classic black dress paired with rose-gold heels. I have one of my versatile and functional oversize purses, also in rose gold, which holds all the things I'll need for this meeting.

"Fantastic," my sisters say in unison.

My phone pings, and I pick it up off my desk and check the message. It's Jackson, letting me know there's been a slight change of plans and that he'll be at Spark House momentarily.

"Why in the world is he coming here?" I mutter.

"What's going on?" Harley asks.

"I have no idea. Jackson is apparently coming to pick me up, which doesn't make a lot of sense if the meeting is in Denver." I sling my bag over my shoulder and blow out an anxious breath.

"Maybe he wanted the time to brief you?" Avery suggests.

"Maybe." It still doesn't quite add up. "I guess now I'll have time to get information out of him about the company we're meeting with." Jackson has been vague about who exactly we're having dinner with. He mentioned that they're in the hospitality business and that it would be informal, more of a preliminary introduction, but that they're interested in learning more about Spark House.

Every time I asked for more information, he would tell me

not to worry about it. That I'm a natural and I should just relax. Easier said than done.

My sisters flank me down the hall. "What are you doing?"

"Walking you out." Harley slips her arm through mine.

I narrow my eyes at her. "Why?"

"Because we're just as curious as you." Harley smiles up at me and bats her lashes innocently.

"You just want to check out Jackson."

"We absolutely do," Avery agrees.

"You get to spend most of the day with him. We should at least get a hit of the eye candy," Harley agrees.

It's my turn to roll my eyes. "You two are ridiculous."

"Are we really, though? Declan will always be a ten in my book, but I feel like it should rain glitter every time Jackson enters a room." Coming from Avery, that's high praise. She hates glitter and thinks the sun rises and sets on Declan.

We step out onto the front porch just as the driver's side door of a very nice hybrid SUV opens and out steps Jackson's driver. His nametag reads Clint, and he greets me as Ms. Spark and opens the rear passenger door. Jackson's head appears, followed by the rest of him.

"Good grief, he's yummy," Harley mutters.

"It should be illegal to be that delicious," Avery murmurs.

"Okay! Time for me to go!" I say in a high-pitched squeaky voice more fitting to the mice in *Cinderella*. Which is sort of how I feel right now—not like the mouse, but more like Cinderella. Except I'm being swept off to a meeting in an environmentally friendly SUV, not a pumpkin-turned-horse-drawn carriage. And I'm not wearing a ball gown either.

My sisters wave hello to Jackson, hug me again, and tell me to have fun and knock 'em dead. I cross the driveway and greet Jackson with a nervous smile and a stomach full of excited hummingbirds.

"Sorry about the change of plans." Jackson smiles and slips his finger under the strap of my purse, lifting it from my shoulder.

"It's fine. Is everything okay?"

His gaze moves over my face, and I feel it like gentle fingers brushing over my skin. "Everything's fine." He passes my bag to Clint and offers me his hand.

This time, I anticipate the jolt of energy that passes through my body when I slip my fingers into his palm. In fact, I breathe out an inaudible sigh at the contact. It's like drinking liquid chocolate—a double dose of caffeine and sinful sweetness.

"I'll see you later!" I call out as I duck into the SUV.

"Don't rush back!" Avery says with a wide grin.

"Take care of London for us!" Harley shouts.

I shake my head and shimmy over to make room for Jackson. The SUV has double bench seats. Jackson slides in and takes the seat opposite me, so we're facing each other.

I buckle in and brace myself as Clint sets my purse on the seat beside me and closes the door, shutting me into the confined space with Jackson.

"Does the change of plans happen to include another estate sale?" I smooth my hands over my thighs and cross my legs.

"I'm afraid not, but I promise this should be just as much fun."

His smile makes my insides feel like a gooey toasted marshmallow. I really need to get a handle on this teen girl style crush I have going on.

Clint turns the SUV around, and we head down the driveway, turning right onto the road leading toward Denver.

I try my best not to fidget, or stare at Jackson, or inhale too deeply. His cologne is mouthwateringly delicious, his crisp dark suit tailored to fit him like a classy second skin, and his dark hair is parted at the side and styled perfectly. Not a hair out of place. Everything about him screams sophistication.

What I like most about him, though, is that under that very polished exterior is a man who likes to genuinely have fun. Estate sales have always been something I enjoy, but with Jackson, it was that much more of an adventure. He's an adventure. I'd forgotten what it was like to authentically enjoy spending time with someone who wasn't one of my sisters. It feels effortless, natural. Which makes the fact that we're stuck in the business associate friend zone that much crappier. Maybe it's better that way, because my romantic relationships tend to fizzle like sparklers in the rain.

We make idle chitchat, with me waiting for an opportunity to ask him to explain what the change in plans are and why he picked me up instead of me driving to Denver.

"Oh, I don't think you ever responded, but the flower arrangement made to look like a soccer ball seems to be perfect for Avery's wedding," he says.

Jackson and I routinely message each other when we're working in our Google Doc. I find it's the one place where I don't feel all awkward about our conversations, and we can have easy chats, and I can poke fun at him with comments about our lists. This morning, he sent me a picture of a bouquet that looks like a soccer ball.

"I'm not carrying a soccer ball down the aisle."

"It's not a soccer ball. It's a bouquet that looks like a soccer ball, and Avery's wedding isn't about you, London. It's about her and her love of sports."

"It's also about Declan. Why in the world were you looking at flower arrangements this morning, anyway?"

"I was looking at some of the centerpiece options from your Etsy site, and I went down a rabbit hole that included soccer ball flower arrangements."

His phone pings with an alert, and he apologizes while he checks the message.

I pretend to look out the window when really, I'm staring at Jackson's profile in the dark glass. At least until I realize that we're no longer headed toward the city. We pass a sign indicating that we're about five miles from a private airfield. "Where exactly is this meeting?"

"Hmm?" Jackson slips his phone into his inside pocket and smiles distractedly.

"I thought the meeting was in the city."

"It is."

"Then why are we heading toward an airfield and not Denver?"

"Because we won't make it to the meeting on time if we drive." He clasps his hands in his lap and smiles innocently at me.

I narrow my eyes. "What city is the meeting in?"

"New York." He busies himself with buttoning his suit jacket. It makes the muscles in his arms flex distractingly.

"Is this the minor change in plans?"

"No. I thought I told you about the location."

"Uh no, Jackson, you failed to mention this meeting was halfway across the country. If this isn't the change in plans, what the heck is?"

"Hmm. Are you sure I didn't mention it? Maybe you weren't paying attention? You have had a lot on your plate recently," he muses.

I'm somewhere between flabbergasted and offended. "I always pay attention. Always. I'm meticulous when it comes to details!"

His smile widens and his eyes twinkle. I want to poke him in one, because he clearly enjoys seeing me flustered. "This is true most of the time. It must have slipped my mind. It's a short flight, and we'll be back early tomorrow morning."

"Early tomorrow morning?" I need to stop repeating everything he says to me. "All I have is my purse. I don't have a change of clothes, or makeup, or a brush. Or anything."

"All of those things have already been taken care of." He's so matter of fact. I can't decide if it's alluring or infuriating or both.

I cross my arms. "What do you mean *they've been taken care of*?" I ask, attempting to imitate his voice.

"I cleared it with your sisters ahead of time. Harley packed you a bag with all of the things she thought you would need for an overnight."

"Wait a second, you pulled my sisters into this? They already know? And you had Harley pack me a bag? That means she had to go through my underwear drawer!"

"Does she have a particularly strong aversion to your underwear drawer?" The way his gaze moves over me is both stimulating and frustrating.

I don't know why I felt the need to mention my underwear,

but now that we're on the topic, I can't seem to stop. "She's my sister. We live together. There are boundaries, and touching my underwear should be one of them. And my underwear drawer has other *things* in it." *Oh my God, London, shut up about your underwear drawer.* I wave a hand around trying to erase my words. "That's not the point. They know I hate surprises!"

"To be fair, I was unaware of your extreme dislike of surprises."

Now I know why my sisters were acting so weird this morning, and why Harley was up so early and told me to go on ahead to Spark House without her and that Avery would pick her up. "What if all she packed were pajamas? What am I going to do then?" I can see her doing something like that. Packing lacy business, thinking she's being funny.

I can tell he's fighting a smile. "Whatever you need, I can have picked up for you. I gave her a list of things I thought you might need. We can go over it right now if you like." He plucks his phone from his pocket again. Apparently he's serious about reviewing the list.

"You made her a list? Were underwear even on it?" I need to stop coming back to that point.

"I thought they were an unspoken essential," he says while smirking. "And like I said, if you don't have something you need, it can be picked up for you."

I pin him with what I hope is an unimpressed glare. "You do realize this isn't how it works for the rest of the world, right? We don't just make phone calls and things magically appear."

"Well, to be fair, London, there won't be any real magic involved. I'll have Aylin go to an actual store and pick these items up."

"Aylin?" What is this hot feeling creeping up my spine?

"My personal shopper. Since our meeting is this evening, I suggested Harley pack you casual wear for the trip home. Is there a store that you'd prefer I send Aylin to?"

"You don't need to send her anywhere if Harley packed me a bag."

"Well, you seem concerned about her packing skills. I want to make sure you have what you need, so I don't think it hurts to be extra prepared."

"I don't see the point in sending Aylin shopping just to be extra prepared," I grumble.

"Would you like to check your bag to make sure you have what you need for the evening?"

"Sure. Yes. I can do that."

We pull into the parking lot of a private airport. I already knew Jackson had his own plane, but I never actually believed I'd fly in it.

As if he can hear my thoughts, he says, "I fly commercial as often as possible, but I'm aware that we're on a tight schedule and I didn't want to tie you up for unnecessary hours at the airport, so we're taking my private jet instead."

"That was considerate of you," I murmur as the car stops close to a small Gulfstream. I stumbled on an article in my Jackson Holt research that focused on the fact that he had a private jet built for him that is currently the most green plane in the US.

The passenger side door opens, and Jackson motions for me to go first. I give him the side-eye, aware all of this is intentional, but I can't call him on it right now. I unfasten my seat belt, gather my purse, and take the offered hand of Clint as I step out into the warm summer day. I breathe in the scent of hot tarmac and jet fuel.

Jackson exits the car, and Clint pops the trunk, revealing two small suitcases, one being my own. Jackson steps back and turns his attention away from the SUV while I unzip my suitcase and check the contents. I also now know where my favorite pajama set went. I was looking for it last night. I'm grateful that Harley did a fantastic job packing for this trip, and I have pretty much everything I could possibly need. I zip my case back up, and Clint steps forward to take it from me, and Jackson motions for me to go ahead of him onto the plane.

I have no less than a million questions about what exactly is happening. Where in the world are we staying tonight? A hotel? His place in New York? Spending the night in the same vicinity will be a test of my personal restraint. He's temptation wrapped in candy bacon and tied with shoestring grape licorice. Which sounds disgusting together, but individually they're delicious.

Once we're in the air, our flight attendant brings us glasses of sparkling water and a small cheese and fruit plate. There isn't much in the way of privacy in here. I'm torn between being impressed and annoyed.

I cross my arms. "I don't understand why you didn't tell me this meeting was in New York ahead of time!"

He sets his water down, giving me his full attention. "Let me ask you a question, London."

I pop a grape in my mouth and motion for him to go ahead.

"If I'd told you the meeting was in New York, would you have been as likely to agree to it?"

"What kind of question is that?"

"A realistic one. Your schedule is always full. You always have a thousand things going on, and you're constantly juggling a million projects. I called your sister to make sure I wasn't taking you away when you were needed at Spark House. I even suggested that I tell you, but she thought it would be better if it were a surprise. And I have to say, I think she was right. If I had told you this was an overnight trip, you would have said you couldn't go."

It's hard to argue with him on that. I definitely would not have agreed to flying to New York, not with how tense things have been with Avery, or how busy we are at Spark House. "I can't believe Harley was able to keep a lid on this. She's terrible with secrets."

"I called yesterday when the person I want you to meet had to cancel their plans to come out here. I wanted to make sure it would all work out okay. I realize it was slightly devious on my part. However, the potential benefit of this meeting definitely overshadows your dislike of surprises. The point of all of this is that I think this introduction will be a really great opportunity for you, and I didn't want you to miss out on it. I've seen you talk about Spark House and know if anyone could sell someone on it, you can. You mentioned wanting to expand without working yourself to the bone and forgetting that you have a life outside of work. This is how we make more time for the things we want, rather than getting bogged down in the minutiae."

"I appreciate the sentiment behind it, and I don't mean to sound ungrateful." I blow out a breath and deflate a little. "I'm just . . ."

"Nervous?" he supplies.

"I don't enjoy curveballs."

"I know. Which is why I predicted that you wouldn't agree to this meeting even if I'd given you fair warning. I decided to take my chances and risk a little of your wrath, which, if I'm going to be completely honest, I actually don't mind being on the receiving end of." He grins.

I roll my eyes and shake my head. "You're too much."

"Better than being not enough, I suppose." There's something in his tone, a hint of vulnerability, maybe.

We arrive in New York in the early evening. We're met by yet another car and immediately whisked off. I wish I could do something with my hands to keep them busy, but instead, I clasp them tightly in my lap and try not to think too much about what tonight will bring. If Jackson has shown me anything, it's that he's full of surprises.

"Is everything okay?" Jackson asks.

"Of course, why?"

"Because I asked you if you're hungry and you made a noise that sounded like a yes, but when I offered you options, all you did was make the same sound."

"I'm sorry." And embarrassed. "I'm just a little nervous about this meeting. Normally I'll review my notes about the company before I meet with a potential sponsor, and I haven't been able to do that because I don't know who they are."

"You won't need your notes for this, but you'll have a bit of time to look them over when we get to my apartment."

"Right. Okay." I want to ask if we're stopping there, or staying there, but I don't want to sound ungrateful for this opportunity. One he's gone to a lot of trouble to secure. "It makes sense that we'd go to your place here since New York is your home." I might as well put on a Captain Obvious cape and call it a day.

We pull into the underground parking lot, and once again, the driver opens the door for me. Jackson's suitcase appears, as does mine, and we head toward the elevators. They're emblazoned with the Mills Hotel logo. Not only do they run some of the most opulent and beautiful hotels in the world, they also own some of the most gorgeous high-end apartments.

My heart is in my throat, and I can feel heat creeping up my spine as we step into the elevator. I'm not sure why I'm this nervous. I've spent lots of time with Jackson over the past few weeks. Enough that I feel as though we're forming some kind of friendship along with our working relationship. My stomach dips when we reach the penthouse floor and the doors slide open, revealing a high-ceilinged hallway with several doors. The two directly in front of us are labeled with *Penthouse A* and *Apartment B*. Jackson heads for the penthouse and I follow. He opens the door by pressing his thumb to the sensor pad and ushers me inside.

The floors are pale gray and polished to a shine. The walls are stark white, and every accent is navy or dark wood. It's stunning and minimalist, and looks more like a model home than that anyone lives here.

"This is beautiful."

"I've been told it lacks personality."

I laugh. "It's clutter-free. Which I can appreciate. Harley is a human hurricane and leaves stuff pretty much everywhere."

"You're kind. And a bit of a liar, which I also appreciate." He smiles and unbuttons his suit jacket.

My stomach flutters. I wish I weren't so affected by him. It would be a lot easier to maintain my composure and keep my head out of the clouds and on my shoulders where it's supposed to be. "I'm not lying. I do think it's beautiful, and I can appreciate minimalism. How often do you stay here?"

He shrugs out of his suit jacket and tosses it over the arm of a chair. I wonder if it will still be there when we come through this room again, or whether one of the people who works for him will make it disappear.

"Maybe a week a month. I don't see the point in adding clutter when I'm not here that often, but I realize that most of the space is impersonal." He checks his watch. "Dinner isn't for an hour yet. Would you like a tour?"

"Sure. That would be great." I'll take any opportunity to dig a little deeper and find out more about the man behind the suits and the worn jeans and old T-shirts.

He walks me through the living room, which is cavernous. One wall is floor-to-ceiling windows with a stunning view of the city, and in the distance is Brooklyn. In the center of the huge room is a white couch, a table, and chairs. All pristine, boxy, and minimalist.

"Can I ask you something?"

"Of course. I'm an open book." He leans against a pillar.

I give him an arched brow.

At least he has the decency to smile and shrug. "Let me amend that. For you, I will try my best to be an open book."

"How many times have you sat in this living room?"

He glances at the couch. "A few."

"So three?"

"Give or take, I suppose."

"How long have you had this place?"

"A few years."

"So this couch gets your attention once a year?" I run my finger along the buttery smooth fabric.

"On the upside, it's going to last for a long time."

"Probably well past its ability to be fashionable," I tease.

"To be fair, this place is four thousand square feet of living space, and I do share it with my friend Trent, who lives in Jersey, so it's very possible he's taken the opportunity to appreciate the view of the city from here." He crosses the room, drops down on the couch, and pats the seat.

I round the arm and expect to sink into it, but it's basically like sitting on a pretty rock covered in leather. Jackson shifts around and stretches out his arm, his expression turning into a grimace. "Well." He taps the edge of the couch. "I think we know why this couch has been sat on so rarely."

"You obviously didn't choose it for comfort."

"I didn't choose it at all. The only rooms in this place that I had any input in were the kitchen, the music room, my office, and my bedroom."

"Well then, skip the rest of the tour and show me those." I stand and wait for Jackson to do the same.

Our next stop is the kitchen, which is a chef's wet dream.

I run my hand over the formed concrete counters, taking in the sleek lines and beautiful white cabinets, the stainless steel appliances, and the amazing prep space. "It's too bad we're only staying the night. I would pretty much give up a pinkie finger to cook a meal in here."

Jackson leans on the counter, watching me as I circle the room. "There's always breakfast."

"How early are we leaving tomorrow?"

"As early as you need. I know you have to be back in a timely manner so you're able to prepare for your event."

"I'm usually awake by five. Even with the time change, there's a good chance I'll still be up early."

"I'm the same way. Always up before the sun rises even if I went to bed a few hours before it comes up."

"I can make Crêpes Suzette. If you have the ingredients, that is." I want to open the fridge and see what's inside. If anything at all.

"I'll make sure we're stocked and have everything you need."

I squeal and clap. "I'm so excited! My kitchen at home is just so . . . basic, and this one is amazing. Can I look in your cupboards and see what all you have? Then I can make a list?"

"You can, but it's unnecessary since I've already sent a request to Aylin, who's gone to pick everything up." He holds up his phone before slipping it back into his pocket.

"Just like that, huh?" I snap my fingers.

He smiles. "Just like that."

"Does everyone say how high when you say jump?"

"You don't. You said yourself you wouldn't have agreed to this meeting if I'd told you where it took place."

"Because it's halfway across the country."

"Hence me tricking you into coming." He arches a brow.

"So you admit that it was all a ruse!"

"I did what I had to do to get you here. I feel no remorse whatsoever, especially not when I'm getting Crêpes Suzette out of the deal."

I can feel my face heating up. "You're too much."

"Still better than not enough."

It's the second time he's said that. There's something in his tone, I can't quite put my finger on it.

"Anyway." He raps on the counter twice. "Let me show you the other rooms that actually have a bit of personality to them." He inclines his head and motions toward the hallway. Even the hallways are wide, the ceilings so high, the clip of my heels echo. He opens a set of heavy wood doors.

Our next stop is the music room. It's stunning and very different from the rest of the house. Nothing in here is white or gray or navy. The colors are warm and inviting, everything trimmed in luxurious wood finishes. But the real showstopper is the antique, wooden, carved grand piano in the center of the room. "Do you play?"

"When I was younger, yes." He slips his hands in his pockets, and I get the sense that I'm seeing a part of his world that not many are granted access to.

"My grandmother used to play. I tried to learn but I have butter fingers." I wiggle them in the air and cross over to the magnificent piece of art. "Is it okay if I touch it?" I'm all breathy, and I can feel the heat climbing up my spine, aware it will invariably make it to my cheeks. I wish I weren't so easy to fluster. "It looks like an antique," I add to explain my request for permission.

"It is an antique. It was my mother's, actually."

"Was it passed down over the generations?"

He gives his head a small shake. "Would you believe that someone was getting rid of it at a garage sale of all places?"

"No! Did they have any idea what it was worth?" I might not play the piano anymore, but I'm certainly aware that this is a gem and could cover my living expenses for at least three years.

"I don't think my parents even realized what it was worth until after we got it home. It took up most of our living room. At the time, we lived in an eight-hundred-square-foot house. They had to remove the sliding glass doors to get it inside, but she loved it, and my dad loved her, so it became a centerpiece, if you will."

Looking at the size of it, I can't imagine that it would have fit easily into a small home. "It's beautiful. He must have loved her very much." I run my fingers along the detailed woodwork. I have the urge to sit down on the bench and play something, although I can probably only remember "Twinkle, Twinkle, Little Star" at this point, which hardly does something like this justice.

"He did. More than anything. He only survived a few days after she passed. Like he'd been waiting for her to go first, so he didn't have to leave her to suffer on her own."

"I'm so sorry. I can't imagine how hard that must have been."

"They fought to stay as long as they could. I think that was the most painful part of it. Watching my parents struggle through treatments, radiation, whatever options were available, eating up their savings, and realizing it wasn't a battle they were going to win. But they hadn't wanted to leave each other. Or me."

He's quiet for a moment before he continues. "But by that time, I was already an adult. Legal to vote. Able to take care of myself. And in all honesty I had been, for a lot of years already. They staggered their radiation and chemotherapy so they were never going through it at the same time, but neither one was really in any shape to take care of the other."

"The responsibility fell on you."

"We had a nurse's aide who would come and help with the things I couldn't or shouldn't, in order to preserve my parents' dignity."

I take a step toward him. "I can't even fathom, Jackson."

"You shouldn't try. I apologize. This is a rather heavy topic and not at all the reason I showed you this room."

"Don't apologize." I reach out and touch his arm, just a brief contact. "Thank you for sharing that with me. I understand what it's like to lose parents far earlier than you'd expect. It leaves scars on the heart. Sometimes we need to share those memories to help them heal."

He gives me a small smile. "I generally don't talk about it. It seems to be a character flaw of mine."

"You're talking about it with me, so maybe it isn't the flaw you think it to be."

He makes a sound, somewhere between a little laugh and a hum. "Come." His fingertips skim my shoulder, and he inclines his head toward the door. "There's more to see."

I fall into step beside him, trying to stay in the moment when all I can think about is the fact that I had the perfect opportunity to offer him comfort that wasn't just verbal. I could have hugged him. Should have, even. Maybe. There's something about Jackson, how easy it can be to lower my guard with him and just enjoy his company, and every once in a while, I get a rare glimpse of vulnerability. That's the side I want to see more of. The side that seems most authentically him. Those little tidbits of information he drops like bread crumbs. Each piece helps solve the puzzle of a man.

"London." Jackson's fingers wrap around my wrist and a buzz zings through my veins, making the hair on my scalp prickle.

I startle and spin around. The floors are polished and slippery. I'm not particularly clumsy, but I don't have the athletic genes Avery does. I stutter-step in order to avoid tripping and end up chest-to-chest with Jackson. I grab onto his shoulder to keep from mashing my face against his tie.

His other hand settles on my waist. "Whoa. You okay?"

"I'm so sorry. I'm not usually a space cadet."

"I'm very aware you're not." He smiles wryly. "But I'm guessing you're a little preoccupied, what with the meeting coming up soon. Maybe we should save the rest of the tour for later. After the business matters are dealt with."

I'd completely forgotten about the meeting, which causes my embarrassment to ratchet up a few notches. "Maybe that would be a good idea." And so would stepping out of his personal space bubble, because right now all I can focus on is the feel of his hand still wrapped around my waist and how I'd like to get closer, wrap my arms around him, and give him the hug I should have back in the music room.

"I'll take you to your accommodations, then."

"My accommodations." I blink twice. "Right. Yes. Thank you."

I step back as he drops his hand and releases my wrist. My blood feels like rushing rapids in my veins. Jackson's smile wavers the tiniest bit, but he motions down the hall, back the way we came. I follow him, making sure I keep a little distance between us so I'm not at risk of touching him. Again.

We leave the penthouse, and he pulls out a keycard for Apartment B. "This will be your room for the night. I hope it suits your tastes."

"I'm sure it will," I murmur and brush by him, my heart thundering in my chest as I cross the threshold and the lights come on, dim at first, and slowly brightening.

It resembles an upscale hotel room, complete with a small kitchenette and a bathroom.

The walls are white, the floors dark wood, the bedframe is feminine, and the comforter is a pale, icy blue. Gray and black accent pillows dot the comforter, and several vases of flowers are placed strategically around the room. The chandelier in the middle of the ceiling reminds me of diamonds and teardrops. "This is beautiful."

"I'm glad you approve." He crosses the room and touches a sensor by the windows. "I entertain business associates often, and I realize it could be awkward to have people stay with me."

The blinds retract, providing a stunning view of the city. The sun reflects off the windows of the skyscrapers, lighting up the backdrop. I can understand from this vantage point why people love New York City so much. The lines and the architecture are incredible from this high up. "Wow, this view is amazing."

He nods. "My bedroom faces the other side of the city, so I get the sunrise, but both views are equally appealing." He rocks back on his heels and glances toward the foot of the bed, where my small suitcase sits. "Everything you need should be there, or in the closet or the bathroom. If you're missing anything at all, or there's something you require, Aylin has left her card for you, so you can contact her directly." He rubs the back of his neck, the first thing he's done to signal anything but poise.

"Thank you, that was very thoughtful."

He smiles faintly and nods, gaze moving around the room before it settles on me again. "I'll leave you to freshen up, and if you want to review anything prior to the meeting, I'm available."

"That would be great."

He leaves the keycard to the apartment on the table and opens the door. "I'm just a text message away if you need anything."

"Thank you, Jackson."

He smiles, and it looks impish. "Thank you for always being up for adventure, even when I keep you in the dark about it." He closes the door behind him, leaving me with a racing heart and more questions than answers.

11

WHAT IS THIS LIFE?

LONDON

I blow out a breath and drop down on the edge of the bed, flopping back. "Holy hell, this man is too much to handle," I mutter. I notice a small note card sitting on the night-stand and pick it up.

It has Jackson's company logo on the front. On the back is the phrase: "Made from 100% recycled paper." I smile and flip it open. The writing is unfamiliar.

Dear Ms. Spark,
If you require any additional items during your stay in New York, please don't hesitate to contact me. I'm at your service for any and all of your personal needs.

Best,
Aylin

Faint buzzing comes from my purse so I rummage around to find my phone. I should not be surprised that it's my sisters, video calling me. I adopt an unimpressed expression and answer. "You two have a lot of explaining to do."

Harley and Avery are sitting at the common table in the office. If I had to guess, Harley is sitting crisscross applesauce. "You can totally thank us later. How was the flight? Where are you staying? Tell us everything."

"The flight was fine. We took his Gulfstream, which was an experience." Small planes are a slightly louder, bumpier ride, but it was still nice. Particularly considering the company.

"But a good experience, right?" Harley wrings her hands before dropping them to her lap under the table.

"Yes, it was a good experience. I can't believe you kept this a secret." Harley usually has a terrible poker face, and she's bad at lying. It's not that she would willingly share a secret, it's just that she can't hold back her excitement.

"It wasn't easy," Harley admits. "Where are you staying? Do you know where you're going for dinner?"

"I have my own apartment beside his penthouse. It's in one of those Mills buildings. And I'm not sure where we're going for dinner. Mostly I'm just trying to stay focused and be prepared for this meeting." Which I still know very little about, so the last part is a challenge.

Harley does me a solid and changes the subject. "Did I do okay packing for you?"

I unzip my suitcase and go through the contents, carefully this time. "You get an A-plus on packing," I tell her. I notice that she's packed my peach chiffon dress and muted gray heels.

"Awesome. I wasn't sure how much time you'd have when you got there, so I tried to be thorough."

"Speaking of time." I check the clock. It's already six thirty.

"I still need to go over my presentation and get ready for dinner."

"Why don't you go over it while you freshen up?"

While I fix my makeup, my sisters listen to me go over the details of the event at Spark House. They also convince me to change into the peach dress. Since I've been wearing the black one all day and flew across the country in it, I agree.

At seven, I leave my room and am about to message Jackson to let him know I'm in the foyer, when I see that he's sitting on the small couch outside the elevator. He pushes to a stand. His hand smooths over his chest, and he adjusts the front of his suit jacket.

His eyes move over me, and he smiles when his gaze pauses at my bag, hanging off my left shoulder. "You look lovely."

"So do you." I shake my head. "I mean you look dashing not lovely. Or handsome. Handsomely dashing." Geez, what is this, 1900? I sound like I just stepped out of the pages of one of my grandmother's beloved historical romance novels.

His grin widens as he crosses the foyer. And once again, he slips his finger under the strap of my huge purse and lifts it from my shoulder. I grip the bag, mortified by the idea that he feels the need to carry it for me.

"I have it."

His eyes twinkle with amusement. "You won't be needing all of this tonight." He tugs the strap.

I tighten my grip on my purse. "But it's a meeting, and I have to present, so I'll need all of these things."

His smile and his eyes soften, and his hands settle on my shoulders, which are mostly bare because this dress has thin straps. The way his thumbs sweep back and forth over my skin is distracting and disarming. "It's not that kind of dinner meeting, London. Tonight, you're just going to enjoy yourself."

"But it's a business dinner."

"It is, but you just need to be you. You don't need this entire arsenal to sell them on Spark House. You can leave this all behind."

The idea of not having my presentation materials gives me heart palpitations. But he's adamant I don't bring it. "I'll just bring my clutch, then."

"Of course." He nods and gives me a moment to root through the bag until I find the small clutch that pairs with the dress I'm wearing. It contains my phone, lipstick, and a small compact so I can freshen up in the bathroom when necessary. I have to leave behind my star strips, but that's inevitable. They were just in the bag because they always are. I leave my purse in my room, and we step into the elevator.

"Are you going to tell me where we're going for dinner?" I ask when we're on the way down to the lobby.

Jackson leans against the mirrored glass, still wearing an infuriatingly delicious smile. "We're not leaving the building."

"Oh?"

"There's a steak and seafood house here. They have a fabulous charcuterie board appetizer."

"Do you have an addiction to charcuterie boards that you need to deal with?"

"No. They just happen to usually have all the things I love on them."

"I'm not eating finger foods during a business meeting."

"You've eaten finger foods multiple times in front of me."

"Because you ordered them."

"Hmm." He taps his lip. "Good point. I'm sure there will be future opportunities."

I don't have a lot of reasons to fly to New York, but I keep that to myself.

When we reach the lobby, I fall into step beside Jackson. Even with heels on, he has several inches on me. I feel very much as if I've just been put under a microscope as eyes shift in our direction when we pass.

As we approach the entrance to the restaurant, a familiar man steps forward to greet us. It's the same man who came into the conference room for Jackson when he crashed my meeting with Mitchell and Tish.

"Trent? What are you doing here?" Jackson allows his friend to pull him in for a half-handshake-half-hug.

Trent gives him a curious smile. "Same reason you are. I'm here for dinner."

Jackson takes a step back, his brow pulled into a furrow. "Are you meeting someone? Why would you come all the way from Jersey to eat here? Do you have a date? I'm staying in the penthouse tonight."

Trent laughs. "Don't worry, man, I'm not here on a date." His gaze flicks briefly to me and then back to Jackson. "I haven't been home. I had a few things to take care of in the city and I ran into Lincoln at the gym. He mentioned dinner, and I'm never one to turn down an invitation. Especially not when it means I get to meet the woman my best friend can't stop talking about." Trent turns to me; his expression holds curiosity and a hint of mischief as he extends a hand. "We haven't been formally introduced, although we have met a couple of times in passing. I'm Trent, Jackson's friend and trusty sidekick."

I take his hand, even more nervous than I was before. It's one thing to be flown across the country for a business dinner, and completely another to meet Jackson's best friend. This whole thing feels like a test I didn't even know I was taking. I smile, hoping it doesn't look strained. "It's such a pleasure to finally meet you. Jackson speaks very highly of you."

"Likewise." His gaze stays locked on mine for a few seconds, assessing before he finally drops my hand. "We should head inside. Don't want to keep the boys waiting."

I have no idea who the boys are. Or who this Lincoln person is.

We're met by the host, who addresses Jackson as "Mr. Holt" and leads us through the empty restaurant. I want to ask Jackson why there's no one else here, at least until I spot the table in the center of the restaurant occupied by two men. They stand at the same time, their movements almost synchronous. Judging by their faces, they must be related. I'd go as far to say they could be twins, but as we get closer, I notice the gray flirting at the temples of the slightly shorter one, along with a few crinkles in the corners of his eyes when he smiles.

"Jackson, man, it's been a hot minute," the shorter one, who's on Jackson's side, extends his hand, and when Jackson takes it, the man pulls him in for a back pat and a hug.

"Nice to see you again, Trent," the other man says before he turns to me. He looks like Adonis come to life and smiles warmly, extending his hand to me. "You must be London Spark. I'm Lincoln, but you can call me Linc."

"I am. It's such a pleasure to meet you, Linc." I wish someone would use a last name so I would have a hope of piecing together why he seems familiar.

"Pleasure is all mine. Jackson has had nothing but great things to say about you and your event hotel."

"Oh, well, that's kind. We're just a small family-run hotel, nothing as elaborate or stunning as this." I motion to our surroundings. "But we've worked hard to get where we are, and we're excited to see it flourish, particularly with our partnership with Holt Media."

Linc's smile turns knowing as his gaze slides from me to Jackson and back again. "Well, he certainly thinks highly of you. I can count on one hand the number of times he's brought someone this far for a meeting with us. Apart from this guy." He thumbs over his shoulder at Trent. "And he mostly comes just for the free food."

"And the excellent company," Trent replies.

"It really is quite an honor." I will my cheeks not to turn red.

The other man turns his attention to me, and Jackson and Linc exchange back pats and hellos. "Griffin. I'm Lincoln's cousin. It's great to meet you, London. I'm sorry you're stuck with just us guys tonight, but you'll get a chance to meet our better halves in a couple of months at Jackson's charity event here in New York, I'm sure." He motions between himself and Lincoln.

"Oh, I don't—"

"How are Wren and Cosy?" Jackson interrupts.

Trent and I both look at Jackson, who is very much focused on Linc and Griffin.

Linc drags his attention away from me, although he too has questions in his eyes.

"Great. They would have loved to have been here, but Wren

volunteers at the hospital once a week when we're not traveling, and Cosy went with her," Griffin says, eyes doing the same volley between me and Jackson.

"She's been doing that for a long time, hasn't she?" Jackson says.

"She has. It's been a passion project, and she misses it when we're traveling."

Lincoln pulls out a chair for me, and Jackson takes the one beside mine. The cousins take the two chairs on either side of me and Jackson, putting Trent between them. Griffin takes the one closer to me and Linc the one next to Jackson. As I settle into my chair, the server appears and offers us sparkling or still water before they ask if we'd like something to drink, and then addresses Griffin and Linc as Mr. Mills and Mr. Moorehead.

Which is when it finally clicks who I'm sitting at the table with.

The oldest of the Mills brothers. Of Mills Hotels. And Lincoln Moorehead, the CEO of Moorehead Media. A hotel mogul and a media mogul. I want to say something to Jackson, like a little warning would have been nice. I'm sitting in a room with some of the most powerful businessmen in the continental US. It's a bit intimidating and awe-inspiring.

There is literally nothing I can do about it apart from tamp down my nerves and try not to drink an entire liter of sparkling water because my mouth is dry from the sudden anxiety of it all. I only allow myself a sip of the pink champagne cocktail—that Linc swears is his wife's favorite drink—every five minutes. It's delicious and almost impossible not to guzzle it. The rest of the time I keep my hands folded in my lap to keep from fidgeting.

The conversation is surprisingly easy despite the company

I'm in. Linc and Griffin seem to love pushing each other's buttons, and it's very clear that Linc, for as gruff as he seems to be, is the more social of the two. Much like Jackson, he has a charismatic way about him that draws people in.

"So tell me about Spark House. I really love the idea of a boutique hotel, but adding the event angle gives it something unique. It must be a lot of work for you and your sisters," Linc says.

"It can be hectic, but we have a great system down, and lots of part-time staff to help with setup and takedown between events. My older sister, Avery, is the one who comes up with obstacle courses or team-building exercises, I take care of the business end of things, and our younger sister is in charge of social media."

"And you own the hotel, is that right? It's completely family-run?" The ice cubes in his glass tinkle.

"We do. My sisters and I are the third generation."

"Have you had it appraised?" Griffin asks.

"It's not for sale." The words are out before I can find a better, less hostile way to phrase it.

The table falls into something that feels a lot like shocked silence, at least until Linc picks the lemon slice off the edge of his glass of water and chucks it at his cousin. Hitting him between the eyes. "Fuck, Griff. This isn't an acquisitions meeting. Dial it in." He turns his attention to me. "I have to apologize for my cousin. He spends a lot of time looking at spreadsheets and not a lot of time dealing with human beings."

"He's not wrong," Griffin mutters, the apology clear in his tone. "We know Spark House isn't for sale. I was just running numbers in my head because it's what I do. I apologize if I took you off guard there. It wasn't my intention."

"It's okay. I apologize for overreacting. My sisters and I are very attached to Spark House."

"And I can definitely see why. Conceptually, it's fantastic," Linc says.

They continue to ask questions about Spark House, how it started, how we took it over when our grandmother decided it was time to retire. Linc is especially interested in the green programs we've put in place to help make it a more efficient and environmentally friendly hotel. In turn, I take the opportunity to ask them all kinds of questions about Mills Hotels and Moorehead Media, which has shifted gears over the past several years, since Lincoln took the helm.

And just like Jackson said, I don't need any of the presentation materials I tend to rely on. It doesn't hurt that both men are charismatic and engaging. Linc is definitely the talker of the two, but they make me feel welcome and included, and very much like one of their equals.

Dinner is long finished, and it's well after ten. Normally I'm in bed by this time, unless we have an event. As the evening wears on, I relax, although I don't accept the offer for a second cocktail, no matter how delicious and tempting it is.

"Jackson tells us that you're not only an incredibly savvy businesswoman, but you're also creative," Linc says after the server sets a teacup in front of me.

"Oh, I don't know about that. I'm just crafty."

"London's being modest. She has her own store on Etsy that she runs in her spare time, which she admittedly has very little of."

"That might be because you're monopolizing all of it these days," Trent says with an arch of his brow.

I can't tell if this is just good-natured ribbing or what. I've never seen Jackson and Trent interact before, apart from Trent reminding him that he had a meeting and Jackson blowing it off to sit in on mine.

"Monopolizing is what you do when you hijack my dinner meetings," Jackson shoots back.

"I'm not hijacking it. I was invited. Anyway, back to this store you have that you don't have the time you need to run because Jackson here is eating it up with meetings on the other side of the country." Trent folds his hands and gives me his attention.

Under the table, Jackson's knee knocks against mine. It's purposeful, and of course he's already aware of how much I don't love having the attention focused on me. When we're talking about Spark House, it's fine. I'm not solely responsible for making it the success it is. Avery is very much the ringleader, and I've had to learn so many different skills that don't come naturally as a result.

And sitting here at a table of multimillionaires, my little Etsy shop that helps pay the mortgage and gives me something to do with the countless tiny stars I compulsively make seems trite and trivial. "It's a hobby. I just do it for fun. The Etsy shop, that is."

"If it creates revenue, it's not a hobby," Jackson argues and then turns his attention back to Linc and Griffin. "Her store has its own cult following. Every time she posts a new item, there's a flurry of social media activity, and she's been featured in several articles on one-of-a-kind blogger sites. And she uses predominantly recycled products."

"What's your store called?" Linc asks.

"Starry-Eyed Treasures," I reply. "And I think Jackson is talking it up a bit."

"I'm just telling the truth. I can't tell you what kind of strings

I had to pull and the favors I had to call in to get London here tonight." Jackson lifts his glass of scotch to his lips to hide his mirthful smile.

"Like keeping the fact that it was on the other side of the country a secret until we were driving to the airfield, and pulling my sisters in on the deviousness," I fire back.

"It worked, didn't it?" Jackson shrugs.

Linc leans back in his chair and swirls his scotch around in his glass, a half smile tipping up one corner of his mouth. "So I gotta know, how long have you two been dating, and why is this the first time you've brought London to New York?"

I almost choke on my tea. As it is, I have to turn my head and cough into my napkin. "We're not dating," I explain. I can feel my face heating up like a Bunsen burner, and not just because I tried to inhale tea instead of air.

"I asked London out, but she turned me down." This time Jackson doesn't even bother to hide his smile. "Trent knows. He was with me when it happened."

"You were high-level compulsive staring at her the entire night. I'm surprised she didn't mace you when you approached her. And now I'm kinda sad I left before you had a chance to embarrass yourself, because seeing you get shot down would have been entertaining," Trent replies with a grin.

I had no idea Trent was with him that day, although the man he was sitting with had his back to us, and I was trying not to pay attention to either of them. "You can't just say things like that without any context!" I shoot Jackson an unimpressed glare before I give my attention back to Linc so I can explain. "I'd just gotten out of a relationship, and he approached me at a bar. The timing was wrong, and now we're working together."

"Interesting." Linc spins his glass on the table. "Did Jackson ask you out *before* or *after* you started working together?"

"Before. By several months. And I had no idea who he was when I turned him down. And then when I showed up for a meeting with two people on his team, he ended up sitting in on the meeting. It took me a few minutes to realize he was the same person who asked me out, which I'll be honest, was incredibly unnerving."

"You didn't seem rattled," Jackson observed.

"I had my game face on."

Linc's grin widens. "Hmm. I suppose we'll see how this working relationship pans out soon enough."

I bite my tongue about the fact that I've already asked him out and he's turned *me* down, so there's nothing to pan out.

"Speaking of, it's too bad you can't come to Colorado for the charity event we're hosting at Spark House," Jackson says.

Thankfully this time I'm not drinking anything, so I don't choke.

"Cosy loves Colorado, so I'm sure it wouldn't be hard to convince her to make the trip. Let me look at my schedule and get back to you?" Griffin says.

I don't know whether I want to kick Jackson in the shins for this dinner or kiss him. Or both.

12

KEEP THE REINS TIGHT

JACKSON

Thanks for calling me out, asshole," I mutter to Linc as I give him a hearty pat on the back. I'm trying to play it off, but honestly, I'm rattled.

"You're as transparent as a jellyfish, my friend," he replies good-naturedly.

"We need to talk," Trent mutters, repeating the same back-pat-hug. "Is she staying in the penthouse or the apartment?"

"The apartment," I reply quietly.

He leans back, his expression reflecting relief. "Good. Okay. I'll see you in the morning. Keep your head on straight tonight." He blows out a breath like this whole thing is causing him anxiety.

I nod and we step away from each other.

Up until now, I thought I'd been doing a good job of keeping the lines between personal and professional entirely separate, but with Linc's observations and Trent's disquiet, I see now that maybe my ability to stay professional has become compromised.

I've been making excuses to see more of her than I would any other company in any of our partnerships. And flying her to New York to meet with my powerful friends so she could pick their brains is a few solid steps outside of my normal.

London, poised and charming as ever, shakes hands with Griffin, Linc, and Trent, thanking them for a lovely evening, and then we're heading for the elevator, back to my penthouse.

London stands about three feet away from me, her gaze fixed on the light above the elevator.

"Did you enjoy yourself this evening?" I try to make polite small talk.

Her gaze darts my way, but she remains facing the elevator doors. "After I got over the initial shock of who exactly we were eating dinner with, yes, thank you."

I'm nervous now, aware that I blindsided her with this dinner. On top of not telling her where the meeting was to take place. At least she has a room to escape to that isn't inside my penthouse.

London steps into the elevator ahead of me.

I hold my card in front of the sensor and the doors slide closed, locking me inside the small, mirrored space with London.

As soon as we're in motion, London turns to me. "Lincoln Moorehead and Griffin Mills? Why didn't you warn me ahead of time that's who we were having dinner with? Why purposely keep it from me?"

"Because I didn't want you to overthink it."

She purses her lips and narrows her eyes.

"I was going to tell you on the way here, but I asked your sisters, and they thought it would be better if I didn't say anything. I didn't want you to psych yourself out."

She props a fist on her hip. "One is the CEO of a media company and the other is a hotel mogul!"

"Griffin's father is actually the hotel mogul, and I'm a CEO and you manage just fine with me," I point out.

"It's not the same and you know it." Her eyes flash with ire. "You set this whole thing up and kept me in the dark about it the entire time." She blows out a breath and pinches the bridge of her nose.

"You're right and I feel like I need to apologize for that. I followed the advice of your sisters, and maybe I shouldn't have. I didn't think through the optics of this for you and how it might make you feel, and I absolutely should have."

"You don't need to apologize." The way she crosses her arms tells me I absolutely do.

The elevator doors slide open, and I motion for her to go ahead of me. She hesitates for a moment and then crosses the threshold. She doesn't make a move past the foyer, though.

I don't like how glaring the power imbalance is right now. "But I do, because I didn't consider how keeping this from you would impact you. I also didn't fully reflect on what I've asked of you on a personal and emotional level. And I realize that we're on my turf, which puts you in an awkward position." I rub the back of my neck.

"Because you usually don't keep who you're having dinner with a secret?" She arches a brow.

"Yes. And until tonight, I've never had a female business associate stay here who I've also asked out." I motion to the apartment door. "Which is something I probably should have considered prior to bringing you here. I need you to know that your place in the Teamology initiative is in no way influenced by how you respond to me constantly forcing you into situations that I know will invariably take you by surprise."

"I didn't think it would be." She arches a brow. "Especially considering we're still working together after I was the one who asked you out last."

"I can't work with you and date you," I remind her.

"I'm aware."

"You're allowed to be pissed off at me." I need to stop being turned on by her sass and her ability to stand her ground.

"Does that mean I need your permission first?" Annnd she's back to crossing her arms.

"Shit. No." I run a hand through my hair. "Of course not. I just mean if you want to give me hell, go for it. Tonight was a complete dick move on my part. Look, I need to be completely honest with you because I think you're under the misguided assumption that I don't want to date you, which isn't the case at all."

She drops her arms. "I'm confused."

"You have a right to be. I like you. I like spending time with you. But I created a business relationship when I got involved with the charity event, and that means I won't act on those feelings or it puts us both in an even worse position. And I'm not willing to jeopardize your place in this initiative or the opportunities this charity event could afford you."

"Oh. I hadn't thought of it from that angle. I just thought you weren't interested anymore."

"This meeting with Linc and Griffin has made it clear that I might not be doing as good of a job at keeping this as professional as I intended. But I wanted you to have this opportunity. They're great guys, and Spark House could gain a lot from having a working relationship with them."

She taps her lips a few times, maybe absorbing my admission. "From the start, you have treated me as your equal. Even in that first meeting when you were asking the hard questions that made you seem like a jerk. But I realized quickly that you were treating me as a peer, and that you've been trying to push me outside of my comfort zone for my benefit. You've been very professional, although it's a bit of a relief to know that this"—she motions between us—"isn't a figment of my imagination."

"It's not. I really am sorry if that's what you believed."

"I didn't know what to believe."

I nod in understanding. It's been a tough line to toe. "It's been an intense evening, so if you would like some time to decompress on your own, we can call it a night, or we can debrief and you can tell me what you thought of Linc and Griffin." I motion to the door of the apartment.

"Would you like time to decompress on your own?" She throws the question right back at me.

"No, but I'm not the one who got put through the gauntlet tonight."

"I wouldn't mind a chance to debrief."

This is good, back to business and away from personal. "It's a nice night. We can have a drink on the balcony."

"Do you mind if I get changed first?" she asks.

"Not at all." I give her the keycard to my penthouse, and she disappears into the apartment.

I use my thumbprint to let myself into the penthouse. I'm

learning that the best way to deflect with London is to bring it back to business when things start getting too intense. Which is ironic since it's the business stuff that tends to get her all worked up in the first place.

I hope she changes into ratty sweats and an oversize shirt because she's been killing me all night in that dress. I scrub my hand over my face. "Only a few more weeks and then the event will be over, and I can ask her out again. And hopefully she's still interested in going on a date by then." Fantastic. Now I'm giving myself pep talks.

I take the time to change out of my suit and into something casual. There's no way I can throw on sweats because they do nothing to hide below-the-belt issues, and those have been happening more and more frequently when London's around.

I check my phone before I put it on the charger.

I have messages from Trent. Actually, I have several GIFs poking fun at my situation. One says: *May the Force Be with You.* Another is of someone drawing a line in the sand and someone else tromping all over it.

It's followed by the message:

Is she safe in the apartment?

I debate pretending I didn't see it, but decide it's pointless.

We're going to have a drink on the terrace. She won't get a tour of my bedroom. She also gave me shit.

Another GIF follows of a woman shoving a man to the ground and dunking a basketball.

She's got lady balls and you've got blue balls. You're a match made in heaven. Stay strong and don't let your hormones fuck this up for you.

I send him back the thumbs-up and crossed-fingers emojis. I can only imagine the shit Trent is going to give me tomorrow.

I toss my dress shirt into the closet and pull a worn T-shirt over my head and jab my legs into my favorite pair of jeans.

Once I'm changed, I head to the kitchen and find the bottle of champagne and the mix I requested to be available when we returned from dinner so I can replicate London's drink. I noticed that she would often reach for it, but then go for her water instead. She also has a habit of rubbing her index and middle finger together, as if she's antsy and looking for something to do with her hands—like make those tiny puffy stars she seems so fond of.

I've just finished making the drink when London calls out hello from the front foyer.

I tell her I'm in the kitchen, and a moment later she appears. I'd like to say that her changing into something comfortable is better, but now she's wearing a pair of navy leggings and a peach shirt that's somehow flowy, but also manages to showcase all of her curves. I should probably go light on the scotch, so I don't make poor choices that will cause me more problems, rather than fewer.

"Oh! Is that the drink I had at dinner?"

"It is. You seemed to enjoy it so I thought you might like another."

"I loved it! I can't believe you have the recipe for it. I might need to get it from you for girls' nights."

"I can most definitely make that happen." I drop a whiskey ball into a glass and pour a modest amount of scotch into the glass, then lead London to the terrace. The breeze is warm and the view of the city is accompanied by the bustle of nightlife in the streets below. The lights on the terrace slowly rise, illuminating the lounge chairs.

"This is amazing." London takes a seat and folds her long legs, tucking her feet under her.

"It is. Very different from Colorado, but this is where I come to relax, when I have the time, anyway."

"I imagine that's fairly rare."

"You would be correct in that assumption." More rare than I'd like. I take the seat across from her, watching her absorb the sights and sounds.

"Thank you again, Jackson. While the surprises were . . . surprising, I've had a wonderful time and I sincerely appreciate all the opportunities you keep giving us." Her expression is earnest as she tucks a few windblown strands of hair behind her ear. "I know I'm taking up a lot of your free time, and I hope other parts of your life aren't suffering as a result."

"The only person I really spend much time with outside of work is Trent, and since we also work together, it's not as if either of us is desperate for a guys' night. Besides, he keeps a full social calendar so his spare time is occupied."

She takes a sip of her drink before she sets it on the table between us. "I'd just hate to think that you're missing out on other opportunities by spending so much time working with me when I'm sure you have other things to do."

"As I've mentioned, I enjoy all this time with you, London."

And I'll feel a lot better about that when the business part of this is over.

She smiles softly. "I feel the same way."

"That's good. I'm glad to hear that. I was worried that I'd pushed you past your limit with this whole scenario."

She nods and gives me a sly smile. "Oh, there were a few moments when I was . . . less than impressed."

"Like throw food at me or squirt lemon juice in my eye unimpressed?"

"More like kick you in the shins with pointy shoes, but"—she raises a finger to prevent me from interrupting—"once I got over the shock of it all, I enjoyed myself. And honestly, if I'd had time to prepare, I would have had a million questions for them and felt compelled to take notes, so I see why you didn't tell me." Her expression grows thoughtful for a moment. "I feel like I get to see a very different side of you here. The man behind the suit, I guess? Which sounds silly, since the first time I met you, you were wearing ripped jeans and a RECYCLE shirt. Very similar to this." She nods at my attire. "I suppose I've been trying to figure out who the authentic you is, or if all of these versions I get to see are you."

"And what have you surmised?"

"That all of these versions are you, just tailored to the situation."

"Is there one you prefer over the others?" It's good there's a table separating us; otherwise I'd want to move closer, get in her personal space. Tuck that unruly piece of hair behind her ear.

She bites her bottom lip and tips her head, obviously thinking through her response. "I like them all if I'm going to be honest.

I like the puzzle pieces, that I get to see how they all fit together and make you who you are. Charismatic, thoughtful, charming, altruistic."

"What about fun?"

She chuckles. "You're definitely fun, and an adventure, and also devious and sneaky, but again, I like that I get to see all of those sides. And I wonder if it would have been quite so easy if I hadn't met you when you looked more like a regular guy than the kind who owns a private jet. I imagine that must be very difficult when it comes to dating," London muses.

"You mean when women find out I can buy a small country?" I don't mean to sound bitter, or jaded, but I worry it comes out with bite.

London doesn't shy away from the subject, not like most women would. Or try to reroute the conversation and avoid sticky topics. "Mmm, yes. I would think it could have the potential to set you up on uneven footing from the start. It would be hard to know at first if someone wanted to be with you because they genuinely like you, or if they were just trying to use you to get ahead. Unless of course you're involved with someone with the same level of wealth." She absently runs her finger around the rim of her glass, making it ring quietly. "And your life isn't really private, is it? People are always interested in what you're doing and who you're dating, I'm sure."

"It can definitely be complicated."

"Money is a blessing and curse, isn't it?" London says gently. "I would think it's easy to be lonely at the top."

"At times, yes, but I have a few very close friends who have been with me long before this became my reality."

"Like Trent?"

"Yes, exactly like Trent." His is a friendship I've held onto tightly. It helps that he already came from a family with a more affluent background than mine. And that we worked together on several projects over the years, as I made my way up a ladder that didn't seem to ever end. He has never once wavered in his allegiance to me and has shown, time and time again, that our friendship is something he values above all else.

"It's clear you two are close. That's what my relationship with my sisters is like. I would do anything for them, and they would do anything for me."

"Which is why you choose to work with them at Spark House."

"It gives me a way to feel connected to my parents as well. But yes, I'm there because of my sisters."

"If you weren't there, where would you be?"

London takes a small sip of her drink and her expression grows wistful. "If I could live on what I make from my Etsy shop, I would take that on full-time. And then just be involved in the creative side of Spark House. I love that part."

I uncross my legs and lean forward. "Do your sisters know that?"

"No." She looks out at the cityscape, fingers going to her lips and staying there for a few moments. "Well, Harley knows how much I love my Etsy stuff. I don't want them to think I don't love doing what we do. Because I really do enjoy it."

"There's a *but* in there, London. What is it?" I ask gently.

Her tongue peeks out and then her teeth sink into her bottom lip before she turns to face me again. "The parts I love aren't the parts that I get to focus on. Avery is amazing at organizing events. It's natural for her and she just . . . loves it. And Harley is a social media guru. She knows exactly what she's doing, but it's not the same for me. I can crunch numbers and make phone calls and arrange meetings, but it all takes so much mental and emotional energy. I just . . . wish it was easier, I guess." It looks as though she's on the verge of becoming emotional. She sits up straight and smiles brightly. "But with all of the opportunities you keep bringing our way . . . who knows? Maybe I'll get to focus more on what I love. And even if I don't get to do it full-time, I get to be with my sisters and that's far more important." There's so much conviction in her words, and a slight hint of defensiveness.

"Do they realize what you sacrifice for them?" I ask quietly.

"It's not a sacrifice. They're my family. They're all I have, and I would trade my dream job a billion times over to preserve the closeness we have. It doesn't matter that sometimes we drive each other nuts. I adore them."

"I can understand not wanting to lose that closeness, but if you have to let your own dreams languish so they can live theirs, is that really better?" I pause to let my words sink in. As someone who has had the freedom to figure out what I love to do, it pains me that she can't do the same. "You always seem to put everyone else ahead of yourself, London. Maybe you need to start putting yourself first."

She takes a sip of her drink, and I'm unsure how she feels about what I said.

"Losing my parents made me aware of just how fragile life is. And then last year when we almost lost Avery." She looks away and takes a deep breath. "It's not just about me. It's about my family. Sometimes we have to make sacrifices for the people we love. And usually those sacrifices are worth it."

We talk a little more, but I can see that she's tired and starting to fade.

She covers her mouth, stifling a yawn. When she drops her hand, she gives me an apologetic smile. "I should probably get ready for bed. I have to be up early, Crêpes Suzette and all."

I nod. "Probably a good idea. I should do the same so I can watch you make them. Unless you're feeling generous and decide I'm allowed to try them."

She gives me a saucy grin. "I could be persuaded to share."

London rises, and I have to avert my gaze so I don't get caught checking her out. She's even more of a temptation than she was before we came out here and had this soul-baring talk.

I remind myself that there are still a little more than two weeks before the event. Once it's over, I'll remove myself from anything business-related so I can finally act on these feelings and ask her out.

London tips her head. "Are you coming in?"

"In a minute. I need to shut everything down and turn out the lights." I motion to the dimly lit apartment.

"You don't have a remote control for that?" she teases.

I do, and someone who will turn them off for me if I forget. And everything is on a timer and motion sensor, but I just smile. "Rest well, London. I'll see you in the morning."

Her face falls slightly, but she smiles and nods. "Of course. You too. See you with the sun." She turns away and pads across the terrace, slipping inside.

I listen for the sound of her leaving the penthouse before I let my head drop back and just breathe for a few minutes. I should have let Trent take over when he offered.

13

ANOTHER CHINK IN THE ARMOR

JACKSON

I wake up at five the next morning to the most amazing smell. It takes a moment for me to remember that London is here and she promised me Crêpes Suzette. Usually, my breakfast consists of coffee and something I can take with me on the way to the office, or whatever is reasonable to eat at my desk while I check emails.

I quickly change into a pair of jeans and a T-shirt, brush my teeth, and comb my hair before I pad down the hall to the kitchen. London's back is turned to me, her long hair pulled into a knot on top of her head. She's wearing a loose, flowy shirt that hangs off one shoulder and a pair of fitted jeans. She looks incredible, but more than that, she looks like she belongs here and always has.

"You are amazing," I say, rather than think.

She gasps and turns around. "Oh! Hey there! I hope I didn't wake you up with all the noise."

"You weren't kidding about being an early riser."

"Not even a little." She points her spatula at the French press. "There's fresh coffee and the crêpes will be ready in just a few minutes."

"Can I do anything to help?"

"If you want to get out plates and cutlery, that would be wonderful. Everything I needed was already set out for me this morning, apart from the dishes we'd eat on."

I have to thank Aylin for making sure she had everything to make this happen. I warm the plates by running them under hot water for a minute, then dry them and set them on the counter next to the cooktop. A tendril of hair has escaped from the knot of top of London's head and she keeps trying to blow it out of her face because her hands are busy.

"Hold on, let me help you."

"It's fine. It's just tickling my nose." She swipes her forearm across her face and blows the hair away again.

"It's annoying the hell out of you. Lift the frying pan and hold still for me."

She sighs, but does as I ask, taking a step away from the stove, bringing her into my personal space. She smells just as delectable as the crêpes she's cooking, like vanilla and something sweet and citrusy.

I take the opportunity for what it is and pull the elastic free from her hair. I grip the satiny strands in one hand and run my fingers from her hairline to the crown a few times, making sure I have all the flyaways and the strays before I fix it with the elastic again.

Without thinking about what I'm doing, I lean in and brush my lips across the nape of her neck.

She sucks in a startled breath and nearly loses her hold on the frying pan. As it is, the crêpe slides off the pan and lands on the floor at her feet. She manages to catch herself before the pan joins the crêpe.

"Shit. Sorry. I wasn't . . . I didn't—" She stumbles over her words.

"It's my fault. I'm the one who should be apologizing." I take the pan from her and turn off the burner, before grabbing the crêpe from the floor and tossing it in the garbage, burning my fingertips in the process.

When I turn around, London is rubbing the back of her neck with one hand, the fingers of her other hand brushing over her lips, her brow pulled into a furrow.

"Sorry about the casualty."

She blinks a couple of times. "Oh, it's fine. It was the last one and there are plenty. Let me plate them." She moves across the kitchen, fingers still on the back of her neck. She opens the wall oven and uses a potholder to remove the glass baking dish.

I managed to make it through last night without crossing the line, and of course I go and fuck it up this morning. I want to address it, but for once, I don't know what to say. And with the way she's going about plating the crêpes as if nothing happened, I can almost convince myself that I only thought about kissing her neck instead of following through on it.

Once the crêpes are plated, we take a seat at the kitchen table that's rarely ever used and dig in. I groan on the first bite, the delicate crêpe and the delicious sweet tart of the orange filling hitting my tongue. "This is incredible. Next time you'll need to teach me how to make these."

She pauses with her fork halfway to her mouth. Her expression reflects mild shock, but she quickly recovers. "I'd be happy to. Harley is the one who taught me how to make them. She's the cook of the family. She used to bake with our mother all the time as a child, mostly so she could lick the beaters when she made icing, I think, but she's amazing in the kitchen."

"Based on this, you're not too shabby yourself."

"I have a few choice things that I've mastered, but Harley can pull anything out of the fridge and turn it into something delicious."

"That must be handy, although I'm guessing you all don't have a lot of time to cook with your hectic schedule," I observe.

"Sundays through Wednesdays aren't quite as busy as the weekends, so she usually has time to put together a few decent meals, and of course, I help when I'm useful. I imagine you must not have a lot of time to make use of this kitchen." London motions to the space with her fork before stabbing another piece of crêpe.

"Not really. And cooking for one isn't particularly exciting. I often have dinner meetings, and on the rare occasions that I'm home before eight, I have someone who prepares meals for me."

London tips her head to the side. "Having food waiting for me when I walk through the door sounds amazing, but I imagine the novelty wears off pretty quickly."

I smile at her astuteness. "Mmm, that it does. Gourmet meals are wonderful, but they're a lot nicer when there's someone to share them with. And you may be surprised to hear that I enjoy cooking, but only when I'm not eating alone, which is rare."

"A bachelor who can cook seems a bit like a mythical creature," she says with a mirthful smile.

I laugh. "That's a terrible stereotype."

"You're right, it is." She props her fist on her chin. "What was the first thing you learned to cook, and how old were you?"

"Toast with butter, and I was four, but I don't think that really counts. When I was six, I learned how to make pancakes. Not from scratch, but from a box where all you had to do was add water."

"Six?" Her eyes flare. "That's so young."

"I had supervision. My parents were both in treatment at the time, and I'd been living on peanut butter sandwiches. Trent's mom came over and realized how dire the food situation had gotten. Neither of my parents had an appetite, and I was limited to what I knew how to make, apart from heating up frozen meals in the microwave. So she would come over every couple of days and teach me how to make something new. We started with easy things, like pancakes from a mix or things that didn't involve a lot of steps."

London reaches out and her warm palm settles on my forearm. "That must have been so hard for you."

"I didn't really know any different. I'd grown up with sick parents and needed to learn how to fend for myself. Of course, Trent's family was always there. And I had other people who would trade off and help, but they couldn't be there all the time, and I learned how to manage. By the time I was in high school, I could make a three-course meal without overcooking anything."

"I'm sure the girls must have loved that," she teases.

"I didn't date much back then, or ever really. My focus was on my family. Most teenagers aren't equipped to deal with that level of trauma, and I didn't want to pull someone else into my upheaval."

"What about the woman you proposed to? I imagine you were fairly close if she was part of your life during such a difficult time."

"We ran in the same circles. Her family was close with Trent's family, and we often ended up at the same events, so we would all hang out together. She was part of my friend group. She was there for me when things got really bad. She was . . . a good friend, and provided a lot of emotional support, and at the time, it was what I needed. But like I said, my headspace wasn't the best when I proposed. I was looking for any kind of stability. It wasn't fair to her." I redirect the conversation, not wanting to talk about that time in my life, not when we've had such a great night and morning.

After breakfast I help London clean up, even though I have someone who normally does that for me. It gives me an opportunity to spend more time with her. Once the breakfast dishes are done, she returns to her room to gather her things and I accompany her to the airport.

"I'm sorry I can't come back with you." I truly mean it. I'd love to return to Colorado, but I have afternoon meetings. As it is, I pushed several back and rearranged yesterday so I could spend the entire day with London.

"I completely understand, and I sincerely appreciate all the time you've already taken out of your schedule for me."

"It's absolutely been my pleasure."

When she steps in and wraps her arms around my waist, I sink into the warm embrace. I don't know if there's ever been a time in my life when I've felt so connected to another person.

There's chemistry between us. It crackles like thin sheets of ice under heavy treads every time I'm near her. I just need to stay on the right side of the line until I can pass the reins over.

Trent is already sitting behind my desk when I arrive at the New York office. "Spill it, Jax."

I set my briefcase down on the desk, very nearly landing on his pinkie. "You're not even going to give me five minutes to get my head in the game?"

"It's ten, two hours later than you usually get here. I think you've had plenty of time to get your head in the game. What happened with London?"

"I didn't sleep with her if that's what you're asking." I drop into the chair opposite him.

"Has anything happened that could constitute crossing the line?"

I tap my lips with my fingers, thinking about the way I kissed the back of her neck and then pretended as though it didn't happen.

"I'm taking this long pause as a yes. Jax, you're setting yourself up for a harassment case if you're not careful. This isn't 1980 when you can sleep with your secretary and everyone pats you on the back like assholes."

"I know that."

"The power dynamic is way off. You said you had this under control, and it's really damn clear to me and everyone else that you don't. That woman looks at you like you're the north star and you look at her like she's your favorite dessert. How do you think this would roll out in the news? Billionaire CEO takes advantage of small business owner in exchange for sponsored ads?"

From his perspective, everything he's saying is right. "I kissed the back of her neck this morning."

His brows do the worm on his forehead. "You what?"

"She was making breakfast and her hair was in her face. I was helping keep it out of the way."

Trent raises a hand. "Okay. There is so much wrong with this explanation, I don't even know where to start. First of all, *she was making breakfast?*"

"She wanted to make use of the kitchen because it's nice."

"Right."

"She stayed in the apartment, not the penthouse," I say, because I already know that's what he's going to ask.

"We'll come back to that. So London made herself right at home and made you breakfast this morning. Did she happen to be wearing a negligee?"

"No. She was wearing jeans and a shirt."

"Were you helping her with her hair because her hands were down your pants?"

I give him a look. "She was flipping crêpes and they burn easily, not that I would expect you to know that since your preferred breakfast is still Eggo waffles. I wasn't even thinking. I just leaned in and kissed the back of her neck."

"How did she react?" I can practically see his wheels turning.

"She dropped the crêpe on the floor."

"Did she call you out?"

I shake my head. "I don't know if she thought she imagined it or what, but I backed right off and she seemed fine. And before you ask, no, I don't think I need to call my lawyer, but I do need to take myself off the Teamology initiative. I should've let you take over the charity event when you first offered."

"Are you serious about this woman?"

"About wanting to date her? Yes."

"Do you want me to be the lead on the charity event?" He taps on the arm of his chair.

"I don't know that there's much of a point with it being so soon."

He nods once. "I reserve the right to step in if I think it's necessary, though."

"I know. And I'd expect nothing less from you."

"I should've seen this coming. You've been spending a lot of time with this woman. I'm going to ask you something, and I don't want you to get all defensive."

"Shoot."

"Are you sure she's genuinely interested and not just playing you? I mean, you're doing a lot for her and her hotel. More than you've done for anyone else who's involved in this whole sponsorship thing. I've been on their social media, and they're looking at a kitchen expansion so they can take on in-house catering and bigger events, which is great, but also expensive as hell. She has to know that there's a benefit in working with you, and you seem to be wearing your heart on your sleeve, which . . . isn't something you usually do."

"That's not how London is."

"Not that you know of. Remember that Jessica woman? She seemed great until she wasn't anymore."

"This isn't the same."

"You were sure she wasn't another one of those gold diggers until all of a sudden she was moving into your place because her lease fell through. I just don't want you to go through something like that again. Jessica was a legal and social media nightmare."

He's not wrong. She seemed great, and stable. Until one night, she was staying at my penthouse and the next, moving all of her things in while I was away on a business trip. That was when I realized she was just looking for a comfy ride.

"She's not going to turn into a Jessica."

"How do you know for sure? You've known her for what? A couple of months at most? You weren't dating Jessica much longer than that before things blew up. Are you sure you don't have blinders on?"

"I'm sure. At least ninety-five percent anyway. I really want to see where this can go, if it can go anywhere."

"Okay. Then let me take over where I can so there's less of a chance of you screwing this up. And you should probably mention this to Selene at some point, so she's not totally in the dark on this one."

"Selene and I haven't been involved in anything but a business capacity in a long time."

He cocks a brow. "What's *a long time*? You know what, never mind. That's not the point. Selene is still your friend, you should give her a heads-up about dating London, just so she's in the know."

"I think it's a non-issue, but if it comes up I'll mention it."

"Whatever you think is best. I hope she's worth it."

14

WHAT IS THIS GREEN MONSTER?

LONDON

I don't know. Should we move that? I think it needs to be over there, where we can make it a focal point." I motion to the sculpture, donated by a prominent local artist, in the middle of the room. I've been amazed by the number of donations, although when people find out the event is being hosted by Holt Media, they tend to want to be part of something special.

"Maybe? But we've already moved it three times. Why don't we wait for Mitchell and his team to get here? They can give us an idea of where things should go," Harley offers.

"Okay. Yes. That's a good idea." And not the first time my sister has made that suggestion. Also, I have a layout for the auction items, but seeing them in three dimensions is different than seeing them on a printout.

It's a strange-looking piece, but I've done my research and I'm very aware that it would most definitely go for a significant sum of money. To be honest, it's a little overwhelming to have all these silent auction items in here, without a human security guard to watch over them. Or maybe some of those *Mission Impossible* laser lights that would signal an intruder.

Spark House has an alarm system, but it seems woefully inadequate considering what is likely more than half a million dollars in donations. This event is shaping up to be very exclusive and good for Spark House on more than a publicity level. The initial social media blast that Holt Media initiated has boosted our following by ten percent already.

Their social media manager, Selene, has been in touch a few times, once by phone, but mostly it's been emails. While our communication has been direct and professional, it hasn't been particularly warm. But then, she's in the business of helping grow business, not becoming someone's best friend. Which I can respect. I'm also a little intimidated by her, and, if I'm completely honest with myself—something I've been reluctant to do—I'm also a little . . . irked by the way she talked about Jackson during our one brief phone conversation. I can't put my finger on why it bothers me, but it does.

Later that afternoon, she arrives. I expect her *not* to look exactly like she does in her social media pictures, but I'm wrong. She doesn't need any filter to look Insta-ready. She has long, thick dark hair, an incredible naturally tan complexion, eyes the color of coffee, full lips, and a body that has clearly been earned through countless hours of training. In short, she's gorgeous. And once again, I experience that odd sensation that creeps up the back of my neck and makes the hairs stand on end. Like a cornered cat. Half of me is desperate for her to like me and the other half wants her to leave. I don't like it. As a result, I'm nervous.

"It's so adorable!" She stands in the middle of the ballroom with her hands on her curvy hips. She does a slow spin and taps her lip. "So much potential."

"Thank you. We like it." I keep my hands clasped in front of me to prevent me from using them to talk.

She comes equipped with an entourage, who she quickly dispatches, moving things around, rearranging the room inside of an hour. Something that took me and my crew almost an entire day. Once she deems the space event-ready, she informs me that she's going to head up to her room.

"I presume that Jackson and I will be on the same floor," she says as she sashays down the hall toward the elevator that will take her to the third floor. She has one of the nicest rooms in the hotel, aside from Jackson's room. The entire third floor is dedicated to executive suites, and we've gone to a lot of trouble to make the accommodations as perfect as possible considering the clientele that we're entertaining this weekend.

"You will." And now that I've seen her in person, I would prefer that they weren't.

"Perfect. I know he'll appreciate that." She affords me a tight-lipped smile.

"Do you work together often?" Jackson has only mentioned Selene in passing—and only in respect to the charity event he's hosting next month in New York—and that she's the Teamology liaison. Selene initially hadn't been slated to attend our event, but apparently she made a last-minute decision to fit it into her schedule, and while Harley loves it, I'm beginning to wish she opted out.

"Mmm. We do." Selene checks her phone, which buzzes several times in a row.

"You've been business associates for a long time, then?" I don't know why it feels like I'm prying.

She lifts her gaze and gives me a quick appraisal, followed by another one of those smiles that seems to be verging on a smirk. "And friends even longer than that."

"Oh? I didn't realize."

Her phone screen goes black, and she gives me her full attention. "Despite being a public figure, Jackson is a private man, so he tends to keep his personal relationships close to the vest. He doesn't love speculation or rumors. It's just not his style."

"Right. Of course. That absolutely makes sense."

"Jackson is very protective of the people who are close to him. Especially those of us who have had the privilege of knowing him before he made his fortune."

"I can definitely understand how important you must be to him, and Trent as well. He needs friends like you to watch out for him." I mean it. Mostly. Although I honestly don't know what to make of the prickly feeling on the back of my neck, or the strange urge I have to tell this woman that I'm not interested in Jackson because of his money. In fact, it's very much the opposite. I like Jackson *despite* the fact that he could basically buy Spark House and turn it into a freaking amusement park should the desire strike him.

Which I sincerely hope never happens.

"He definitely does. Jackson has a soft, generous heart, which is why he needs people like me and Trent around to keep him in line." She smiles, so I do in return, but it feels a lot like I'm being given a warning.

"Soft heart or not, I can't imagine he's gotten where he is today without a shrewd business sense." Normally I'm not combative, or even the kind of person to incite conflict of any kind, but I don't love that this woman, who is very much the reason Spark House has had so much social media attention, is also the bug in Jackson's ear.

I'm also confused by Jackson's behavior since I went to New York. First he tells me he's interested in dating me, and then all of a sudden, it's Trent who has seamlessly taken over the event without a peep from Jackson. It doesn't make sense. And I still don't know if I imagined his lips on the back of my neck or if it actually happened when I was in his place in New York.

Selene throws her head back in a laugh. "Jackson would tell you his success is attributed to a little luck, his ability to tell people what they want to hear, and having the right people behind him. Anyway, I've taken up more than enough of your time, and I'm sure you still have much to do before tomorrow night. It's been a pleasure meeting you, London. This really is a lovely event hotel. It's obvious you and your sisters have put your heart and soul into making it what it is. I'm looking forward to seeing what kind of sponsorships we can secure for you once the guests see what you've set up for them."

"Thank you. Enjoy your evening, and if you need anything, don't hesitate to call me or the front desk directly."

"Absolutely. See you in the morning." And with that, she steps onto the elevator, her attention already on her phone again.

I wait until the doors close before I let my shoulders sag and blow out a breath. I don't have time to fixate on Selene, though, because she's right, I have a million things to do before tomorrow night and not nearly enough hours left in the day to complete everything on my mental and physical checklist. Not to mention that Jackson is supposed to arrive in just a few hours, and I want everything to be as perfect as it can be before his arrival.

Two hours later, I'm in the ballroom adjusting centerpieces and making sure everything looks perfect for tomorrow night. Once I'm done in here, I'll go back to the office and review my checklist, answer any pressing emails, and make a new list for tomorrow morning.

"How you hanging in there?" Harley hands me a glass of sparkling lemon water, which I down too quickly and finish on a hiccup.

"Nervous. Excited. This is kind of a big deal, and I don't want to let Jackson down. Or Selene, since she's the one who's going to be promoting this event and we kind of need her on our side." I make a face. One that probably isn't very becoming.

"She's fantastic, isn't she? I really hope I get a chance to talk to her tomorrow night. I have so many questions, but I don't want to fangirl all over her."

"Hmm. Maybe she was just preoccupied when I met her." I rearrange a centerpiece on the head table, adjusting the flowers. Then I move a few of the stars that frame the bowl so there aren't two blue ones beside each other.

"Why do you say that?" Harley asks.

"She was . . . standoffish with me, maybe? I don't know what to think of her. She made it sound like she and Jackson are really close, but he's only ever mentioned her in a business capacity." I tap my fingers on the table. "I don't know why, but she sort of irks me."

"I can tell you why she irks you." Avery smirks at Harley as she comes into the room.

I glance between them. "What do you know that I don't?"

"You're jealous."

"Jealous? Why in the world would I be jealous?"

"Because she's a friend and business associate of Jackson's, and she's made you believe she knows him in ways you don't. I'm guessing that irked feeling is actually jealousy because you have the hots for Jackson."

"That's not true."

"Uh, yeah, it is." Harley nods her agreement.

"Jackson and I are friends and business associates." Even I don't believe what I'm saying, and I get confirmation that they don't either a second later when Avery and Harley give each other a look.

"Whatever you say, London."

Jackson finally arrives just after five. My stomach is full of butter-flies and my nerves are in high gear. The jar full of puffy stars on my desk is a testament to that.

I haven't spoken to Jackson much since I went to New York with him. In fact, it's been Trent who has been in my Google Doc, commenting on the color-coded lists and discussing any of the last-minute adjustments we need to make for the charity event.

"How was your flight?" I ask, barely resisting the urge to pepper him with more questions before he can answer the first one.

He's dressed in a suit and his phone is in his hand. He slips it in his pocket and smiles, but for some reason it looks a little stiff. "The flight was fine. How is everything here?" He glances around the office. My computer monitor is framed with Post-it Notes.

"Good. Great, even. Would you like to settle into your room?"

"Why don't we have my bag brought up and you can show me the auction room before I head up?"

"Absolutely." I don't know how to read him right now. He's

usually so much more relaxed, although this is a significant charity event and the only other time I've seen him in full-on business mode was the day he sat in on my meeting with Mitchell and Tish.

I call for the bellhop to take his bag to his room, and he falls into step beside me. I don't love how tense things feel right now, and I don't know how to make it better.

I open the door to the auction room and motion for him to go ahead of me. "Selene has already been in and shifted a few auction items around, but I wanted you to have a look and give it your seal of approval."

His brow furrows. "Oh? When did Selene arrive? I thought she wasn't supposed to be here until later tonight."

"A few hours ago. She's on the third floor. Your room is down the hall from hers." I wait for a reaction to that news.

He makes a sound, one I can't quite decipher, and then moves deeper into the room. He makes a few suggestions regarding the auction items, moving a couple of them back to where I originally had them. I show him the dining room next, expecting a comment about the centerpieces, but all he does is pick up one of the gold puffy stars on the table and flip it between his fingers. "Everything looks good."

"I want to ensure Spark House does the charity justice, so if there's anything you think needs my attention, let me know."

"I think we're in good shape." He pulls his phone from his pocket and glances at the screen. "I have a few things I need to deal with, so I should probably settle into my room."

"Would you like me to show you where it is?"

"Oh no. You don't need to worry about that. I'm sure you have lots to take care of." He smiles, but once again it looks stiff.

"Right. Okay. I'll just get your keycard and meet you by the elevators?"

"That's perfect."

I leave him standing in the hallway and grab the keycard to his room and meet him at the elevator. "You're in room 303 and Selene is in 306."

"Okay. Thank you." He slides the card into his suit pocket.

"If you need anything, you can call the front desk or text me. I'll be here for a few more hours before I head home."

"I'm sure I'll be fine. I'll see you in the morning." The elevator doors slide open, and he disappears inside, leaving me more confused than ever.

15

THIS LITTLE SPARK

LONDON

I sleep like garbage. It's often the case the night before an event, but even more so this time because my interaction with Jackson keeps playing over in my head.

The last time I saw him, he admitted to wanting to date me, and since then I've hardly spoken to him. I understand that he's shifted things to Trent, but I didn't expect him to avoid me like the plague.

And that uncertainty hangs heavy like a cloak around me as I get ready for the day and head to Spark House.

Not long after I arrive, a frazzled Selene sashays through the lobby, suitcase in hand. She spots me and shifts course. That sensation my sisters claim is jealousy takes over and I force a smile. "Good morning, Selene."

"I wish it was." Her smile looks far from genuine. "I have to apologize, London, but I have an emergency situation that requires my presence back in New York."

"Oh no, I'm so sorry. I hope it's not serious."

She waves the comment away. "Nothing that I can't handle, but unfortunately, I'm unable to deal with it remotely. I have faith you'll pull off a wonderful event. Mitchell has my notes. I'll be in touch sometime next week." She leans in and air-kisses both of my cheeks, and then she's off with two women speed walking after her. That prickly feeling at the back of my neck leaves with her.

The rest of the morning is filled with last-minute details, putting out small fires, and managing the reservations as guests begin to arrive. The majority of the charity attendees are local, with only a handful coming from out of town.

It's the first time I get to see this version of Jackson—the self-made multimillionaire CEO. He's very much the same man I've come to know: poised, articulate, and charismatic. I just wish I knew why he was being so remote with me.

Dinner is to be served in less than half an hour, and I'm in the middle of making sure we have enough of the vegan and vegetarian menu options with the catering staff when Jackson pops his head in the kitchen. He's dressed in a black tux and looks edible. "Hi, London, I'm sorry to interrupt, but Griffin and his wife just arrived, and she's asking to meet you. When you have a minute, can I steal you?"

Harley pops her head right behind him. "Hey, sorry to interrupt, but there's a man named Harmon who's looking to speak with both of you." She holds out two fingers, one pointing at me and the other at Jackson.

"Can you handle the vegan and vegetarian menu options, and then I can meet Cosy and say hello to Harmon?" I glance from the caterers to Harley and Jackson.

"Yup. For sure, I can do that."

"Great. Thank you."

Jackson holds the door open, and I fall into step beside him. "How are you holding up?"

"Good. Great. You?" I run my hands over my hips in part to make sure they're dry.

"Also good. Everyone is very impressed. The guests are excited to meet you and your sisters."

"I'm used to fading into the background at these things, not being in the limelight. That's usually Avery's strong suit."

We run into Griffin and Cosy first. She's a petite woman with dark hair and an impish grin. "This place is amazing. Have you ever had a live band here before?"

"Do you mean instrumental? For a wedding?" I glance at her hand and am almost blinded by the rock decorating her finger.

"No. More like a rock band."

"Why don't you get London's contact information, and you can email her about this instead of trying to plan your own event while we're in the middle of one, sweetheart?" Griffin leans against the edge of the bar, swirling his ice cubes in his glass, wearing a knowing smirk.

She gives him a look that would bury a lesser man. "It was one freaking question, Griffin."

"Thirty seconds after you introduced yourself, Cosy." He turns his attention to me. "I'll be contacting you by email next week because my wife is in love with this place and basically wants to move in. And don't worry, I've already told her it's not for sale."

"I have a soft spot for Colorado," Cosy admits.

"I completely understand. I can't imagine living anywhere else," I tell her.

Harmon slips into the small circle and introduces me to his wife, Lucile.

She takes my hand in hers and gives me a warm smile. "This place is truly magical. Jackson told me that you and your sisters run the hotel, and I must admit I didn't expect you to be so young! What an amazing accomplishment."

"Well, Spark House has been in our family for three generations, so we've had a great foundation to work with."

"I think it's very noble to follow family tradition. I have to tell you, London, the centerpieces are absolutely delightful. Are they made in-house?"

I explain that I create the prototype and that we have a team who replicate them, often using recycled goods.

"Do you ever make them for events outside of Spark House? Or sell them?"

"Oh yes! Actually, I have an Etsy store, and often we'll put a few up for sale after the event is over. There's a link to my site on the website under my profile."

"Wonderful! I'll be sure to have a look after the event."

Avery makes her way through the crowd and is pulled in for introductions. She excuses us, citing that we're needed, but that we'll be back to mingle a little later. I allow her to thread her arm through mine and guide us toward the closest exit. "Is everything okay?"

"You've been gone for an hour, and it's just me and Harley running the show."

"I'm sorry. I didn't realize."

"I know, which is why I came to get you. Once dinner is done we can socialize." She sounds stressed.

We get the dinner situation sorted and trade off shoveling whatever food we can into our mouths before we're on duty again.

Over the course of the evening, my sisters and I are introduced to one influential business associate after another. Even with all the research we've done, it's a challenge to remember everyone's name and what business they're associated with.

By the end of the evening, the auction has raised over one million dollars. It's an incredible success, and we have no less then twenty-five new business cards and a lot of interest from guests who would like us to host their own events, from birthday parties to team-building programs. It's overwhelming and amazing in equal measure.

By midnight, the guests have disappeared to their rooms, and Avery and Harley are making sure the auction items are properly tagged and secured, while I head back to the office to shut down the computers and ensure everything is in order for tomorrow morning. I grab my purse and dig around for my phone, intending to send Jackson a message before I leave. I barely had a chance to speak with him tonight, and I'm hoping I'll get an opportunity to at least debrief about the event, and maybe find out what in the world is going on with him. I'm about to pull up his contact, which has several missed messages attached to it, when the sound of footfalls momentarily distracts me. "I'll just be another minute or two, and then I'm ready to go."

"Not without saying good night, I hope."

I fumble my phone and it clatters to my desk. "I was just about to message you."

Jackson stands in the middle of the office, his bowtie hanging loose around his neck, his tux jacket open, one hand tucked into his pocket. His gaze is hot as it moves over me. "Are your sisters still here?"

"They are. Somewhere. Maybe in the kitchen." Possibly eating leftover dessert, as they like to do.

He crosses the room. "You were amazing tonight. I truly love watching you shine, London."

"Thank you for making this possible." I'm aware that on the grand scale of things, this is a small, intimate event and that most of his charity events make twice as much, or more.

"Based on the discussions I had with many of the guests tonight, I have a feeling Spark House is going to be very busy for the foreseeable future."

"You've opened so many doors for us."

"You opened all your own doors, I was just here to hold them for you." He comes around my desk and stops when he's right in front of me. "I'm sorry if I've been off since I arrived, but I needed to be able to remain professional until the event was over, and the only way I felt that was possible was to keep my distance."

"Is that why you basically ghosted me since New York?"

He frowns. "My intention wasn't to ghost you, London. After our time together in New York, I realized I needed to take a step back, and now that the event is over, I'm letting Mitchell and Trent take over where Spark House and Teamology are concerned. I don't think my involvement will be necessary after the success of tonight."

"Oh. I see." I'm finding it very difficult to swallow past the lump in my throat. I knew this would happen eventually, and I'm honestly surprised that he's been so involved in the first place. I'd hoped that it had less to do with the actual charity event and more to do with me. "I'm sure your time is better allocated elsewhere, and I sincerely appreciate all you've done for me. I mean for Spark House."

"That isn't what I wanted to tell you, London. That was just the preamble."

"Oh."

He gives me a small, gentle smile. The kind I've learned he adopts when he finds my reactions amusing for whatever reason. I'm not finding this particular conversation all that amusing right now. "Maybe I wasn't as clear as I should have been in New York. I'm not stepping back because I don't want to be involved, I'm doing it because I need to let someone less personally invested take over."

"So you ghosted me the past few weeks because you're too invested."

"I can't work with you anymore because I have feelings for you that are not related to business or in any way platonic. But now that this event is over, I'd like to officially ask you on a date."

"Officially?"

"Well, according to Trent, we've already been dating for the past two months, give or take, and I've just been too much of an idiot to realize it."

"How do you mean?" I tip my head.

"How much time have we spent together over the past two months?"

"Well." I rub my fingers together. "A lot, but it's been business-related."

"The truth is, I don't attend estate sales with my other business associates. And while I might have clients stay at the apartment in New York, I usually don't fly them out for an overnight and clear it with their sisters first. You made me crêpes, London. Would you do that for any of your other business associates?"

"No, but—"

He gives me a wry grin. "Like it or not, we've been unofficially dating for months now. And I'd like to make it official."

"Official how?" My stomach is a whirl of excited butterflies.

"Official in that I'll take you on the date that we've both been trying to get each other to go on. I would like to treat you like the queen you are, and if all goes well, at the end of our date I'll finally find out what your lips taste like." We both take a step closer. "If you're amenable to a date, that is."

"That depends."

He arches a brow. "Oh?"

"Is this the date that's going to include a hot air balloon ride?"

"Hot air balloon ride?" he echoes.

"When you approached me and my sisters at the restaurant the first time, you mentioned a hot air balloon ride."

"Ah. Yes. I did do that, didn't I?" A slightly embarrassed grin curves the right side of his mouth. "I hadn't factored that into my plan for tomorrow, but I'd be willing to see what I can do about that."

"Actually." I pick imaginary lint from the lapel of his jacket. "I have a small fear of heights." I hold my finger and thumb two inches apart. "So maybe we could hold off on the hot air balloon ride, for say, a half century or so."

"You do realize that I'm going to make it my mission to get you in a hot air balloon eventually, right?"

"Not if you want future dates you won't." I give him a saccharine smile.

He chuckles. "So as long as tomorrow's date does not include any heights, apart from elevator rides, are you amenable?"

"I am." I nod. "And I'd also like to state that I'm confident the date will go well and that the kiss you're hoping will happen is already highly anticipated."

"I'm very pleased to hear that." His breath breaks across my cheek, and a moment later I feel the press of his lips, soft and warm, leaving a promise of more lingering on my skin. "What are your plans tomorrow?"

"I usually arrive fairly early so I can oversee takedown and make sure I'm around to say goodbye to all the guests."

"What time would you be free?"

"Around two in the afternoon or so. Then I'll have some Etsy orders to take care of." Last I checked, I had at least fifteen orders to fulfill.

Jackson frowns. "How long will that take?"

"A few hours maybe."

"Is it something I can help you with?"

"I guess it depends on how crafty you are." I smooth his lapels for a reason to touch him.

"Hmm. Maybe I can just supervise, then."

"It won't be very exciting," I warn.

"I don't care if it's exciting. I want to spend time with you. And after your Etsy orders are done, I want to take you out for dinner." His gaze darts to my mouth and then back to my eyes. "I'm looking very forward to our first official date, but let's not tell Serious London because I rather like Fun London, and I'd like her to be the one who shows up tomorrow night."

I roll my eyes and grin, but I'm honestly worried that Fun

London is going to do a disappearing act because Jackson is so intent on calling this a date. "I'll try to keep Serious London on lockdown."

"I would greatly appreciate that. I hear she's not quite as adventurous as this Fun London I like so much." His smile is full of mirth.

I swallow hard and whisper, "What if I'm not a fun date?"

"We've been on at least a dozen dates so far. The only thing that was missing was the label and me getting to kiss you at the end of each one." He tucks a loose tendril of hair behind my ear, even though I didn't feel one. I don't mind. I appreciate the contact. "You're a fabulous date, London. Every time we've done something together, it's been more fun than the last."

I meet his amused gaze. "Can I be honest about something?"

"Absolutely." The humor in his expression fades, and he regards me with mild concern.

"What you said in regard to finding out what my lips taste like." I bite my lip, nervous that I'm going to mess this up.

"What about that?" He nods solemnly and his eyes dart to my mouth.

I run my hands over his suit jacket-clad shoulders. "I was wondering, since you've pointed out that all of these business meetings you've organized over the past couple of months have been more like dates, if maybe waiting until tomorrow night to find out what my mouth tastes like is a little pointless."

"Interesting. I've actually wondered that myself." He cups my cheek in his palm.

"I suppose if we're both wondering the same thing, then maybe it would make sense to just throw caution to the wind and find out *before* the date."

"That seems like something Fun London would definitely do."

"It does, doesn't it?" I bite my lip.

"And we both know how much I like Fun London." He bows his head, lips an inch from mine.

I tip my head up and push to my tiptoes. At the same time, I slip a hand around the back of Jackson's neck and tug, just a little. His lips touch mine, a barely there caress. He comes back again, lingering this time. We tilt our heads, lips parting at the same time, tongues stroking out to meet each other.

One of his hands stays on my cheek, but the other arm wraps around my waist, and he pulls me against him. I loop my arms around his neck and slide my fingers into his thick hair. He had it cut recently, the back shorter than usual.

I feel like I'm freefalling into heaven. His mouth is magic, his lips soft like satin. His kiss is both tender and commanding, and I find myself wanting to get caught up in the wave of bliss and ride it all the way to his hotel room. And then ride him.

I can't remember a time in my life when a kiss had the ability to undo me entirely. And this kiss definitely possesses that quality. I want to get closer, put my hands all over him. It's as though this one single kiss has lit a fire inside of me. One I didn't even know existed.

Jackson's hand—the one cupping my cheek—slides into my hair, gripping the strands and anchoring there. His thumb rests against the edge of my jaw, and he applies the tiniest bit of pressure. As if he's making a silent request for me to tip back farther and open wider for him, without breaking the intensity of the kiss.

So I do.

He groans into my mouth, the sound low and primal.

His other hand eases down my side and rests on my hip. His

fingertips dig into the fleshy part of my ass and he rocks into me. And for the very first time, I feel him.

I'm relieved I'm not the only one so affected by this kiss.

If we were sitting, or even lying down, and I wasn't wearing a floor-length gown, I'm one hundred percent sure that I would be straddling his lap, grinding up on him shamelessly. I can count the number of times I've been that worked up on one hand.

All I drank tonight was sparkling water. I needed a clear head, and my lack of sleep over the past few nights would have been exacerbated by even the smallest amount of alcohol.

I grip the lapels of his tux and roll my hips, wishing that all these layers of clothing could magically disappear.

"Whoa! Wow. Yup. Okay. Wasn't expecting that." Avery's shocked voice shatters the spell, and I tear my mouth from Jackson's. The hand in my hair loosens, but the one on my hip stays where it is, keeping our lower halves connected.

He backs up just enough that my eyes don't cross when I look up at his gorgeous, flushed face. "That was absolutely worth the wait," he murmurs.

"Oh hell yes! I so called this! Avery, you owe me a hundred bucks!" Harley shrieks.

Jackson arches a brow, and I push on his chest. It's either that or I pretend that my sisters aren't in the room and we go back to making out. I'll be honest, I consider that a viable option for a second or two.

"Could you not have just backed out slowly and quietly?" I ask my sisters, my face heating with embarrassment.

"Obviously the answer to that is no, otherwise we would have done that in the first place," Harley says with a smile. "Hi, Jackson. Thank you for making me a hundred dollars richer and also for using Spark House for this event, and for digging on London. We owe you. I make great cookies if you want to put in a request."

The corner of Jackson's mouth twitches, and his fingers brush my hip. "You're welcome, and I love oatmeal raisin."

"Ah, I knew you were a good egg."

He turns back to me. Taking my hand in his, he lifts it to his lips with a wink. "Until tomorrow."

He nods to my sisters, who smile and wave at him like a pair of overly enthusiastic teens at a boy band concert, and then he's off down the hall, one hand in his pocket, the other at his lips. None of us say anything until the sound of his footsteps fade out. As soon as the ding of the elevator filters down the hall, Harley squeals and rushes over, pulling me into a huge, rib-crushing hug.

"Oh my God, oh my God, oh my God. I just knew this was going to happen!" She releases me and steps back, jumping around like a toddler at Disney. "That was your first kiss, wasn't it? It looked so intense!"

"It looked like you two were about thirty seconds away from getting naked on the floor," Avery deadpans with a smile.

I touch my lips, the memory of his on mine making them tingle. "He's taking me out for dinner tomorrow night."

"I vote you go home with him," Harley says.

"Who says he'll invite me back to his place?" I sincerely hope he does. He bought a house in Denver recently, but I've yet to see it. He obviously could have opted to stay there during the event, but he wanted to be able to mingle with the guests.

My sisters look at each other and then me as if I have two heads. "Uh, if that kiss is anything to go by, you'll be lucky to make it through the main course without tearing each other's clothes off."

16

FAN THE FLAMES

LONDON

Jackson and I end up spending the majority of the following day together. He helps with takedown, which is mostly tackled by our weekend employees, and once the guests have departed, we sit in the office and manage emails—me on my desktop and him on his laptop. It's strangely natural. It's also fraught with sexual tension because we're sitting in the same room where he kissed me last night.

"I already have half a dozen emails from guests wanting to book us for events, and Selene emailed this morning to say that Moorehead Media is very interested in sponsoring Spark House, and there's a florist who would like to partner with us," I tell him as yet another email alert hits my inbox.

He rolls his chair around the other side of my desk so he's beside me. He's dressed casually today in a pair of jeans and a collared black polo shirt. He's also wearing a pair of running shoes.

Ones that have clearly been around for a while based on their scuffed toes. He extends his arm across the back of my chair.

He's not even touching me, and still my body warms to his proximity and my mind starts to wander toward last night and the kiss we shared.

"I definitely think a partnership with Fendley's Florists would be fantastic, particularly with how many weddings you have slated for next year. And I know you'll be hearing from Griffin early next week. Cosy is in love with this place, and he's working on a surprise birthday party for her for next year."

After dinner last night, I was able to sit down with Cosy and chat for a while. She's gorgeous, full of fire, and an absolute hoot. I learned all about how they met and fell in love in the most unconventional way.

"That's a huge compliment coming from a family of hotel moguls." I turn my head and find Jackson's lips temptingly close to my own.

Our gazes meet and lock, and as if by magnetic force, our heads tip and we lean in at the same time. I allow my eyes to flutter shut as his lips brush over mine, once, twice, a third time. Each time we connect, a wave of desire washes over me. I part my lips and he takes the invitation, tongue sweeping out to dance with mine. After what might be a few seconds or maybe several hours, he pulls back.

"How much longer before you're done here?"

"I can be finished right now." It comes out a husky whisper.

"If you finish right now, will you have a million things to catch up on tomorrow?"

"I have some Etsy orders that need my attention, but I can't imagine getting anything done when all I can think about is your mouth," I tell him honestly.

"Hmm. I understand your predicament and I have a proposition for you."

I want to ask if it includes skipping the whole dinner date entirely and just making a meal out of each other, but I bite my tongue and nod instead.

He raps on the edge of the table three times, his gaze flitting between my mouth and my eyes. "This may sound incredibly presumptuous and forward, but I'd like you to keep in mind that we've basically been dating minus the good-night kisses for the better part of two months and that you've already almost spent a night at my place, even if it was in a different bedroom, so what I'm about to ask you would absolutely be reasonable had either of us been aware that we've been sneakily dating without realizing it up until now."

"Unless I missed something, there wasn't a proposition in there," I say with a half smile.

"That was my preamble, the proposition is forthcoming."

"Right. Okay. Fire away."

"If I could be so bold, I would like to suggest that we stop at your place and pick up any of the things that you might need to work on those Etsy projects. That way, after dinner, when I ask you if you'd like to come back to my place, and then later, I ask you to spend the night, you won't have to worry about rushing through your projects or turning me down because you're concerned about work."

I arch a brow. "You're feeling pretty confident about this date, aren't you?"

"Confident, no. Hopeful, yes." He skims the edge of my jaw

with a fingertip. "Well, maybe there's a hint of confidence in there, but I'm attributing that to your admission that all you can think about is my mouth. Especially since I'm suffering from the same plight."

"Hmm. You're very set on dinner out?"

"Do you have qualms about dinner?"

"Not qualms, per se."

His brow furrows. "Concerns, then?"

I nod.

"What concerns you about dinner?"

"I'm not sure how easy it's going to be to focus or engage in meaningful conversation when I'm aware that we'll eventually end up back at your place." And based on the sound of things, in his bed, naked.

His gaze sparks. "Consider it extended foreplay."

I sigh. It seems silly that I'm resigned to going out for dinner, but what I would really like is alone time with Jackson. "Let me pack up my things."

Less than two hours later, Jackson and I are walking up the driveway to his house in Denver. It takes two trips to get my Etsy things inside. It can be an elaborate setup. I half expect him to jump on me the second we're inside, but it appears— unfortunately—as though he's found some personal restraint and is employing it.

"How are plans for your sister's wedding coming along?"

Apparently, we're engaging in small talk. "Things are pretty good."

"Are the bridesmaid dresses all picked out now?"

"They are, and I'm happy to report that we won't be wearing maroon and blue dresses."

"That is excellent news."

"It really is. We were concerned for a bit."

"Reasonably so." He sets my bag at the foot of the stairs. "Would you like a tour?"

This is very different from his penthouse in New York. Instead of a monochromatic color scheme, the living room is decorated in soft creams with pops of color. The furniture looks inviting and cozy. There's a huge barrel chair with an incredible number of throw pillows in the living room off the front entrance.

"This is lovely." I turn to Jackson, whose eyes are already on me.

We stare at each other for all of two seconds before we take simultaneous steps closer. His arm circles my waist, and I loop mine around his shoulders. Our mouths connect and Jackson groans while I sigh.

Unlike the last time, we're not in the middle of my office, so we don't need to worry about interruptions or someone walking in on us. Unless he has people taking care of this place like he does in New York. I decide before we get too heated that I should address that one issue.

I disengage long enough to mutter one sentence, "Are we alone?"

"Completely."

That's all the reassurance I need, so we go back to making out. Like we're ravenous high schoolers. I want to climb him like a tree. And since he's right, we've basically been dating for the past two months, I figure it doesn't hurt to be a little brazen.

He breaks from my mouth to kiss his way along the edge of my jaw and down my neck. Our breath comes in quick pants.

"Jackson?" I tip my head to the side to give him better access.

"Mmm," he mutters against my skin as his hands roam over my curves and he palms my backside.

"What time are our dinner reservations?"

"Not until seven."

I'm not entirely sure of the current time, but we left my place at around three thirty, so at the very latest it's closing in on five. That's two more hours before we sit down for a meal and at least four before we're back here, and that's me being conservative on how long dinner is going to take.

If we make out for ninety minutes and then I have to sit in a restaurant and be attentive for several more hours, I think my brain may liquify and my vagina could explode.

Before he can glue his mouth back to mine, I cover it with my palm. "Would you like to show me your bedroom?"

He blinks three times. "Now?"

"Yes."

"You wouldn't prefer to wait until after I take you out for dinner?"

I swallow down my nerves and lay it all out for him. "I've been thinking about what you said last night, and again today. If we've been unofficially dating for two months, it's really a wonder that we've made it this long without tearing each other's clothes off. In the interest of not embarrassing ourselves with overt and inappropriate public displays of affection, I think it might be wise for us to indulge ourselves before dinner, instead of after. In all honestly, we should already be naked, and I should be bent over that couch." I point at the piece of furniture.

"That's very fair and also reasonable, and I will most definitely keep bending you over the couch in my back pocket should I need to get creative later." Jackson threads his fingers through mine and tugs—not toward the couch.

I practically have to jog to keep up with his long strides as we ascend the stairs.

We pass two half-closed doors, and I follow him into the one at the end of the hall. I don't even have time to take in the room before Jackson cups my face between his warm palms and kisses me again.

We're a flurry of hands, tugging, unbuttoning, groaning, sighing, and laughing as we struggle to undress each other and still keep our lips locked. I've never been this frantic to get a man out of his clothes.

Jackson in a suit is a glorious sight, as is Jackson in pretty much any clothing combination. I even imagine he'd look good in a kilt. But Jackson naked is a sight to behold. He's athletic and deliciously toned. Not too bulky, not too lean.

We kiss and touch, and all the while, Jackson backs me up until we reach the bed. He fumbles with the comforter, tugging it down, and pushes throw pillows out of the way. I have my doubts that he chose them or put them there, since I'm assuming he doesn't even have to make his own bed.

I also consider that since this house is new, I'm the first person to sleep in this bed with him. No other woman has kissed him in this room, or made him groan the way he is now. And I find I like that idea. Knowing that I'm the only woman who has been here, and that every time he climbs into this bed, the echo of this experience will be there.

As with everything Jackson does, he's slow and careful and pays very close attention to detail. As his mouth and fingers explore the dips and curves of my body, he pauses when he elicits a particularly breathy sigh or a soft moan.

"You are absolutely perfect," he murmurs as he kisses his way along my collarbone, up the side of my neck, and back to my mouth.

"So are you." I run my fingers through his hair and ease my hand down his back, between his shoulder blades.

"I can't tell you how glad I am that I found you again." His gaze is soft, expression earnest.

"Me too. And I'm also very glad that you hoodwinked me into all those nonofficial dates."

"I feel the same way. About everything." He skims a nipple gently, wet from his mouth, and continues to trail lower, circling my navel. "I don't think I've ever wanted anyone the way that I want you, London. I would have lived in the friend zone for another six months if that's what it took, but I have to tell you, I'm very, very glad it didn't. It was killing me trying to hold back and not slip up."

His fingers glide lower until he dips between my thighs.

"Oh my God, yes, please." Our little admissions cease as he explores, touching me, making me sigh and squirm and moan. Lust, hot and thick and overwhelming, blankets me, and I pull him over me, wrapping my legs around his waist.

We grind against each other, bodies slick and hot, and when neither of us can take it any longer, he sheaths himself with a condom and eases inside.

In all my life, I've never been with someone who makes me feel so connected, not just physically, but on another level. As though we've truly become one. He moves over me, and I shift, rolling my hips, meeting every slow thrust. I feel as though I'm spiraling up, and when I orgasm, it's the headiest sensation, radiating through my center, all the way to the tips of my fingers, and makes the hair on the back of my neck rise, as though I've gotten too close to an electric current.

I'm grateful that I come first, because it means that I get to watch Jackson as he reaches his own peak. He doesn't pull out or roll off me. Instead, he braces himself on his forearms and kisses me, long and languorous, in no rush to break the connection.

And I realize that this is the spark I've been missing all along. And now that I've found it, I want to nurture it and turn it into a flame that will never extinguish.

17

SO THIS IS CHEMISTRY

LONDON

We end up being half an hour late for our dinner reservations. The benefit of going on a date with Jackson is that the restaurant doesn't give away your table when you don't make it on time. We're escorted to a small, private room, completely isolated from everyone else at the restaurant. It's gorgeous and decadent and the nicest restaurant I've ever had the pleasure of dining at.

I'm also famished and half-drunk on the afterglow of sex.

Jackson orders appetizers and we settle in. We're seated in a high-back booth, beside each other rather than across. His eyes roam over my face like a caress.

"What are you thinking about?" I take a sip of my drink. I'm also parched, and I probably need to chug a gallon of water.

"That I'm on the fence as to whether your proposition was a good idea or not."

"Oh?" I arch a brow. "Have you made a list of pros and cons in your head?" I'm only being slightly cheeky.

His eyes narrow slightly, but his smile is full of amusement. "You know me too well already."

"Well, we have been on a lot of dates, so I suppose it makes sense that I can predict your reactions. Also, I'm feeling very much the same way. I thought it was bad enough knowing what an amazing kisser you are, but now I know you're proficient at everything, which is both a blessing and a bit of a curse. As much as I'm glad that I'm very relaxed, I'm also very keen to get dinner over with so I can get back in bed with you."

"I feel the same. I thought it would settle the craving, but all it's done is magnify it. The torture of knowing is worse than the anticipation of finding out."

"Exactly."

He holds his hand out and I slip mine into his. "We should probably stop talking about this."

"That seems wise." I give his hand a squeeze and withdraw mine from his grasp, aware that the contact only serves to heighten the awareness of his proximity and what it does to me.

We shift the discussion back to last night's event and who Jackson thinks will be the best sponsors for Spark House.

"The charity event next month in New York would be another great networking opportunity. And obviously a good excuse for us to spend time together. Do you think you'd be able to sneak away overnight to attend? It's on a weekend, which I know is a challenge for you, but it's at a Mills Hotel, and you'll have a chance to speak with some of the people you met last night. It would be a great opportunity to meet new potential clients and grow Spark House even more."

"Selene will be there, won't she? It's unfortunate she had to leave in such a hurry. I hope everything is okay." I sincerely mean the last part, despite my relief at her not actually being at the event.

"I'm sure it is. She has a big event she's covering in New York this week and probably shouldn't have tried to make the trip to Colorado. But at least she was able to see Spark House, which is good." Jackson's gaze shifts away and he focuses on his drink.

"Do you work together often?" That foreign hot feeling creeps up the back of my neck. The one I don't quite know what to do with, even though it now has a name.

"She manages projects for Holt Media on occasion."

"So you have a business relationship, then?" I press.

Jackson regards me for a few long moments. "She's a family friend and a business associate. I've known her for a long time."

"Right. Okay." I swallow down the lump in my throat. "Thank you for being honest." Now that I've met Selene, I can unfortunately say that she's even more stunning in person. And she lives in New York, where Jackson's home base is, while I'm a three-hour flight away.

"Hey." Jackson skims the edge of my jaw and takes my hand in his again, bowing until his lips touch my knuckles. "Wherever you're going in your head, don't. I'm fully invested in you and me, and while I realize all of this is very new for both of us, let me be clear that it's only you that I want."

"I believe you," I whisper.

"Good."

"I have a question, though." I fidget with the napkin on the table.

"I'll do my best to answer."

"When you say you're fully invested in us and that it's only me you want, does that mean we're dating exclusively?" My mouth is bone dry.

"Unless you don't want to be exclusive." I can't read Jackson's expression, but there's something in his tone—it reminds me of the way he is in the boardroom, when he turns off his emotions and goes into business mode.

"I would prefer exclusivity. I just . . . My whole life is in Colorado and yours is mostly in New York. How is that going to work? Can a relationship survive that kind of distance?" Part of me wishes I'd kept my mouth shut because it feels like I'm ruining what should be a nice dinner.

"Have you ever had a long-distance relationship before?" Jackson asks.

I fold my napkin into a square. "Daniel traveled often for work, but that's not a great example because he and I weren't a good fit. In fact, I don't know if I have any good examples because I'm starting to think I haven't made the best choices in my past relationships."

"How so?" Jackson props his chin on his fist.

"I think I've always played it very safe. Or maybe that's not totally accurate. I think losing my parents impacted how close I would allow myself to get to another person. And my sisters were always going to be the top priority, so my past boyfriends were like . . . hobbies, I guess?" I tap the edge of my wineglass. "That sounds awful. I didn't want to get too invested. Daniel was easy to date because he wasn't around a lot, and he didn't interfere with my job or my relationship with my sisters."

"I don't think that sounds awful. It sounds a lot like self-preservation and what I tend to do. Or had. Until you came along."

"I don't think I had a chance to put my guard up with you because we were in a working relationship, so it couldn't be more than friendship. And now, well, I'm invested. It's a bit scary."

"As I already mentioned, I'm also invested." Jackson reaches out and brushes my bottom lip with his thumb, and I realize I've been biting it. "I'm very concerned that you're going to do damage to those lips, and I'm selfishly worried that I'll have to be exceedingly careful when I kiss you later."

I free the skin from my teeth.

"Thank you." He exhales a deep breath. "It's also a distraction, and makes it a challenge for me to think." He takes my hand in his again. "I'll be spending more time in Colorado while I'm setting up the office in Denver. And I'm hopeful that I'll be able to fly you out to New York in between those visits. And of course we'll have video chats, and Google Docs, and messages." He winks.

"That all sounds doable." As long as Avery doesn't give me shit for wanting a day off here and there to spend with Jackson. I imagine I'll get some pushback, but again, this could be an opportunity to get Avery to finally agree to hiring on some extra help. And with the new sponsorship and potential new clients, it's likely going to have to happen sooner than later. Not to mention the kitchen expansion seems to be more necessary than ever.

"I think so. I'm aware of the challenges that come with long-distance relationships, and that this solution isn't permanent, but I'm hoping for now, we try this? I want you to be honest if you're finding it at all difficult, or if it's not working for you, and I, of course, will do the same."

"I can do that." I exhale a sigh of relief.

"Good." He kisses my knuckles again. "Now about the charity event in New York. I would love it if you would submit one of your creations for the auction."

I give him a look. "Seriously, Jackson? As if I'm going to put one of my Etsy trinkets up against sculptures donated by some of the most sought-after artists in the country."

"Last year Cosy submitted one of Griffin's high school art projects and someone bought it for fifty thousand dollars."

"That must have been some high school art project."

"It was supposed to be a sculpture of a flower, but it ended up looking a lot like female anatomy. We've had everything from specialty cakes, to trips to Bora Bora, and anything in between. One of your pieces would be a wonderful contribution and another way for you to gain more recognition, not just for Spark House but for the things you're passionate about as well."

His arguments are valid, even if the idea makes my stomach feel like it's trying out for the circus with all the flipping it's doing. "Okay. I'll submit something. When do you need it by?"

"In a few weeks?"

"That should give me plenty of time."

"Excellent. If you need more time, just let me know. I'll plan to pick it up at least a few days before the event."

"I can just bring whatever it is with me, if I can manage to make the event, that is."

"It's an excuse for me to come see you, and I'm more than happy to talk to your sisters and convince them that you attending the charity event in New York will only do good things for Spark House."

"I think they might see through you, considering what they walked in on last night."

"Hmm. You do make a good point. Still, if you run into issues convincing them, know that I'm here to help."

The server brings our appetizers, putting an end to that conversation, at least for now.

Two hours later, we're back in the car, heading for Jackson's house. We were chauffeured to the restaurant, which means the moment we're in the back seat and the divider whirs closed, our lips are locked. We take a short break when we arrive at Jackson's. I can't look the driver in the eye as Jackson helps me out of the back seat. I also stumble a step or two because my legs are wobbly, thanks to Jackson's wandering and very adept fingers.

The moment he closes and locks the door, we're back at it. My dress ends up in a heap on the floor in the foyer, Jackson's clothes make a path to the living room. One of his buttons rolls under the couch in my zeal to get him out of his shirt.

This time, we don't make it back to the bedroom. Instead, I end up bent over the back of the couch, as I suggested earlier. I can see our reflections in the mirrored glass, and I watch him, completely enthralled and very aware that I'm falling for this man, and fast.

18

DON'T RAIN ON MY BONFIRE

JACKSON

hy the hell are you smiling? I just wiped the floor with
your ass twice in a row." Trent swipes a towel across his
forehead to mop up the sweat.

I'm not a big squash player, but every once in a while, I need
to change things up, and Trent loves to kick my ass at the game,
so I let him, since it's usually me kicking his ass at most other
sports.

"I just confirmed my date for the charity auction." I set my
phone down and use the towel draped around my shoulders to
wipe the sweat dripping down my temple.

"Your date? Aren't you going with Selene?"

"Why would I do that? I'm taking London."

He arches his brow. "Does Selene know you're taking London?"

"I'll probably tell her the next time I talk to her."

"You should do it soon, since that event is coming up, and Selene won't appreciate being left in the lurch." He shoulders his way out the door of the squash court. "You two always show up together. Officially or unofficially, you're typically each other's plus-one when there's a charity auction. Apart from Colorado, anyway."

I fall into step with him as we walk down the hall to the locker room. "That's because I haven't been dating someone when we've had something like this."

"Is this official now that her event is over?"

"We're seeing each other, yes."

"Wow, you're moving fast on this one. The last time we talked, you were taking her out on a date, and now you're what, a couple?" Trent looks shocked in a way I didn't expect.

"I told you I wanted to pursue her, and you were the one who pointed out that I've basically been dating her this entire time with all the stuff we've been doing together. I like her a lot." I follow him into the locker room.

"Yeah, but 'a lot' as in you want to get her naked as often as possible, or 'a lot' as in you want to call her your girlfriend?"

"Uh, both?"

"Oh. Wow. And you're sure she's not just using you for all the golden opportunities."

"I know you're just looking out for me, but London isn't like the Jessicas of my past." I don't want to get dragged into the paranoia of it all either.

"You've only known her for a few months. She could be pulling the wool over your eyes."

I hold up a hand to stop him. "She's not."

He scrubs a palm over his face. "I get that you're into her, Jax, but she turned you down when you asked her out the first time."

"Yeah, but then she asked me out again."

"After you started working together and she knew who you were. And now you've introduced her to some of the most influential people in the country. I don't want to jump to conclusions, but it seems a little convenient."

"She was in a relationship at the time." I've explained this to him before, so I don't know why he feels the need to push this angle.

"What if that's what she wants you to believe?"

"Look, I need you to stop feeding the paranoia. I haven't been this interested in someone in a long time, and I don't want to mess this up by letting your worries dictate my actions. I'm not asking her to move in with me or marry me, for fuck's sake! I'm taking her to the charity event. That's it."

Trent blows out a breath. "Shit. Sorry. Look, man, I'm not trying to be an asshole. I just don't want to see you get duped again. You're usually very cautious and very private, and you've been neither of these things when it comes to London. I hope you're right, but if you're as serious about her as you seem to be, you need to give Selene a heads-up. When was the last time you brought someone other than Selene to an event?"

He has a point. "I think she's been dodging me since the Colorado event."

"Why would you say that?" Trent stops rummaging in his duffel.

"I've left her a couple of voicemails that have gone unanswered, and her PA is the one responding to emails. I figured she was just busy with whatever she's got going on, but now I'm wondering if that's it. We haven't been together in a long time, not since before Peru."

"Together as in . . ." Trent lets it hang.

"I don't need to spell that out for you." I arch a brow. "Before that, it was probably closer to a year. She was dating that soccer player. Whatever his name was. Anyway, that's beside the point." I wave the comment away. "The last time, which was more than half a year ago we agreed that it was the *last time*."

"Who put that on the table? You or her?"

"I don't know. It was a conversation and we came to a mutual agreement that it was better for us not to go there anymore."

"Right. Okay." Trent rubs between his eyes, like this conversation is making him uncomfortable. "Do you want me to talk to her?"

"Let me try one more time. If she's still avoiding my calls, I'll take you up on that."

"Okay. I've always got your back, you know that. Except in the shower, you can loofah your own back."

I chuckle and clap him on the shoulder as I pass, heading to the showers. "And I appreciate that."

As promised, I attempt to contact Selene, but again, my texts go unanswered and my call goes to voicemail. I would prefer to speak with her directly, but she's not leaving me with much of a choice. I leave a voicemail letting her know that I have a plus-one for the Mills Hotel charity event and that I wanted to give her time to plan accordingly. I also request that she call me back, but I'm not holding my breath on that.

The next morning Mitchell shows up at my office door about three minutes after I sit down at my desk to review the charity event from the weekend and go over the one we're hosting next month at the Mills Hotel.

"I'll reach out to Selene's stylist so we can color coordinate your attire," Mitchell says.

I flip a pen between my fingers. "That won't be necessary. Selene isn't my plus-one for this event."

Mitchell looks up from his tablet, his expression reflecting surprise. "Oh?"

Over the years, there have been a handful of occasions in which Selene has not been my plus-one at events that we both attend. Usually, it's a result of Selene being involved with someone, rather than the other way around. Where Selene tended to date high profile people, I kept my relationships—what few I'd had—fairly low-key.

"London will be my plus-one. I'll reach out directly and inquire about her dress so we're able to coordinate."

"London Spark, sir?"

"That's correct. If you can connect with her regarding the flight to New York, that would be great. And if we need to use the private jet, we can, but see what's available on commercial flights first."

"Would you like me to arrange hotel accommodations as well?" He types furiously on his tablet.

"That won't be necessary. London's accommodations are already taken care of."

Mitchell has been my right-hand man for years. So when I'm met with silence, I finally look up from my calendar.

"I know you have questions, so go ahead and ask them."

"No questions. You're quite taken with Miss Spark."

"I am."

"That's good. It's about damn time."

19

DOUSE THE FLAME

LONDON

Jackson left for New York yesterday morning. He's already messaged asking about my schedule for the rest of the week. He's determined to fit in a visit. And a sleepover. Dating someone who lives halfway across the country seems daunting, but when they have their own jet and own shares in an airline, it certainly makes the distance a whole lot more manageable.

We have a huge event this weekend, and I still need to make the centerpiece prototype. Beyond that, I have more than twenty Etsy orders to catch up on, and I have no less than six conference calls scheduled with the guests from the charity auction. To say I'm a little overwhelmed would be an understatement.

I spend the first couple of hours of my day managing emails, then switch gears and head out to the barn to create a centerpiece so the staff can get started on those tomorrow, then come back to the office, where my sisters and I gather around my desk for the first two conference calls.

At the end of it, we have two more events to plan for later in the year.

Avery is ridiculously excited about one of them because it's a team-building conference, which means she'll be able to design an obstacle course.

Harley and I leave Spark House together at six thirty and stop to pick up takeout on the way home. I grab my laptop and set it up at the table beside my dinner plate and pull up my Etsy orders.

"Holy crap."

"What's up?" Harley shoves a forkful of pad thai in her mouth.

We had an early lunch of leftovers from the dinner event this weekend, so we're both starving.

"This can't be right."

She covers her mouth with her hand. "What can't be right?"

"Between this weekend and now, I have another twenty-five Etsy orders." I scroll through the new orders, mentally trying to figure out if I have enough stock to fulfill all of these, or if I'm going to need to rush order supplies.

"That's amazing!" Harley leans across the table to check out my computer screen.

"Yeah, amazing," I echo.

I'm already wiped out from the weekend, and from staying up late with Jackson. Now I'm looking at several evenings of work on top of everything else. This is more than double the orders I'm used to managing.

"I can help if you want. I know you usually like to do it all on your own, but this seems like a lot."

"I might have to take you up on that."

We finish dinner, and I get out everything I need for the first batch of orders. On the upside, I have enough to fulfill all the current orders. Before I get started, I reorder more of the stock I need to complete the new ones, so I can have them all sent out by the end of the week. And then Harley and I set up an assembly line and tackle each project, one at a time.

The joy I usually experience is diluted with anxiety over the sheer number of orders, and the fact that I'm already tired and trying to figure out how I'm going to get the rest of these done and still manage to find time to spend with Jackson when he's back in town later this week.

"We need to pick out a dress for you for that charity event in New York. Maybe we can look at sites tomorrow night," Harley suggests.

"Jackson has already asked about my color preferences, and Aylin reached out this week asking about styles, so I'm not sure that's necessary. And I'll probably have to work on these tomorrow night." I motion to the computer screen with all the pending orders.

"We'll get them done. One step at a time," Harley assures me.

"Thanks, I really appreciate it. There's no way I'd be able to do all of this on my own."

"You know I don't mind. Plus, you've been working so hard with all the calls for new events, it's a wonder you've had any time to sleep at all. Oh! Did I tell you that one of the guests this weekend is some kind of fashion designer and she offered to provide us with bridesmaid dresses?"

"What? No! Who is it?"

"Maxine Delacour. Her dresses are beautiful. I can't believe all the opportunities coming our way. It's wild."

"I know. It's a little overwhelming, you know?"

Harley nods. "It's a lot. How are you feeling about being Jackson's date to the charity event?"

"I'm nervous, obviously. And excited. I'm a little worried about perception, though."

Harley pauses her flower petal curling. "How do you mean?"

"I've met all of these amazing people, and it's been wonderful, but I worry it's going to start to look like nepotism. Or worse, that people are going to think I'm only with him because of all the strings he can pull for me." Maybe that's one of the reasons Selene seemed so . . . standoffish with me.

"Anyone who knows you, knows that you would never do that."

"I know, it's just . . . I'm surrounded by all of these unbelievably wealthy people and we're . . . average. And there's nothing wrong with average. It's an adjustment, that's all."

"I get it. But Jackson is very down to earth, at least from what I've seen, and if anyone can handle this, it's you."

As if he can sense us talking about him, my phone buzzes and his name appears on the screen. I answer and put him on speaker phone.

"I'm sorry I'm calling so late. Meetings went long today."

"No apology necessary," I tell him. "But you should know you're on speaker phone and that Harley is in the room with me."

"Hello, Harley," Jackson says.

"Hey. Your timing couldn't be more perfect. I need a bathroom break." Harley waggles her brows and jumps to her feet, practically skipping her way down the hall.

"We're alone now," I tell him.

"I wish. I miss you. I can't wait until Wednesday. How was your day?"

"It was busy but good. We booked two more events this after-noon from guests who attended the charity dinner, which is ex-citing, and now I'm catching up on Etsy orders. How about you?"

"That's great news about the bookings, although I'm not surprised. I've had a lot of calls from the guests telling me how much they love Spark House, so I expect those will continue. Are you very behind on the Etsy orders?"

"A little, but it's nothing I can't handle. And Harley is giving me a hand, so we'll get it done."

"Have you brought up hiring people to Avery again?"

I sigh. "Yeah. When I did, Avery accused me of trying to blow off work because we're dating now. It didn't go over well."

"Hmm, well eventually, that will have to change if you keep growing, won't it?"

"You know that. I know that. Harley knows that. Avery does not know that."

Jackson makes a noise, but doesn't comment otherwise. "Anyway, I know Aylin has already been in touch, but I wanted to talk to you about your attire for the charity event. I have a few designer friends who would love the opportunity to outfit you. Would you be interested?"

"Um, sure?"

"Unless you already have a dress."

"I don't have a dress yet."

"Great. I'll send you an email with links to their exclusive websites. Once you've narrowed it down to your top three choices, let me know, that way I can coordinate with you."

"Okay. I can do that."

"Wonderful. I'll talk to you tomorrow. Don't stay up too late."

"I won't."

I end the call, and Harley appears in the doorway, smirking. "That takes care of dress shopping, doesn't it?"

"We can look at them together." I yawn so long and hard that tears form in the corners of my eyes. "But maybe we should look tomorrow." I rub my eyes, blinking several times as exhaustion sweeps over me.

"Seems like a solid plan."

I know better than to try to keep going when I'm this tired. I'm bound to make mistakes and then I'll have to redo things. No point in doing something twice.

I spend the next two days working double time, juggling conference calls, organizing dates for new events, setting up for our event this weekend, and trying to stay on top of my Etsy orders.

On Wednesday morning I go into work extra early to get a handle on emails and make sure everything is ready for the event on Friday night. By eight thirty I'm fighting to keep my eyes open, having stayed up until midnight. I decide to close my eyes for a few minutes and am startled awake by Harley.

"You need to see this!" She holds her phone in front of my face, too close for me to be able to make out what's on the screen.

I blink several times and wipe the drool from my cheek. "What's going on?"

"I don't know, but our IG inbox is literally full of hate messages."

"Hate messages? About what?"

"You and Jackson."

"Me and Jackson? Why would there be hate messages about that?"

"I don't know, but people are losing their minds."

I take her phone and scroll through the messages. There are an unbelievable number of them. Even worse are the death threats and the hate messages on our IG feed centered around a photo of me and Jackson at this weekend's event that Harley must have taken and decided to post.

It looks like a candid shot. We're standing next to each other. His head is tipped down, mouth close to my ear, and I'm smiling at whatever he was saying. There's nothing racy or untoward about the image, but we look very much like we're in our own little bubble.

The comments are horrifying. I'm being called a boyfriend stealer and a homewrecker. The threats are the worst. Someone says they're going to torch Spark House, someone else says they're going to shave my head.

My stomach rolls and I break out into a cold sweat. "What is this about? Why are people so upset?" I ask my sister.

"I don't know. I'm trying to figure it out. Is Jackson involved with someone else?"

"Not that I know of." I try not to overreact. But it's difficult.

Jackson lives halfway across the country. I only see him once a week at the very most, and that's if his schedule allows it. Although he mentioned wanting to spend a week in Colorado after the charity event in New York, working remotely so we could have more time together.

I could very easily be his side piece and not even know it.

I hate that this is where my head goes.

"Has Avery seen this yet?" I ask as Harley pulls up the chair beside mine and commandeers the keyboard, quickly pulling up our social media account on the big screen. It's not isolated to our hotel IG account. It's on every platform and on my personal account, which Harley manages as well.

Harley finds a hashtag and clicks on it. We're brought to a whole bunch of images. All of them of Jackson, with Selene.

"Oh God." My stomach rolls as I take in the screen full of images. "He said she was a family friend and business associate."

"I mean, it's possible, but there are a lot of pictures of them together."

"There really are," I agree.

And some of the images hint at intimacy, especially with the way Jackson's arm is wrapped around her waist, and his lips are at her ear in several of the images, very similar to the one Harley took of him and me.

"I think I need to find out what's going on." Especially since Jackson is supposed to be in Colorado this evening and we have plans.

I screenshot several of the most heinous messages. I don't send them to Jackson, though. Instead, I send him a message asking if he's available to talk. He calls me right away.

"I can't wait to see you this evening. I was thinking we should just order in, that way we can make the most of our night together."

"That's probably a good idea considering I'm likely to be stoned if I'm seen in public with you." I don't mean to be sarcastic, or to start the conversation with dark humor, but I'm a little shocked and frankly pretty darn concerned about what I'm seeing.

"I'm sorry, what?"

There's no point in tiptoeing around the issue. "Are you and Selene romantically involved?"

"I thought we already discussed this." His tone is gentle and concerned.

"We did. But I'm beginning to wonder exactly how honest you were with me about it considering the concerning number of hate messages I've received in the past twenty-four hours."

"Hate messages? What's going on, London?"

"I think you need to tell me. I'm sending you screenshots now. If you're involved with someone else, you should have told me instead of stringing me along."

"I'm not seeing anyone else. That's not how I work, London. You're the only woman in my life right now," he assures me.

"No offense, but those words seem empty in the face of all of this contradictory evidence. Check your text messages. I've sent you a few of the most disconcerting screenshots."

He sucks in a breath and utters a curse. "I'm so sorry, London. This is not at all what it looks like. I'm leaving for the airport now. I'll be in Colorado in four hours. Can I come get you so we can talk this out? I promise, you're the only person I'm involved with, and I'll explain when I see you."

There doesn't seem to be any other option, so I agree.

The next four hours are horrible. Harley and I spend two of them scrubbing our IG account of the scathing, horrible comments from Selene's followers. We have to tell Avery about the hate messages, and she voices the fear we all have—that this is going to damage Spark House and all the gains we've made recently.

Dealing with a social media firestorm is emotionally draining and ridiculously frustrating.

At three in the afternoon, Jackson's driver picks me up and takes me back to his place in Denver.

He meets me at the front door. All I have with me is my purse. He pulls me into his chest, wrapping his arms around me. I stiffen and don't make a move to hug him in return.

He releases me and steps back, his expression reflecting his concern. "I'm so sorry. I know how this looks, and I should have been prepared for it. I've been in touch with Selene's team. They're going to call off her fans. They can be like rabid dogs sometimes."

"I thought you said you were just family friends and business associates." I don't hide the hurt or the accusation.

For the first time, I notice that despite the fact that he's in a suit, he doesn't look entirely put together. His tie is loose and pulled askew. The top button of his shirt is undone, and his hair looks like his hands have been in it a lot.

"Come in so we can talk?" He runs his hand through his hair and nods to the living room.

The last time I was here, we had sex on that couch. Well, I was leaning over the back of it. But that memory is one I can't seem to get out of my head, and I'm thinking it would be a good idea not to sit on a piece of furniture on which I've had an orgasm for this particular discussion.

"Can we sit in the kitchen, please?"

"Of course." He doesn't question me, just motions me ahead of him. "Have a seat. Can I get you something to drink?"

"Just water, please." I take a seat at the island.

He opens the fridge and pulls out a bottle of water—reusable, obviously. He pours us both a glass. "I'll be right back." He gives me a small, slightly strained smile and leaves me in the kitchen.

I sip my water and take a deep breath. I need to have some faith in the man I've gotten to know over the past several months.

But the hate messages, death threats, and everything I've seen today raises a lot of questions, like how honest he's been with me about Selene.

He returns less than a minute later and slides a small package toward me. It takes me a moment to realize it's star strip paper. "I don't know if it's a good thing or a bad thing that you thought to get me these."

He smiles, but it looks more unnerved than anything. "I know it calms you, and I thought maybe you would appreciate having the distraction. I'm sure you must have a lot of questions."

I nod and open the package. Freeing a strip, I start folding. "You said Selene is a family friend."

"She is."

"But you've been involved with her. Romantically."

Jackson grips his glass of water and nods. "In the past, yes. But it was casual. She was the friends with benefits." He sounds cha-grined. "We both have very busy lives and travel a lot for work. It was convenient and worked out for both of us. It wasn't this." He motions between us.

"So you were what? Fuck buddies? How long ago was that? And if you're friends with her family, does that mean you see her outside of business events? How does that even work? How can you be friends with someone you previously slept with?" I don't know if I want the answers to these questions. I tear another strip free, bite the tip of my tongue, and give him time to respond.

He rubs his thighs and exhales a slow breath. "Selene and her family were part of my support system when I lost my par-ents. I wasn't in the best place emotionally, not for a long time after that. We never dated, but I won't lie, we were close. And eventually some lines were crossed. She's been part of my life for many years, and when we weren't seeing other people, we would sometimes be physically involved. Mostly when a lot of drinks were involved, not that it's an excuse, but it wasn't frequent, and we were never in a relationship."

"You still work with her now, though. And you're still friends."

"We do and we are. We're both very capable of separating business and pleasure. Whenever either of us was involved in another relationship, we would always respect those boundaries."

"How could she be okay with you seeing other women?" I muse. I don't know if I'm asking him as much as I'm trying to understand myself.

"We weren't dating. It was more about the convenience. I *want* exclusivity with you. It's why I asked for it, hoping you would want the same."

I rub my temple. "When was the last time you were together?"

"It's been months."

"How many months?"

"Before I went to Peru. It's been more than six and after that, we agreed that it would be best to stay on the friend side of the line."

"Why, what happened?"

"It ran its course. We're better as friends."

I nod. Absorbing that information. I drop another star on the counter. "And she's going to be at the charity event in New York."

"Yes. She works for Mills Hotels. She'll be covering the event."

"Does she know about us? What exactly are we?" I whisper the last part.

"I've been trying to get in touch with her, but I'll talk to her before the event. Her team is aware of the situation on social media, and they're going to set the record straight. As for exactly what *we* are, I consider us a couple, and when I introduce you to friends and associates, I would like to be able to call you my girlfriend." He swallows thickly, glancing away before his gaze returns to me. "I'm so sorry this happened, London, and that you were blindsided. That wasn't my intention. I should have realized that photos of us together would invariably garner media attention. I didn't anticipate the backlash. I haven't had someone in my life that I've dated publicly in a very long time. You're kind of a big deal." He smiles wryly. It makes him look boyish and ridiculously handsome.

"I still don't understand how she could be okay with you seeing other people." I don't think I'm successful at keeping my disdain out of my voice.

"She and I were comfortable with each other, and it made sense until it didn't anymore. But she and I don't have the emotional connection you and I share."

I nod, but I honestly can't imagine being okay with sharing Jackson, which I suppose tells me everything I need to know about my feelings for him.

He takes my hand in his. "Are we okay?"

"Yes. I think so. I just didn't know what to think of all the homewrecker messages." All I can hope is that Selene's public post about the status of her relationship with Jackson, dispelling the myth that I'm a homewrecker and a boyfriend stealer, will calm her rabid fans.

"Those never should have happened. Selene's fans can be very protective of her. I should have taken into consideration how much media attention my dating you would create."

"I guess I should have expected it as well. You're basically famous. And in the eyes of the public, this must look very much like a Cinderella story."

"Except you don't need a fairy godmother to turn you into a beautiful princess." He squeezes my hand. "Please tell me if you think this is going to be too much for you, London. I'm already in over my head with you, and I don't want to put you in any situations that are going to jeopardize that. My life is very much public, no matter how much I would like it to be otherwise. I can do my best to insulate you from the media, but my lack of public relationships has always been fuel for speculation."

"Which makes me a point of interest."

"Correct. If you don't think you're ready, you can skip the charity event and we can wait on officially going public with our relationship."

I shake my head. "I don't want to wait. I can handle it." I'm not sure if that's true, but I don't want to hide what we have either.

"Are you sure?" His expression is both hopeful and nervous.

"I'm sure." I squeeze his hand. "How many times have you been let down by the women you dated in the past?"

"My life isn't typical, and it can be a challenge to be my partner."

"Everyone can be a challenge."

"You know what I mean."

I nod. I do know what he means. Or at least I've had a taste of it with this whole hate-message shitshow. "I promise I'll tell you if I'm struggling in any way with the attention."

"I have a team watching social media and addressing the threats. I don't know how you'd feel about additional security measures, but if you're okay with it, I'd like to have your system looked at to make sure Spark House is secure enough. And I think it would be wise to make sure visitors provide identification if they're working on site."

"Is that really necessary?" I ask, taken aback.

"I'd rather err on the side of caution when it comes to you and your safety," he says gently.

"I don't know if additional security would be in our budget," I reply honestly.

"Don't worry about that. I'll cover everything since I'm the reason this is happening. And if there are any more negative messages or backlash, I need you to let me know so we can address it immediately."

"Okay. I can do that."

He lifts my hand and kisses my knuckles. "I was very worried today, London. I have to tell you, a three-hour flight has never seemed so long before. I wanted to be here the moment you called, and I hated that I couldn't fix things right away, or that you felt unsafe. I didn't like that you were kept waiting and wondering. I know how awful that can be."

"It wasn't my favorite either, but we're fine now." I realize he needs the reassurance in much the same way I did.

"Good. That's good." He takes my face between his hands and tips my chin up, covering my mouth with his. "I missed the way you taste."

We don't make it to the bedroom before we're naked and I'm wrapped around him, absorbing his apology through touches and moans.

20

INTO THIS LOVE I FALL

LONDON

Jackson has to head back to New York early the next morning, and my night off means I have more Etsy orders I need to catch up on. I'm definitely burning the candle at both ends. I immerse myself in work, preparing for our event this weekend. It's a bachelorette party, so it's intimate, with only thirty guests.

That should mean less work instead of more, but the bride-to-be keeps changing her mind on linen colors, so I've had to change the tables three times. On Saturday morning I arrive at Spark House extra early so I can manage a few last-minute things and spray a bunch of picture frames for my Etsy orders.

Harley finds me passed out on the table, streaks of gold and silver spray paint on my face. "You need to get more than three hours of sleep a night." Her fists are on her hips, her lips mashed in a line.

I scrub a hand over my face and blink several times. My eyeballs feel like rusty eggs. "I think we need to put our foot down and go with majority rules on hiring extra administrative help. This isn't reasonable. We can't even have outside interests or hobbies anymore without sacrificing sleep. It's ridiculous."

"I know. You're right. Maybe if we find someone first, it'll force her to agree," Harley says.

"Maybe. I get that this is her baby, but she can't run it without us. If I have a freaking nervous breakdown, she's going to find out real fast how impossible this place is to run with no backup."

"We'll be fine after this weekend," Harley tries to convince herself, but we both hear how hollow her words are.

"Really? Because my eyes are so bloodshot, it looks like I was hotboxing a bathroom and eye toked an entire blunt."

"They aren't that bad."

I give her a look that calls out her blatant lie.

"Fine. We're spending tomorrow morning sleeping in, and then you're letting me help you tackle whatever orders you have left."

"Okay." I could use the sleep and I could also use the help.

"And we're getting you some eyedrops so you don't look like you've been frolicking in a field of burning marijuana."

"That's fair."

I make it through the bachelorette party, but it's a struggle. I'm very glad that Avery is the face of these events, although I'm getting a lot better at the whole peopling thing considering the number of events and dinners I've been to with Jackson over the past few months.

As soon as Harley and I get home, she confiscates my phone, gives me a dose of melatonin, and sends me to bed. I pass out hard. So hard, it's nearly eleven by the time I finally open my eyes.

I pop out of bed, horrified that I've wasted those important hours on sleep. Despite all the hours I've spent unconscious, I'm still bleary-eyed. If I didn't have a pile of orders to tackle, I could probably go back to bed and sleep for another six hours.

I rub my eyes and amble down the hall toward the kitchen, yawning all the way. I need coffee, and then I need to get my ass in gear. Thankfully there's already a fresh, mostly full pot on the counter. My mug is sitting beside it. I drop in a spoon of sugar and a dash of cream and fill it within half an inch of the rim. The first sip is always the best.

I sigh, wishing I could go back to bed with my coffee and lie there for the next hour, answering emails, but I have orders that need my attention.

I head to the living room, which is where I usually set up when I'm filling orders and come to an abrupt stop when I find my sisters in there. And my stuff is already set up.

"What are you guys doing?" I ask and then yawn. I clearly overslept.

"Harley invited me over for blueberry cream cheese French toast, but it was all a ruse to get me to help out." Avery motions to the empty plate with blueberry smears on it and the mountain of puffy stars.

"The brunch was incentive, not a ruse." Harley gives Avery the side-eye before turning back to me. "We printed all your orders and the shipping labels. All the boxes are ready to go, and we set up an assembly line so we can help put things together. If you want us to."

"You didn't have to do all of this." I feel a little guilty that they're picking up my slack.

"We know we didn't have to," Harley says with a smile. "We wanted to. Well, I wanted to, and Avery wanted French toast casserole."

I glance around the living room, which is literally covered with my craft supplies. "You know, I sort of expected business at Spark House to pick up, but I didn't realize my Etsy store would too with this Holt Media connection."

"It's great all the way around."

"We're booked all the way into late fall next year. Maybe now is a good time to look at hiring on someone to help with the administrative stuff," Harley says absently.

"We don't need to do that. We're handling it." There's a bite to Avery's tone. "Maybe you should hire someone to help you with this stuff if you're feeling too overwhelmed. Like a student or something." Once again what I want or what I enjoy doesn't matter.

When we took over for Grandma Spark, she left Avery in charge, despite our unanimous decision rule, but there are times—like right now—when it feels a lot like she's abusing that power. I don't want to start a fight when she's here to help, so I leave it for now. "Yeah, maybe."

"Did you know you have over two thousand reviews and a four-point-eight-star rating?" Harley interjects as she curls another flower petal with a pair of sheers and sets it with the others.

"I do?" Last I saw, I had a thousand reviews, although I'm usually looking at my orders and everything else takes a back seat.

"You totally do. You should have some French toast and drink your coffee before you start tackling this stuff," Harley suggests.

"Wanna cut me another piece too?" Avery calls out as I head back to the kitchen.

I cut two pieces and return to the living room, dropping into one of the chairs that isn't covered with my projects. "Can I have my phone back? I should probably check for new orders."

"I did that an hour ago, so you should be up-to-date. Also, Jackson messaged early this morning, so I messaged him back to let him know you were sleeping in and we were hoping you wouldn't be up until closer to noon."

"You messaged him back as me?"

"No, I messaged him on your phone, but told him it was me. Don't worry, I didn't read your text messages. Although, I did see the preview and from that one sentence it seems like that man is a smitten kitten."

"He's a smooth operator, I'll give him that." I balance my plate on my lap and slide my fork through the crunchy, buttery, French toast concoction. I hum in contentment as the flavors hit my tongue.

"Things are okay, though? You believe him when he says there's nothing going on between him and Selene?" Harley asks.

"I can't imagine that he would still want me to come to the charity event if they actually were together. He gave me the option to skip it, but I have that piece going up for auction, and honestly, I think it would drive me batty if I didn't go, knowing that Selene was going to be there."

"You don't trust him?" Avery asks with a frown.

"It's not that." I stab another bite of French toast with my fork. "I just don't like that they have a history, and he would be at the event and she would be there, and I wouldn't. I can see someone taking pictures and posting them on social media of the two of them together. And then there would be all this speculation, so I told him I'm going. Which I think is the right thing to do. I'm nervous, but I'll deal with it."

"So basically, you're jealous and you're willing to deal with whatever media crap comes your way so you can stake your claim on him."

"I'm not jealous."

"Haven't we already gone over this before?" Avery cocks a brow.

"I just don't understand how that woman could be happy sleeping with Jackson and it not being anything more than that!" And now I sound indignant. Maybe because I am. "I find it offensive that this woman has been with my boyfriend and never truly appreciated what she had. He's the whole package and more! He's kind, caring, attentive, understanding, and he's the first man to give me multiple orgasms. Who willingly sleeps with other people when they already have someone so amazing? Someone who takes what they have for granted! That's who." I stab the table with my finger and leave behind a sticky fingerprint.

"Tell us how you really feel." Avery grins.

"I want to make sure that woman knows he's off-limits."

"So, like I said, you're jealous."

I pause my ranting and frown.

"There's nothing wrong with being jealous, London. It doesn't make you a bad person. It just means you have strong feelings for this guy. And it seems pretty mutual," Avery assures me.

"Is this how you felt about Declan and all of the women he brought home? I would have lost my damn mind. Or at the very least torched their shoes."

That makes Avery laugh. "I didn't love Declan bringing home

all of those women, but we were both lying to ourselves about how we felt. And neither of us were in a place mentally or emotionally to make it work, so it's a lot different. But yeah, there were times I wanted to scratch a woman's eyes out. But mostly I was glad that none of them stuck around long enough for Declan to get attached."

"I don't get how you managed to stay *just friends* for so long. Every time I'm in the same room as Jackson, I want to tear his clothes off. The two months of being business associates was pretty much torture, and now that I know what he's like in bed . . ." I sigh. "It's like there's this constant . . . ache for him?"

Avery smiles and so does Harley, but she looks a little wistful.

"Oh yeah, that's normal. At least that's how Declan and I are. It was so much more intense at the beginning when we started sleeping together, because, well . . . we were exploring this new side to our relationship, and we'd spent a lot of years forcing each other into the friend zone even though the feelings were there already. When we finally gave in to them, we were ravenous for each other. Like you can never really get enough."

"Yes! That's it exactly! I can't get enough of him. Every time we go out for dinner, I want to rush through the meal so we can get back to his place and into bed." Just thinking about it makes my body warm. "When I'm not with him, I'm thinking about being with him, and I would gladly forgo sleep in order to get more time with him."

Avery nods knowingly. "It sounds like you're falling for him."

And I realize, in this moment, that she's right.

That's why my heart pounds when he calls or messages. Why my stomach flutters every time he calls me beautiful. Why I crave him so desperately.

What's even more startling is the knowledge that based on how intensely I feel for him, this is the very first time I've ever been truly, hopelessly in love with someone.

It's as elating as it is terrifying.

21

THE BITTER CRACKLE OF TRUTH

LONDON

I'm sorry I couldn't come get you, but I promise as soon as you land, I'm all yours for the next twenty-four hours." Jackson's voice holds both apology and excitement.

"You don't need to be sorry about not wasting an entire day on a plane so I don't have to fly alone." I think it's sweet and slightly ludicrous that he would have even considered doing that in the first place.

"Time spent with you is anything but a waste, London. I'll meet you at the airport at noon, then I have big plans for you."

If I wasn't in the back seat of a car on the way to the airport, I would most definitely ask if those plans entail being naked and horizontal, but since I'm not alone, I bite my tongue. "I can't wait."

"Me either. I've missed you this week. I'm clearing my schedule in New York so I can spend a week in Colorado."

"I can't wait for that either."

Jackson blows out a breath. "Okay. I need to go. I have meetings and I need to get a handle on myself. Have a safe flight. I'll see you soon, London."

"See you soon."

Four hours later, I'm in the back of another SUV with Jackson beside me. "We have a bit of a busy afternoon ahead. I've scheduled a little pampering for you when we get to my place."

"Oh? What kind of pampering?"

"A massage, facial, hair, nails, makeup."

"Oh. How long will all of that take?"

"Probably a few hours. Are you okay with that? I can cancel if you're not interested."

He looks disappointed by the prospect, and it's clear that he wanted to surprise me with something nice. Wanting to give him the satisfaction of doing something sweet is the only thing that outweighs my need for alone time with him.

"How soon after we get to your place will the pampering start?"

"The massage therapist is scheduled to arrive at one."

I check my phone for the time. It's already noon, which means we won't have much time alone, if any at all. "How long is the trip back to your place?"

"At least thirty minutes with traffic."

"That's enough time," I murmur.

"Enough time for what?" Jackson's brow furrows.

I hit the release button on my seat belt and straddle his lap. For a moment, he looks shocked, but I fuse my mouth to his and he responds quickly. His hands slide up the outside of my thighs, under my skirt, pushing it up.

"Can the driver hear us?" I whisper-groan.

One of his hands leaves my thigh and music filters through the speakers. He turns up the volume a few notches. "Not anymore."

"Excellent." I unclasp his belt buckle and pop the button on his pants. "Do you have a condom handy?"

"There's one in my wallet."

"Perfect. I have a great way to keep ourselves entertained on the way back to your place."

His eyes darken with lust. "I see Frisky London has come out to play."

"Is she your favorite?" I slip my fingers under the elastic of his boxer shorts, skimming the head of his erection.

His nostrils flare and his eyes flutter closed. He tips his chin up and exhales a low groan before he cracks a lid. "Every version of you is my favorite, but this one is particularly enticing."

"Hmm." I wrap my palm around him and smooth my thumb over the crown. "You know, after that time you took me to the estate sale at Harmon's, I fantasized often about what it would have been like to make out with you in your car."

"Did you now? Tell me more about that." He unfastens the buttons on my blouse, one at a time, fingertips skimming the edge of my lace bra.

"It was hard to focus on the conversation and I kept wondering how much of a pretzel I'd have to turn myself into to get into this exact position."

"We can absolutely find that out the next time I'm in Colorado."

I continue stroking, my rhythm faltering when he reaches the last button on my shirt and cups my breasts in his palms, thumbs brushing over my nipples, the sensation muted by the lace. "You are exquisite." He drops his head, lips sweeping along my collarbone, teeth nipping at the swell of my breast before he covers the peak with his mouth and sucks gently.

I thread the fingers of my free hand through his hair, holding him to my breast. "I've never had sex in a car before," I admit.

His gaze lifts, eyes hooded with desire. "That's about to change."

He tugs my blouse free from my skirt and carefully removes it, hanging it from one of the hooks on the window.

"You are beyond sexy," he murmurs, fingers drifting along the edge of my bra, then dropping to my thighs and running up the outside of them, pushing my skirt higher until he exposes my matching panties. His hands shift course, and I suck in a gasp when his thumbs sweep along the seam of my panties.

His tongue drags along his bottom lip as he slips a single finger under the lace at my center and skims my sex.

"Jackson," I whimper.

"So soft," he murmurs, and withdraws his hand. He brings his finger to his lips and licks the pad. "And so sweet." He wraps his hands around my waist. "I think I need another taste of you."

I shriek when he lifts me off his lap and sets me on the seat beside him. "Shh, we don't want Clint to know what we're doing back here." His mouth covers mine before I can respond and he shifts, laying me out on the back seat, one of his knees settling between mine. He props himself up on one arm and his free hand smooths up the inside of my thigh, fingers dipping under the lace of my panties to stroke my sex. I arch and moan against his lips. His tongue strokes out to meet mine, but he breaks the kiss a moment later and trails more down my neck and over my collarbone. He pulls the lace cup down, freeing a nipple, lapping at it before he continues his descent.

"Jackson." I grip his hair when he reaches my navel.

"Mmm." He pushes my skirt up until it bunches around my waist.

"What are you doing?"

"What does it look like?" He lifts his gaze and one side of his mouth turns up in a mirthful smile. "I'm turning you into a delicious appetizer."

I laugh, and then sigh as he drags my panties down my legs and sets them on the back of the seat, then drops his head and strokes at me with his tongue. I cover my mouth with my palm and thread my fingers through his hair, as he laps at me, bringing me to orgasm with his mouth, and I bite my palm to keep from making too much noise.

He fumbles with his wallet, dropping it on the floor and I snatch it up, find the condom, and pass it to him, my hands too shaky and my coordination too off to be able to help. He rolls it on, and settles between my thighs, entering me on a slow stroke.

When our hips meet, he drops his forehead to mine and exhales on a low groan. "You really have the best ideas. I was worried about having to wait until the end of the night to get inside you."

"At least now my dress has a hope of making it from my body to the floor in one piece later." I pull his mouth to mine and he moves over me with slow strokes that gain speed as he gets closer to release. I have to brace my hand on the door behind my head to keep from sliding up with each thrust. And when I come, again, I turn my face into his neck to muffle my moan.

I barely have my blouse buttoned again when the car comes to a stop. As it is, I have to rush to put my panties back on and smooth my skirt down, while Jackson tries to hide his wrinkled shirt behind his suit jacket before Clint opens the passenger door. If he has any idea what happened in the back seat, he hides it well.

As soon as we arrive at Jackson's New York penthouse, the pampering begins. It starts with a massage and a light facial. Then my hair is twisted into an intricate updo while another woman gives me a pedicure. A selection of cheese and fruit is brought in for me to nibble on, and Jackson disappears, telling me he'll see me in a bit, when I'm ready for the event. The team of men and women make small talk with me while they work on my makeup, talking about fantastic bone structure and how easy it is to accent natural beauty.

I've gone for manicures before and had my hair done for weddings, but I've never been pampered to this extent. I feel a lot like Cinderella getting ready for a ball, except instead of a fairy godmother, I have four different millennials primping and pampering me, turning me into a princess.

I'm ridiculously grateful that I took advantage of the ride from the airport, because by the time they're finished with me, it's already after four in the afternoon. While the charity auction doesn't start until seven, the cocktail hour begins at five thirty. The Mills Hotel where the event is taking place isn't far from here, but with rush hour traffic, it's bound to be another half-hour drive.

Once I'm deemed event-ready, I'm led to a room where my dress for the night hangs, along with shoes and a clutch. It's a designer number, and I don't want to even consider how much this dress would cost to buy. Sitting on the vanity is a box, a small peach-colored card fixed to the top with my name in Jackson's writing on the front.

I pick the card up and slip it out of the envelope.

A *little something beautiful for my beautiful someone.*
~*Jackson*

I open the box to find tissue paper dotted with fresh rose petals. I carefully peel it back and discover a matching bra and panty set in the same color as my dress. Everything is the palest peach. I slip into them, unsurprised to find that they fit perfectly.

My dress has a side zipper, so I'm able to manage getting into it on my own. Once I'm ready, I step out of the dressing room. I expect to find my prep team waiting on the other side, but in their place is Jackson.

He's standing in the middle of the room, hands clasped in front of him. He's wearing a black tuxedo that fits him like a glove. His pocket square matches my dress. He's gorgeous and he's all mine.

"Hi," I breathe.

"Hi, yourself." He crosses the room and takes my hands in his as his gaze moves over me. "You're stunning." He brings my hand to his lips and presses a gentle kiss to my knuckles. "There's just one thing missing."

"Oh? What's that?"

He leads me over to one of the mirrored stations and turns me around so I'm facing it. His lips find my shoulder and sweep up the side of my neck and his arms encircle my waist. He pulls me against him, his chest to my back.

"Jackson, we have to leave soon," I say in a breathy whisper.

"I'm aware. I just want a minute with you before we go. And I have something for you."

"You already gave me a gift. I'm wearing it under my dress." I tip my head, giving him better access to my neck, should he want it.

"There's one more." His lips brush the shell of my ear.

"I hope whatever that something is, it won't ruin my hair or my makeup."

He smiles against my skin. "I have more restraint than that."

"That's almost a pity."

"I managed to spend two months with you and I only slipped up one time."

"When was that?" I meet his gaze in the mirror.

"When you stayed here the first time and made Crêpes Suzette in the morning."

"You fixed my hair." I tip my chin down. "And kissed the back of my neck? I thought maybe I'd imagined it."

"That was when I knew I was in trouble. You were so tempting, I lost my head. I promise not to do that until we get home tonight." His lips leave my skin, and he raises his hands, revealing a box in one of them.

He holds it in front of me and meets my gaze in the mirror. "Go ahead and open it."

He doesn't let go of the box but holds it in his palm, allowing me to flip it open. A stunning necklace with a pale pink crystal heart is wrapped in a diamond-encrusted shooting star. I've never seen anything like it.

"This is too much," I breathe.

"Always better than not enough." He kisses my shoulder again. "I'm trying not to overwhelm you, but when I saw it, I thought of you in this dress and felt they would go perfectly together. Can I put it on for you?"

"Yes. Please. It's beautiful." I bow my head so he can fasten the necklace, and I'm not disappointed when his lips press against the nape.

"There you go."

I look at my reflection in the mirror. The heart sits just below the hollow of my throat. I turn to face him and smooth my hands over his chest, looping them behind his neck. "Thank you so much, Jackson, for everything."

"Absolutely my pleasure, always." He drags his fingers gently down my cheek. "I want to kiss you, but I know if I do, it will be hard to stop."

"I know exactly what you mean." I lick my lips in anticipation. All I have on is a little gloss. My makeup artist told me she didn't want to mess with natural beauty despite my eye rolls. I tug on the back of his neck, and he gives me a wry smile but dips down and brushes his lips over mine.

"We should go."

"The sooner we go, the sooner we can come home, and I can model the other gift for you."

He groans and chuckles, then steps back, out of my personal space. "This is going to be one hell of a long night."

The drive to the hotel feels like it takes forever. Especially with the way Jackson keeps kissing my shoulder and finding reasons to touch me.

I'm shocked when we reach the hotel, and the entrance is roped off. Paparazzi and bystanders line the street. "What's going on? Why are all these people here?"

"It's a charity auction. Some of the people attending are famous."

Up until now, I've only been to private events and dinners, so I'm unaccustomed to this kind of fanfare. "Like you?"

"No, more like movie stars."

"Movie stars are attending? Will I know any of them?"

I can't imagine what my expression must be, considering the way he throws his head back with a laugh. "It's possible, yes."

"Why didn't you tell me that before? What if I start fangirling all over someone famous and make an ass out of myself?"

"You didn't fangirl over me." His voice is laced with sarcasm and humor.

"I didn't even know who you were when I first met you!"

"You know I'm kidding, right? I'm not famous."

"You're not exactly low-profile, either. And you didn't even look remotely the same. Besides, if I had recognized you and realized who you were, you might have reconsidered approaching me the way you did, and then we wouldn't be here, with me freaking out over the possibility of famous people looking at my Etsy creation."

He plasters his mouth to mine, which startles me, and is probably the point. I think I'm halfway to an actual nervous breakdown. I sink into the kiss and Jackson. One of his hands curls around mine, and his lips turn up in a smile despite the fact that we're kissing.

I pull back and realize I'm fisting the lapels of his tux, and he's gripping the door handle with his free hand, preventing the driver from opening it.

"To be continued." He kisses the tip of my nose and releases the door handle.

He exits the vehicle first and holds out his hand. I slip my fingers into his palm and step out on the red carpet—which I've just noticed. He threads his arm through mine, and I grip his forearm tightly. He bends so his lips are at my ear. "This is the most overwhelming part. Just smile and try not to look directly at anyone who shouts at you because they'll blind you with the flash. I've got you, London."

"I trust you."

"Smile and hold for the count of five. Then we head for the doors."

"Got it."

His lips find my temple and the flurry of flashes reminds me of a lightning storm. Media shout questions. I hear Selene's name and my own and Jackson's, but he urges me forward, and I cling to him as we walk briskly across the carpet and up the steps.

"We turn now and wave, then head inside." He practically has to yell for me to hear him over the shouts and questions that we're apparently not answering.

And a moment later the din is shut outside. "Wow. I would hate to be famous if that's what life is always like. You can never have a bad hair day, can you?"

Jackson laughs and gives my hand a squeeze. "You can, but everyone and their best friend will know about it. You did great."

We're greeted by the staff and escorted to the ballroom by two bodyguards. I spend the next hour being introduced to one influential person after another.

It doesn't matter that I employ all the tricks I've learned over the years on how to remember people's names, there are just so many new faces, and time and time again, he introduces me as his girlfriend. It's all a bit overwhelming. And I worry that people are going to make assumptions about why I'm with him or think that I'm using him for his connections and wealth.

Just before we sit down for dinner, Jackson is approached by a couple who look to be in their early to mid-sixties. The woman gives me an assessing glance, one I've been on the receiving end of a few times this evening, although it's usually from women closer to my age.

"Jackson, darling, it's been too long. You haven't been by for dinner in ages." She air-kisses him on both cheeks.

"It's been a busy last few months," he replies.

"We need a round of golf soon, son. Martina is right, it's been far too long. Are you traveling next week? We could arrange a brunch."

"I've been spending a lot of time in Colorado lately. I'll have to look at my schedule."

"And who might your friend be?" The man nods in my direction.

"Excuse my poor manners. London, this is Frank and Martina Angelis. Frank and Martina, this is my girlfriend, London Spark."

"Girlfriend? I didn't realize you were dating." Martina gives me a practiced, stiff smile and extends her hand, gracing me with one of those limp-noodle handshakes.

"We've only been seeing each other for a couple of months. It's a pleasure to meet you, Martina."

"Ah. I see. Well, it's a pleasure, I'm sure. Enjoy your evening. We'll be in touch, Jackson." Martina turns to her husband and slips her arm through his. "Come, Frank, let's find our table."

"We should do the same." Jackson settles his palm on my lower back and guides me in the opposite direction.

I don't have a chance to ask him about Frank and Martina, or who they are and whether I'm being overly sensitive about their reaction to me, because the moment we take a seat, Jackson and I are pulled into a conversation with our table mates. I'm very pleased to find that we're seated with the Mills brothers and their wives. After a round of introductions, Cosy takes the seat next to mine, and Amalie and Ruby force their husbands to sit next to each other so we can sit together. "They're going to talk business the entire night, and you'll be stuck in the middle, having to pretend you care about stock markets and hedge funds." Ruby rolls her eyes.

"Also, Amalie and Lex aren't allowed to sit beside each other at these events because they're horrible about public displays of affection," Cosy tells me.

Amalie, who is sandwiched between Cosy and Ruby, shrugs. "It's not untrue."

The women are incredibly easy to talk to. As we chat, I notice a woman across the room in a red dress looking in our direction. It takes me a moment to figure out why she looks so familiar. And then I realize it's Selene. She's stunning, poised and polished, and she's talking with the couple Jackson and I met just before we sat down for dinner.

It's then that I put together the fact that there's a family resemblance. She's clearly their daughter. And now I wonder if I wasn't all that off base in thinking I received a cool reception from Martina and Frank, and that limp handshake was purposeful.

I want to ask Jackson about it, but it's clear I'll have to wait until later. I excuse myself to the bathroom after dinner, and Jackson heads to the bar to grab us drinks.

"I'll meet you in the auction room?" I ask.

"Perfect. I shouldn't be too long." He kisses me on the cheek, and I head for the bathroom at the other end of the room.

I take a minute to collect myself. I know at some point I'm going to have to talk to Selene, and the thought makes my stomach churn. That uneasy feeling is only amplified when I overhear a group of women talking in the lounge on the other side of the bathroom. There's a wall between us, and I'm hidden by the vanity, but there's an echo in the room, making their conversation less than private.

"Can you believe he had the nerve to bring that woman with him to another event? It's like he's throwing it in Selene's face."

"I know. She's livid. Did you see her in the bathroom earlier? She's barely holding it together. I wouldn't be the least bit surprised if she confronted him about it. Personally, I'd like a front row seat to that. You know how she is when she's fired up."

"Mm-hmm. I sort of feel bad for that woman he's with, though. She seems like she's completely in the dark about the entire thing."

"Who is she even?"

"Some nobody. A pet project maybe? You know what Jackson is like, he's a bleeding heart. I heard she lost her parents to some kind of horrible disease. It's probably a lie, and she just used that as a way to lure him in."

"I don't know about that. I heard she lost them in a car accident."

"Drinking and driving?" another woman asks.

"Who knows? He has such a soft spot for charity cases. Always looking to save people, or help them climb the ladder. I mean, look at Selene. She wouldn't be where she is if he hadn't pushed her straight into the limelight."

"Well, it wasn't as if her family didn't have influence."

"But Jackson is the one who really put her on the map."

"Even after she refused him."

"Wait. What? Since when?" another woman asks.

"It was a long time ago. I shouldn't have said anything, so that stays here."

"My lips are sealed, but that's a juicy piece of news. I had no idea." There's a murmur of agreement from the other women.

"I bet she regrets saying no now," another one says.

"Mmm. When was the last time Jackson brought anyone other than Selene to an event? Never. I can't think of one time."

"Me either."

"I wonder if that woman is half as clueless as she seems. I don't think she even realizes the attention she's drawing or how much gossip there is around her."

"Did you see the necklace she was wearing, though? That's a Delacour original. That has to be worth at least a quarter of a million dollars. I heard she runs a bed-and-breakfast in Colorado."

"Can you even imagine? Her dress and that necklace are probably worth more than her little B-and-B."

One of the women scoffs. "I bet she's from some little nowhere hick town. And if that's the case, her shoes are probably worth more than her shack in the mountains."

That earns her a chorus of laughter. I'm grateful when their group moves on and leaves the bathroom. I swallow down the bile rising in my throat. My head swims with questions. All of them having to do with Selene, because as much as I'd like to believe those women were just spewing vicious rumors, I'm beginning to realize there must be more to his relationship with Selene than what he's told me. Otherwise, their reaction doesn't make sense.

22

THIS UNWANTED REALITY

As soon as dinner is over, I head to the bar for a drink. The silent auction is still running for another hour, and then they'll announce the winners for each item. With such a great turnout, we should have a sizeable check for the Cancer Research Foundation at the end of the night.

London excused herself to the bathroom. I'd be lying if I didn't consider abandoning my spot in line at the bar to accompany her there.

I don't love that I've caught Selene glaring daggers at her more than once tonight, or the number of whispers and looks that have been directed at our table, and more specifically myself and London. But following her to the bathroom is a little on the right side of overprotective, and I'm sure I'm just being hypersensitive.

She had a wonderful time at dinner with the Mills wives. Those women are as thick as thieves, and despite their being married into one of the wealthiest families in the country, they're grounded and very down to earth. They're also a lot of fun. Which I thought London would appreciate tonight. Hence the reason for the seating arrangement.

I usually sit with Trent and often Selene and her family, but I thought it best to avoid that awkwardness. I tried calling Selene again, but my messages went unanswered. I'm assuming she heard the voicemail I left her about taking London, but I can't be sure. Trent assured me that he'd speak to her, but I don't know how that conversation went.

Trent appears beside me and hands me a glass of scotch. "Where's your date?"

"In the bathroom, where's yours?" It's a joke; he rarely brings dates to events. In fact, Trent rarely dates at all.

"I need to talk to you, in private," he says quietly.

"Why? What's going on?"

He keeps a smile plastered on his face and shakes his head once. "Not here, too many eyes and ears. Let's take a walk."

I glance toward the bathroom. I don't want to leave London on her own for too long, but based on Trent's expression, something is going down and it doesn't look good. I follow him out of the crowded ballroom and down the hall. He makes a right into a small, empty alcove.

"How did you know this was here?" I ask.

"That's not important. So you know how I said I would tell Selene about you and London being a thing?" He makes a face I don't like.

"Please tell me you actually had the conversation you said you were going to. She's been dodging me for weeks."

"Well." He scratches his jaw. "I tried."

"What does that mean, you tried?"

· "I just couldn't go through with it. She was asking all these questions, wanting to know if this was just you doing another favor for London. She got emotional, and I thought she was going to cry, and you know how bad I am with women and tears, so I wasn't quite honest about how involved you were."

He jokes about being allergic to tears, but he quite literally breaks out in hives when women cry. It's a stress reaction, but still, it's a hell of a reaction. I knew I should have dealt with this myself. "So you said nothing?"

"I told her that you were bringing London, which she knew since she heard your voicemail, but I didn't mention the girlfriend part, which is how you've been introducing her all night, and the PDA has been pretty over-the-top."

I don't acknowledge the last part. "Why didn't you tell me this until now?"

"Because I didn't realize how upset she was going to be."

"I don't get why she's upset at all."

"Well, she was pretty much fuming all through dinner. It's a wonder she still has teeth in her head with the way she was grinding them. I tried to pull her aside and talk to her, but she's mad at me now too. Saying I had to have known and now she feels like an idiot."

I blow out a breath and look up at the ceiling. "I don't get it. Why aren't I allowed to have a life or a girlfriend?"

"You're allowed to have both, but Selene feels blindsided."

I throw my hands in the air. "Why would she feel blindsided when we already agreed that it was better to be friends ages ago? She's been avoiding my calls ever since the Colorado event.

How could I have a meaningful conversation with her when she won't even respond?"

"I don't know, but based on what she said, it seemed like she thought you would come to her eventually if she ignored you long enough?"

"What the hell is the point of that? Since when does she play these kinds of games? This isn't her style at all." At least not that I've experienced before.

"I wish I could explain it, but I can't. I'm worried about the optics of this. The way she's acting sets up London to look like the villain."

"That's the last thing London needs, especially after Selene's fans went after her."

"I agree, which is why I think you need to talk to Selene and figure out what the hell is going on."

"How am I going to do that? It's not as if I can leave London to fend for herself while I deal with Selene." I rub my temple. "I still don't understand why she's so upset about this. This hasn't been an issue before now."

"I know you said you agreed to stop sleeping together before you went to Peru, but what did that conversation actually look like? Who initiated it, you or her?"

I frown and think back, trying to remember. "I think I did? It had just started to feel like we were a habit neither one of us was willing to break and I didn't want to put our friendship at risk. Plus with the Teamology start up, we were working together a lot more. I didn't want it to complicate things."

"And she was fine with that?" Trent asks.

"She agreed that it was the right thing to do."

"Maybe she didn't think it was permanent? Maybe she thought after the roll out things would go back to the way they were?" he suggests.

"What am I supposed to be? A mind reader?"

"Did you ever sit down and talk about the limitations of what you were doing? For a long time it seemed like you two were blindly trucking along, using each other for comfort. At least that's how it looked from the outside." He rubs the back of his neck. "I'm not trying to overstep here, but maybe you need to give her some closure so you can both move on?"

"What is this, high school? Things were always very clear between us, so I don't know how I got here." I tap on the wall, trying to get my head around this whole thing. "Why wouldn't she say something?"

"I don't have an answer to that. But I do know that no one wants casual forever. Maybe she's been holding out for more, and you're not going to know that until you've talked to her." Trent pulls his phone out of his pocket and checks the time. "You have a long history and it's not simple. Right now, she feels like you're rubbing salt in the wound by parading London around and calling her your girlfriend."

"I wish I'd realized this before I brought London to this event."

Trent gives me a sympathetic look. "I didn't see it either."

We both blow out a breath and I pinch the bridge of my nose. "I need to find Selene."

"It's probably a good idea. London will be fine, the Mills wives will keep an eye on her."

I leave Trent standing in the middle of the hallway. I'd like to find London first to make sure she's okay, but before I can do that, I run into Selene. She's standing at the edge of the room near the balcony.

"Hey, do you have a minute? I think we need to talk." I incline my head toward the door leading to the balcony behind her.

Her jaw tics, but she turns and sashays to the door, pushing through it. I glance over my shoulder as I follow her outside, but I don't spot London anywhere in the room. I can only hope that Trent is right and that she's found the Mills women.

Selene moves to the far side of the balcony, into the shadows. She crosses her arms, her expression is flat. While I'm aware she's intentionally putting out an angry vibe, I've known her far too long not to be able to see the hurt that flashes behind her eyes.

"Where's your *girlfriend*?" she hisses in a low whisper.

"With the Mills wives." At least that's what I'm hoping.

She scoffs. "Of course. How perfect for her. I can't believe you have the nerve to bring that woman to this event. Do you have any idea how humiliating this is for me?" Her eyes glint with ire. "Have you heard what people are saying? I understand wanting to help the less fortunate, I really do, but you're taking this way too far."

I realize that Trent is more right than I wanted him to be. And that the conversation Selene and I had about staying inside the friendship lines wasn't received the way I intended. Trent has a point that for a lot of years I stayed where I was comfortable, and I'd thought Selene was fine with the way things were. But based on how upset she is, that's not the case.

23

THIS ONE MISSING DETAIL

LONDON

I leave the bathroom with my heart in my throat and go in search of Jackson. I stay close to the perimeter of the room, avoiding the guests as best as I can. I spot Cosy, Amalie, and Ruby on the other side of the ballroom, but one of the women who was in the bathroom is with them, so I avert my gaze and continue to search for Jackson in a sea of tuxedo-clad men and women in ball gowns. I push through one of the doors leading to the balcony, suddenly feeling light-headed and overwhelmed.

I truly feel like a version of Cinderella tonight. But not the one who has to leave the party at midnight because the spell my fairy godmother spun for me will come undone. Instead, I feel like I no longer belong. As if I'm somehow stepping on toes without even knowing it.

I gulp several deep breaths of fresh air, trying to clear my head, and step back into the shadows.

I glance around the mostly empty balcony and consider sending Jackson a text feigning illness so I can slip out the back door and head to his place, but I don't have a key or the entry code.

"Why are you doing this to me?" a woman asks quietly, sounding forlorn.

I don't want to eavesdrop on someone's private conversation, so I take a step toward the door, scanning the balcony, hoping that I'll be able to escape unnoticed. At least until I spot the woman the voice belongs to.

It's Selene. And she's not alone. Even in the dim light, I recognize Jackson's profile, and as a slight breeze picks up, the scent of his cologne wafts in my direction.

Selene's arms are crossed, and she looks like she's on the verge of tears. Neither of them notices me as I sink back into the shadows. If I hadn't overheard that conversation in the bathroom, I would turn around and give them some privacy, but I feel like I'm missing vital pieces of information. I have a feeling I'm about to find out if the things Jackson has glossed over have been intentional or not.

Jackson slips his hands in his pockets. It's his signature move when he's trying not to fidget. "This isn't about you, Selene. I didn't expect you to be so upset about me bringing a date to this event, especially when it's never been an issue before. You've brought plenty of dates to events in the past."

She throws her hands in the air. "There was always a reason and most of the time it had to do with business! You were never serious about any of them before!"

"That's unfair."

"Is it really? Before tonight, you have never brought a woman to an event that I've been present at. Especially not one hosted in a Mills Hotel. Not once in the past decade. And over the past three months, you've been seen everywhere with this woman! And you're flying her all over the country! What are you doing?"

"I'm introducing her to new clients. You're the one who suggested I bring her on board as a potential client for sponsorship."

"I suggested *your team* bring her on board. I didn't think you would make her your personal project. How much longer is this going to go on? Have you even told her about us?"

"She's aware that we were involved in the past."

Selene's eyes go wide. "In the past?"

"We haven't been together in months."

"Because of her!"

"Last time we agreed that this should stop." He motions between them.

"I thought you meant while we were starting up Teamology. How much longer are you planning to be with her?"

"Since when do you act like a jealous girlfriend?"

"I am a jealous girlfriend!" she whispers angrily.

Jackson recoils, his expression reflecting his shock. "We have never had a label, Selene. You turned *me* down, not the other way around."

She throws her hands in the air. "Because you asked me to marry you for the wrong reasons. We weren't even dating at the time! You were emotional and looking for a lifeline. I wanted to be it, but for the right reasons, not because you didn't know how to move on after your parents died. I thought if I waited long enough, you would ask again when the time was right."

He staggers back a step, as if her words are a physical blow he didn't expect. "Why would you allow me to believe that you were fine with casual when you weren't?" His tone softens, and his voice is thick with emotion as he continues, "You never once told me that you wanted more from me. Why wouldn't you say something? Why keep me in the dark about the way you felt?"

"I thought we would evolve naturally. I thought you would see that we were meant to be together, and you just had the timing wrong, Jackson." She takes a cautious step forward. "I honestly believed you just meant it as a temporary break. Nothing seemed like it had changed until that London woman came into the picture."

"I had no idea, Selene." He runs a rough hand through his hair. "I don't know how I didn't see this. I didn't realize it was me you were waiting on." He gives her an imploring look. "I'm with London now."

"I didn't want to push for something you weren't ready to deal with." She puts a hand on his chest and looks up at him.

I slap a palm over my mouth to stop my gasp from escaping. Everything Jackson has told me over the past several months— his failed marriage proposal, failed relationships because he refused to open up and let people in, all of it makes sense. The woman he proposed to is the same woman he's had a friends with benefits relationship with for who knows how long. And to Selene, I'm just a placeholder. I'm both devasted and angry, because Jackson has unwittingly put me in the role of the other woman in Selene's eyes, and apparently in the eyes of a lot of other people here. Something I never wanted to be.

I back up a step, needing to escape. I hit the back of my head on a wall sconce and hiss in pain. They're at a stupid height.

Both Jackson and Selene turn in my direction.

"London?" Jackson takes a step toward me.

I watch Selene's expression shift from hurt to anger.

"Don't." I point a finger at Jackson. "Stay away from me."

He raises both hands, as if he's trying to calm a cornered animal. Which is very much how I feel.

"London, I can explain."

"Explain? You *lied* to me."

He shakes his head, taking another step toward me and away from Selene. The way her expression crumbles cracks my already aching heart.

"I didn't lie," he says softly. "I told you I'd proposed before."

I swallow down the bile rising in my throat. "Yet you very consciously omitted the fact that the woman you proposed to is the same one you've had a long-standing relationship with. Regardless of whether you put an actual label on it, Jackson, that's exactly what it was. How convenient that your lack of label worked to your advantage when I came along. You made me the *other* woman." I turn to Selene. "I'm so sorry. I had no idea about the extent of your history."

I turn back to Jackson, who looks like he's the one who just had his heart stomped all over. The goddamn nerve. I reach behind me, searching for the clasp on the necklace, struggling to get it off because now it feels like it's choking me. "We are done. Don't call me, don't text, and don't have anyone contact me on your behalf. You clearly can't be totally honest with me, and without that trust, there's no way we can be together." I toss the necklace at his feet, spin on my heel, and avoid making eye contact with any of the people I pass on the way out of the ballroom.

I head straight to the airport wearing a ball gown.

24

THE LOGIC OF THE HEART

LONDON

I walk through the door to my apartment in Colorado at five thirty in the morning. I took a red-eye from New York and had to stop in Atlanta for a two-hour layover. I put my phone on silent to avoid the calls and messages from Jackson.

I managed to keep it together until now. But as soon as the door closes behind me, I sink to the floor and bury my face in my hands, letting the tears I've been holding back since I walked out of the Mills Hotel and hailed a cab to the airport finally fall.

I got a lot of looks at the airport and on the plane. I'm extremely grateful for virtual payment options, since all I had in my clutch was my ID, my phone, lip gloss, and a packet of mints.

I don't know how long I sit there on the kitchen floor, sobbing into my hands, but my nose is running, my hands are wet, and there are discolored drops all over my dress, likely because my makeup has run from my tears.

"London? What are you doing home? Oh God. What happened?" Harley's hand touches the top of my head, and then she's on the floor with me, wrapping me up in her arms.

I sob even harder, falling apart, feeling the weight of this pain like knife wounds to my heart. "He lied." I manage to get those two words out, but everything else is swallowed up by the pain.

And so I cry.

And cry.

And cry until every part of my body hurts right along with my heart. Until every breath is a gasp. Until there are no tears left to shed. Until I feel empty.

Eventually, I'm too dehydrated to cry anymore. The last time I shed this many tears was the day we lost our parents. I never thought my heart could ever hurt as much as it did then, but I feel this agony like grief. A loss like no other, because Jackson still lives and breathes, but he's not who I thought he was. He had so many opportunities to be honest with me, but he wasn't.

"I'm so sorry." Harley sets a coffee mug in front of me.

"I was falling in love with him." I shake my head. "I fell in love with him, and now I don't even know if his heart already belongs to someone else."

I explain what happened between hiccups. What I overheard in the bathroom, and then the conversation between Jackson and Selene on the balcony when they didn't know I was there. How I knew he'd proposed in the past to someone, but that he'd left out the very important detail that he'd been sleeping with that very same woman on and off for years. They might not have given it a label, but it didn't make it any less of a relationship. "Maybe it wasn't serious, but maybe it was." I pick up a strip of paper and can't find it in me to start making a star, because now I associate those with Jackson too. "And now I'm the other woman and driving a wedge between two people with a history I can't compete with. And frankly don't want to."

My phone buzzes on the counter. I turned it back on when I arrived home. The messages have been relentless. There are several voicemails from Jackson and plenty of missed messages, but there are also a ridiculous number of email alerts and social media comments. I'm terrified to look, in case it's another round of death threats and hate messages from Selene's fans.

"Do you want me to deal with this?" Harley asks.

"Please. I can't right now." I push my phone toward her, and she keys in the passcode. She and Avery have always had access to my phone, just like I have access to theirs. Although I don't think I'd ever want to read the content of Avery and Declan's messages.

"Do you want me to respond to Jackson? There are a lot of messages, and he's expressed that he's worried. I can tell him it's me and that you're home safe and would prefer that he doesn't contact you right now?" Harley offers with sad eyes.

I nod once and feel myself crumpling, tears I didn't think myself capable of shedding streaming down my face and landing on the countertop.

As soon as she sends the text, my phone rings and Harley sighs. "She doesn't want to talk to you right now."

I try to breathe, to shut off the thoughts and feelings, but they crash over me in waves, pulling me under, dragging me down with the undertow. I feel like I'm struggling for air, every inhale a gasp and a sob.

"Do you hear that? This is your fault. You did this, you heartless sonofabitch. Leave her the hell alone." My phone clatters to the floor.

And then I'm wrapped in a set of arms that aren't the ones I want. "It'll be okay. I'm so sorry, London. I'm here. I'm sorry."

"I never want to fall in love again. It hurts too much." I wonder if my heart is too broken to fix anyway.

The hate mail and messages I expect don't ever come. But in the days that follow me walking out on that charity event, life changes yet stays the same. Selene posts about the auction and my piece is featured prominently. I find out it went for over twenty-five thousand dollars, and the event raised over two million dollars.

It's bittersweet considering the way my life feels like it's fallen apart, and I'm standing in the rubble, trying to hold myself together while everyone else moves forward.

In the wake of the event, my Etsy shop orders have more than tripled, and my social media following has skyrocketed. It's amazing and overwhelming, and a much-needed distraction from the constant ache in my chest.

Like a true masochist, every morning when I open my laptop, I go to the Google Doc I share with Jackson. Trent took over for a while, but I notice he's been removed and now it's just shared with Jackson again.

The icon in the top right corner shows me that he's in the doc. The chat bubble pops up and a message appears.

Every star you see in the night sky is bigger and brighter than the sun.

I don't respond, but the next morning I check again.

The universe is not made of atoms. It's made of tiny stories.

Every day there's a new message. And every day I read it and shut the document before I'm tempted to respond.

In the week that follows the event, the things I left at Jackson's New York penthouse are delivered to Spark House. And not by a mail carrier. It's Mitchell who brings them, and Harley and Avery who collect them for me. I send out the dress in return, and despite Mitchell's insistence that it's meant to be kept, he gives in and takes the dress, probably because Harley told him it would meet a terrible end if it stayed here, and I didn't need any additional reasons to cry. My sisters have also intercepted every single email, message, and phone call from Jackson and Holt Media, taking it over entirely for me so I don't have to deal with anything related to him. I know it can't go on like this forever, but it will until I can think about him without crying. This is the way it's going to have to be.

Harley brings my suitcase into the office, her bottom lip between her teeth.

"Thank you for handling that for me." I can barely get the words out without choking up.

She nods sadly and continues to chew on her bottom lip. "He's in the car. He wants to know if you'd be willing to speak with him. I said you wouldn't be, but he wanted me to ask and make sure before he leaves."

I hold onto the edge of the desk, willing my body to stay where it is and not go running into the mouth of the lion. I breathe through the pain, wondering how long it takes a broken heart to mend itself. Hoping that this horrible ache will eventually subside. I remind myself that I've suffered greater losses and survived them. But this feels different. The pain isn't the same.

"I can't," I croak.

"I'll tell him." She turns and walks down the hall.

I breathe and count to sixty, no longer fighting the fresh tears of hopelessness. And I try so hard to stay where I am, but my stupid, broken, and masochistic heart wins the fight. I push away from my desk and move on unsteady legs to the window that looks out on the front drive.

I stand behind the curtain and peek through the narrow gap. There's a black SUV in the driveway. And standing beside it is Jackson. He looks every bit as gorgeous as he did the last time I saw him, but as I drink him in like the idiot I am, I notice the dark circles under his eyes, how it looks as though it's been a few days since he last shaved. He's wearing a worn long-sleeve shirt and a pair of tattered jeans with holes in them. Not the purposeful kind either.

He runs a hand through his hair, sending it into further disarray and bows his head, his back expanding and contracting on what looks like a sigh.

Harley stands there, hands on her hips, head tipped back, and chin jutting out.

His lips form the word *please* and she shakes her head.

I feel a sob bubbling up, one I'm powerless to keep inside.

"London?" Avery's soft, worried voice comes from behind me. She laces her fingers with mine.

"I'm sorry," I whisper.

"You have nothing to be sorry for. I know it's hard. We're here for you." She steps in closer, her chest against my back, her chin resting on my shoulder.

"I didn't realize it could hurt like this. I don't know how you managed to go on every day when you and Declan broke up. I'm sorry if I wasn't there enough for you."

She wraps her arms around me. "You were there, and you were everything I needed you to be, and Harley and I are going to be everything you need, as much as we can."

Harley turns and walks away, and Jackson stands there in the driveway, his face a mask of agony that matches mine. He rubs at his eyes with the heels of his hands, and Mitchell gets out of the SUV. He puts a hand on Jackson's shoulder and says something to which Jackson finally nods. He rounds the hood of the SUV, but as he opens the door he looks up, and his gaze moves across the outside of Spark House, stopping at the window I'm hiding behind.

His eyes are full of the same pain that makes my heart squeeze.

I step back and let the curtain fall into place.

"Why does it hurt so much when I know walking away is the right thing to do?"

"The heart is stupid. It doesn't like logic. It gravitates to the things that make it feel intensely, even if those things will eventually cause it pain."

Harley appears a few seconds later, and I'm engulfed in a hug from both sides.

And again, I fall apart.

When I get home, I do something stupid. I take my suitcase to my bedroom and lock the door. I feel beyond pathetic as I set it on top of my comforter and lay my forehead on the hard plastic while I wrap my arms around it.

I have never felt this level of hurt over the loss of a relationship. It makes me question how closed off I've been up until now. I try to convince myself to get Harley and make her look through the suitcase before I do, in case Jackson has left a note in here. I'm even more terrified that he hasn't. I close my eyes and there he is, standing in the driveway looking as broken as I feel.

Is he going back to Selene?

Did he realize I was a mistake?

Does he want me still? Do I want to be wanted? Why can't I just let go?

I didn't ask Harley about the conversation outside of Spark House with Jackson, and she didn't offer any information. I have no idea what he wanted to say, or why he was there in the first place.

I unzip the case and brace myself as I open it. Everything is folded neatly, mostly the way I left it in New York, but with the few things I'd taken out sitting on the top. One of those small jam jars they give you at restaurants sits between my brush and my makeup bag. It's not filled with jam, though. It's a small collection of paper stars. I recognize the paper as mine. With a hand that trembles, I lift it from the case and shake the stars around. A makeshift snow globe without a scene or snow.

I set it on my nightstand and run my hands over the folded clothes. And then I lift the shirt I'd been wearing last week when I arrived at his place and bring it to my nose. As I hoped, it carries the faint scent of his place, and even more faintly, a hint of his cologne, telling me that it was he who packed up my bag and he who put the stars in the jar.

Under the shirt is an envelope with my name on it.

I don't know how long I stare at it, all the while breathing in his scent on my shirt. But eventually I set the shirt down and pick up the envelope. I run my fingers over my name, written in Jackson's pretty cursive. I don't have the restraint necessary not to open it.

It isn't sealed, so I flip it open and withdraw the single sheet of paper.

London,

    I don't have words to express how much our time together has meant to me. If or when you're ready, I'm here to talk.

                              Yours,

                              Jackson

I want to be able to read between the lines to know what talking looks like, but I can't. So I tuck the note and the jar of stars in my nightstand drawer. I don't know when I'll be ready to talk, if ever, in the wake of what feels like such a massive betrayal.

I don't know who I feel worse for right now. Myself or Selene. I suppose if this makes him realize she means more to him than he led me to believe, then I have my answer.

An hour later I leave my room and decide it's time to move forward. I can't wallow in misery like this. First of all, I don't have time. And second, I'm so miserable, I don't even want to be around myself.

I throw myself into my Etsy orders—lord knows I have enough of them to tackle—and when I'm not at work planning events, I'm at home, putting together orders and doing everything I can to avoid thinking about Jackson and the letter still sitting in my nightstand.

It's two weeks post-breakup, and every morning when my alarm goes off, I open the Google Doc, and check for Jackson's message. Once I've read it, I drag my depressed butt out of bed. I force myself to shower, to put on makeup, to put effort into getting dressed. I choke down breakfast that tastes like sawdust.

I feign cheerfulness when I take phone calls and force a smile when I meet new clients, but every day feels like an uphill climb through emotional sludge, and no matter what I do, I can't make my heart forget to love him. I don't understand how I can feel this strongly about someone after only a handful of months. It doesn't seem logical or reasonable for my heart to ache this way or feel this hollow.

It's a Monday, and I'm sitting at my desk reading emails when Harley clears her throat.

I glance up and she holds out a tissue.

"What's that for? Did something happen?" My stomach twists at the thought that something happened to Avery. Again. Or Grandma Spark. She's been enjoying Europe and her new boyfriend, and I can't see her coming home until we're close to the wedding.

"Nothing happened." She gives me a sad smile. "But you're crying."

I touch my cheek and my fingertips come away wet. I don't know what it says that I didn't even realize it was happening, or that I've been staring at the same email for probably twenty minutes, processing nothing.

Harley takes a seat in the chair across from mine. "Maybe

you need to just hear him out, at least get some closure so you can move on, if that's what you want to do."

I shake my head. "I can't." I can't handle seeing him. I can't deal with him in three dimensions. I can't let him see how much this has affected me.

Harley sighs and passes me another tissue before she covers my hand with hers and squeezes. "I know this is hard for you and that you feel very betrayed, but there are two sides to every story. Don't you want answers?"

"Yes. No. I don't know. I don't want to love him, but I do. I don't know if I'm strong enough to say no to him if he wants me back, or if I can deal with the other side of the coin. I feel like I need to apologize to every single guy I've ever dated and broken it off with. I feel like I've been purposely choosing the wrong guys so I couldn't get hurt, and now I feel like I finally met the right guy, but he hasn't been transparent about his past, and I don't know if I can trust him to be honest with me." I dab at the corners of my eyes, trying to get a handle on my emotions, but it's pointless. Once the tears start, I can't stop them from coming. "I had no idea it could hurt this much to lose someone you love. The only comparison I have is when our parents died. And somehow, even though Jackson is still very much alive, it almost hurts worse, if that makes any sense."

Her smile is sad and knowing. "It does. Because he's still out there and you're still here, and those feelings haven't gone away."

"When does it get better?"

"I don't know. But avoiding the pain isn't going to help make it go away. If nothing else, talk to him so you can start to mend your heart. You have to tend to the wound so you can heal."

25

WOMAN TO WOMAN

LONDON

Gifts start to show up a little more than two weeks after I left New York. First, it's little things—a package of new star strips in designs that are impossible not to fall in love with, treats from the bakery we stopped at before the estate sale. Then a framed photo of me and my sisters at the Spark House event that was clearly inspired by my Etsy store. After that, a pair of earrings made from my puffy stars arrives. It would be so much easier if they were gifts I could send back, but they're thoughtful and they're wearing me down.

That scares me because I'm afraid to open my heart back up just to have it slashed to ribbons again. And maybe that's the real issue. That I'm avoiding a conversation with Jackson because either way, whether or not we're done for good, he has the ability to cause me a great deal of pain. Which is something I've spent my adult life shying away from.

It's a Tuesday and it's started like every other day: me waking up, checking the Google Doc. Except today there was no message from Jackson. I've had to fight with myself not to check again. Needless to say, it hasn't been a great morning. Has he given up on me? Did I make him wait too long?

Avery comes rushing into the office, clearly flustered. "Hey! I'm so glad you're here, I need a favor."

"Okay. What's up?"

"I have a meeting with the Williamsons at noon, but there's a problem with the alterations on my dress and I need to go to the boutique so they can do whatever they need to do to make sure it fits. She was mostly speaking in dress lingo, and she seemed kind of panicked and insistent that I needed to come right away. I wouldn't ask if it wasn't an emergency. Please, London? I'll love you forever."

I honestly don't have the energy to get mad at her, or tell her again that we need to hire someone else to help us out. I've started to put together a list, so I have ammunition for the discussion that definitely has to happen, sooner rather than later. I haven't been in a place emotionally to stand up to Avery after everything with Jackson. It's a problem. One I need to deal with. But not right now. "Am I just going over the event details at this point? Can you send me your notes so I can read them over first?"

"Absolutely. They requested to walk through the venue one last time and make sure it's going to be accessible without any issues. I want them to be reassured that everything will be taken care of."

"Of course, I completely understand." And I do, but I'm also aware that they're chatty, and that going over everything will be time-consuming because they won't want to miss any of the finer details. Which means I'm going to lose a couple of hours to a meeting I didn't plan for. And the Etsy projects that are waiting for me at home are going to have to wait a little longer. If things keep going the way they are, I might need to go on hiatus for a week or two so I can get caught up.

"I know it's not super convenient, but I figured you'd be able to manage it. I'd ask Harley, but this isn't really her area of expertise."

"I'll take care of it. Do you think you'll be back in time to help set up the ballroom for tomorrow night?"

"I'll do my best. Hopefully whatever the dress issue is doesn't end up being a big deal and doesn't take too long."

"Right, okay. Well, I guess Harley and I can take care of it if it comes down to it." I try to keep the annoyance out of my voice. I know the wedding is both stressful and exciting, but it's eating more of her time rather than less these days. And it's been three weeks. I shouldn't feel like my heart is constantly in a meat grinder at this point.

"Thanks, London. I owe you one." She leans down and gives me a quick hug and then she's off.

I realize after she's left that she didn't, in fact, pull the file for me, so I have to go through Avery's folders, and she doesn't use the same labeling and filing system I do. It takes me twenty minutes before I finally manage to locate everything I need. I pull up the information for the meeting, including the list of things I need to cover when I meet with the Williamsons and the map showing the accessibility features in Spark House.

I've just finished putting everything together when I catch the clip of heels coming down the hall. Avery never wears heels; they were a rarity before the accident and after it, an impossibility. Harley usually prefers flats unless we have a formal event.

So I'm not surprised when a woman who isn't my sister appears at the office entrance and knocks.

I push back my chair and round the desk, calling out, "Come on in."

I'm shocked speechless when I realize it's Selene.

She gives me a small smile. "Hi, London. I know you weren't expecting me, but I wondered if you had a moment to talk."

I don't know what to do with my hands, so I clasp them behind my back. "I'm not seeing Jackson anymore. I haven't spoken to him since the charity event."

She nods once, her smile turning sad. "That's what I wanted to speak with you about."

I don't want to be rude, and my knees feel suddenly weak, so I motion to my desk. "Would you like to sit?"

"That would be great." She follows me across the room and takes a seat in one of the chairs across from my desk.

"Can I offer you something to drink? Sparkling water? Still? Coffee? Tea? A shot of tequila?"

She chuckles. "The tequila sounds appealing, but water would be wonderful. Still please, if it isn't too much trouble."

"Not at all." I pour us both a glass and take the seat opposite her, rather than putting the barricade of the desk between us. As she lifts her glass to her mouth, I realize her hands are shaking.

Selene sets the glass on the table beside her and folds her hands in her lap. "I'm not entirely sure what you overheard at the charity event, but I need to explain my side of the story."

"I never would have dated Jackson if I'd known that you were involved. I had no idea how extensive your history was. And I wouldn't have attended the charity event either. I can't imagine how you must have felt. I never wanted to be the other woman."

She gives me a small, apologetic smile. "You aren't the other woman, London, you are the *only* woman."

I shake my head. "But you and Jackson. He proposed to you!"

Selene runs her fingers along the handle of her purse, her expression reflecting a hint of embarrassment. "When he was twenty-two years old."

"You were still romantically involved," I say softly.

"But only because I pushed us to be." Selene clears her throat and glances out the window. "I've never seen Jackson as broken up as he is right now, and that's my fault. I didn't realize how invested he was in his relationship with you. I never told him how I felt about him. I knew he only saw me as a friend, but I continued to pursue something more. It wasn't fair to him."

"I don't understand."

"Jackson asked me to marry him at a time in his life when things were very unstable. I knew he wasn't asking for the right reasons, and I didn't want to start a life with him that was tainted by loss and desperation on his part. I was never his girlfriend, so to get married? It seemed crazy. And as much as it hurt to say no, it was the right decision. We stayed friends, and eventually well . . . our relationship shifted. Jackson was very clear about it being casual, and I agreed, but I'd always assumed eventually, we would be more, and he would ask me to marry him. But for the right reasons."

"I overheard that part. I knew that he had proposed to someone, but I didn't realize it was you. Or that you'd been involved for all those years."

"That's what I'm trying to explain. We weren't involved. Not in the way that you're thinking. Yes, we slept together occasionally, but I was always the person initiating. Jackson didn't come to me. I went to him. I kept trying to make us something we could never be. Yes, it was only when neither of us were with anyone, but I made it easy for him. I never asked for more and never told him I wanted more. There were years when we truly were just friends, so when he said we should stop sleeping with each other I thought it was just temporary. He'd said it once before, very early on, but I assured him back then that I wasn't looking for commitment." She pauses and looks up at the ceiling. "I should have realized this time was different, especially when he started spending more time with you."

"It doesn't make the emotional connection you two have any less real," I say.

"You're right. Which is why sleeping together was easy. We're comfortable together. We know each other well. But we don't have that spark. If we did, we would have been more a long time ago. I was holding onto an idea, not a reality. And I finally see it now. I want someone to love me the way Jackson loves you, London. And he does. Very much. He's so broken up over this. I don't want to be someone's second choice, and that's what I would always be for Jackson. I love him, and he will always be part of my life, but only as a friend. So please, London, talk to him. I don't think I could live with myself if my misplaced expectations and feelings are the reason you never talk to Jackson again."

26

HOLD ON TIGHT

JACKSON

I'm only half paying attention to what Mitchell is saying. I've been in Colorado for four days, and my focus has degraded exponentially since I've been here. Not that it was much better back in New York, but knowing that I'm this close to London and she's still out of reach brings with it a level of pain I've only ever experienced once before.

My phone buzzes in my pocket with a call. This isn't unusual. I field phone calls all day long. Normally when I'm in a meeting, I'll just ignore it. But for whatever reason, this time I don't. I pull out my phone and glance at the screen, assuming I'll send it to voicemail. Until I see London's name and her gorgeous face—the photo I've assigned to her contact—flash across the screen.

I hit the answer button and bring the phone to my ear. "Hello? London?"

Mitchell stops speaking. I cover the receiver and hold up a finger, signaling I need to pause. "I'm sorry, I need to take this."

Mitchell looks like his head is going to explode. It's a reasonable reaction considering we're in the middle of a meeting with half a dozen people.

"Hi, do you have a minute to talk?"

"Yes. I absolutely have a minute. Is everything okay? Are you okay? How are you? I miss you."

So much for keeping my cool.

I push my chair back from the table and stand, excusing myself from the room and Mitchell's slightly horrified expression.

"You weren't on the Google Doc this morning."

That was not what I expected her to say.

"I had an early morning conference call with someone in Europe, so I haven't had a chance to log on."

"Oh."

"Is that why you called?" I hope she doesn't hang up, not after waiting weeks for the chance to talk to her again.

"I'm . . . I won't lie, the last few weeks have been pretty awful. Selene came to see me today."

I feel like I need to sit down again. "What? Why? Are you okay?" Since the event, Selene and I have sat down and talked things out. For once she was completely honest with me and I think we're in a better place now. As friends.

"It wasn't bad. Her visit, I mean. She explained where she was coming from and where she was at emotionally and how she'd perceived your relationship with her. I don't know if you're in New York, or if you'll be in Colorado anytime soon, but—"

"I'm here. Right now. I'm in Colorado. At my office."

"Oh. I had no idea. Can I meet you there?"

"We could meet at my house if that would work for you."

"Yes. Okay. I think I can be there in an hour?"

"Perfect. Drive safely, please."

"I will."

I end the call feeling slightly more hopeful than I have in the past several weeks. Which I realize might be stupid since I have no idea why London was calling me in the first place—whether she wants to try to work things out, or if whatever Selene said to her only solidifies her reason for walking away from me in the first place.

I remember that I've walked out on a meeting, so I pop my head back into the conference room. I've known Harmon for a lot of years, both professionally and personally, so I'm hopeful that my walking out right now isn't going to damage either relationship. I apologize, tell him I have a personal emergency that needs my attention and that I'll call him tomorrow. I also make a mental note to send him and his wife a gift to make up for this.

Then I'm heading to the parking garage so I can get to my place before London does.

Less than an hour later, London arrives. I open the front door and there she is, wearing a pale dress, looking beautiful, nervous and tired. I want to pull her into my arms and just hold her. But I'm still uncertain of the direction this conversation is going to take, so I stay where I am.

"Hi." I don't even know if the word comes out with sound, or if I just thought it.

She gives me a small smile. "Hi."

"Come in. Would you like to sit? Can I offer you something to drink?"

"I would like to sit. And water would be wonderful."

"I'll be right back." I berate myself for not having water already available. I'm so eager to get back to her that I nearly spill it all over the counter.

I take a seat across from her, at the other end of the couch, not wanting to crowd her.

"Thank you for agreeing to talk." London takes a sip of her water and sets it on the coffee table.

"Before you say anything, I want to apologize for not being entirely forthcoming about my relationship with Selene. I should have told you about our complicated past."

"Why didn't you?"

"At the time, because it was in the past. At least it felt that way for me. Selene and I never dated. I never looked at what we had as more than friendship, which I see now was a mistake."

"Did you think I would be upset if I knew that you were still friends with her?"

"Honestly? I don't know if I even took that into consideration. Mostly I just don't like talking about it because it was a dark time in my life."

"She told me she was always the one who pushed your physical relationship."

I rub my jaw. "That's not fair to her. We'd had chemistry, and this might sound callous, but it was convenient and easier to appease those needs with someone who didn't expect more from me than it was to try to put myself out there and meet someone new, especially considering my experiences with some of the previous women I'd been involved with. It doesn't matter if she sought me out, I was a willing participant and she shouldn't shoulder the blame. My romantic relationships have never been easy, maybe in part because I didn't want to experience that kind of rejection again, and it was so closely tied to the loss of my parents, that those two things almost felt synonymous with each other," I tell her, coming to realize that it's exactly why I couldn't and wouldn't entertain getting serious. And why talking about it with anyone hasn't been something I've ever been open to. The painfulness of it has been too deeply intertwined. "I was too afraid to really put myself out there. At least until you came along."

"I think I understand what you mean. You were already comfortable with each other. It was easier not to put your heart on the line with someone new, and since you'd already put your heart on the line with Selene and survived it, sleeping with her allowed you to take care of your personal needs, without the fear of getting attached again," London says.

"It sounds really awful when you put it that way."

"It doesn't sound awful. It sounds like survival," London says with a small smile, giving my words back to me. "And somewhat familiar. Although I never had an ex I could go to when I wanted my needs to be met, I do have these." She raises both of her hands and wiggles her fingers, then maybe realizes what she's insinuating and clasps her hands in her lap.

"I consistently chose men I would never fall in love with. I don't even think I realized that was what I was doing until I met you. And then I had all these feelings I'd never really experienced before. Not with this kind of intensity, anyway. I mean, I'd never even been jealous until Selene. I had no idea what to do with that feeling. When I went to the bathroom at the event, there was a group of women talking about Selene, and being . . . catty bitches."

I sit up straighter. "What women? What were they saying?"

"I don't know who they were, but they were gossiping, just being generally nasty. But they mentioned your relationship with Selene. And then when I overheard the two of you talking on the terrace, I just couldn't handle any of it. I thought you didn't trust me enough to be completely honest. And then I didn't know what to believe. And I realize I should have given you a real chance to explain, but I felt like I'd been strung along."

"If I'd realized what Selene was holding onto, I wouldn't have crossed that line with her, and that's on me. I feel bad that I put you in that position. Omissions are the same as lies, and as embarrassing as it might be, I should have told you the truth. Selene and I talked last week. We both realize we made mistakes, but we also agree that we're better off as friends."

"And is she okay with that? Just being friends?"

"She seemed almost relieved. She told me that seeing how I was with you, and how broken up I was over you not speaking to me showed her what she wanted and deserved. If that makes sense?"

"I think it does. You have a lot of years of being tied to each other one way or another. And it's not as though you can just disappear from each other's lives. You run in the same circles and know all the same people. And you work together on projects."

"All of that is true. Although depending on where you're at and whether you'd be willing to give us another try, if you need me to avoid Selene, I can and will do that."

London gives me a small smile. "You don't need to avoid her. And I don't think that's fair or reasonable. I believe you when you say you're not interested in her romantically anymore, and I believe Selene when she told me she needed to let you go."

"Does that mean you're willing to give me another chance?"

"If you can be honest with me, even when it's hard, then yes, we can try again."

"I promise that I'll be open with you. I don't ever want to put you through something like this again. I hated that I hurt you and I couldn't fix it."

"This isn't going to be easy." She motions between us. "Especially with you being in New York more than you're here."

"Well, I'm hoping that's going to change a little, and that I'll be able to work remotely. And I'm hopeful that with Spark House doing as well as it is, you'll be able to hire on some additional help so you can work less and play a little more."

"That's a conversation I'll be having with Avery sooner rather than later."

I shift closer on the couch and extend my hand, palm up.

London mirrors the shift and places her hand in mine. She exhales on a sigh. "The last few weeks were awful. It felt like my heart was constantly in a meat grinder."

"I'm so sorry. I wish I'd handled things differently."

"Honestly? Me too. I felt so blindsided. I was terrified to talk to you, the hurt was already so hard to handle and I didn't feel like I could manage with more of it. And not just for me, but for my sisters, who had to deal with my moping around."

"I'm so sorry I put you through this. I'm sorry I put us both through this." I squeeze her hand. "Trent will be very glad I'm no longer too morose to do anything but stare at walls. And I'm sure Mitchell will be happy that I can focus on something other than what an idiot I've been."

London laughs and I smile, thankful for her compassion and forgiveness. "We were quite the pair. I guess we better make sure the other one knows exactly where they stand, so we don't end up in another morose situation again."

"In case you were unaware, I'm painfully in love with you, London, and I don't plan to ever mess things up like this again, because I don't want to have to go weeks without seeing your beautiful face."

"I love you too. So much it's a little scary."

"I promise I will do my best to ensure I never make you feel the way you've felt the last few weeks. Honestly, I don't think I can personally handle more time in that state either. I've been a mess."

"Me too. I did a lot of ugly crying."

"I did a lot of sulking." I reach up and sweep a finger along the edge of her jaw. "If it would be okay, I'd love to seal that promise with a kiss."

"That would be more than okay."

We lean toward each other. I should know better than to think I'll ever be able to stop at a single kiss with London. The moment our mouths connect, it's like a spark being ignited into a flame. Need, the kind that's built up over the weeks of separation takes over, and we practically tear each other's clothes off. I lose two buttons on my shirt and the zipper on London's dress gets caught so she has to pull it over her head.

Neither of us suggests moving to a bedroom. I want to slow things down, to savor every moment of having her back in my arms, but London has different plans.

"We can take our time later. I just need you inside me." She straddles my lap, naked and gorgeous, and tears the condom open and rolls it down my length. I grip her hips as she braces her hand on my shoulder and guides me to her entrance. Our eyes lock as she sinks down, taking me in, joining us.

We both exhale the same relieved breath. "I missed you," I tell her.

"I missed us. And this feeling." She threads her fingers through my hair, and tips my head, bringing our lips together.

We stay like that, mouths fused, as we move together, hands roaming, bodies melding, reacquainting ourselves with each other as we revel in this connection we share.

I'm so glad I have her back.

And I plan to never lose her again.

27

STRAWS AND CAMELS

LONDON

My clothes are strewn all over Jackson's living room floor. So are his. We're still wrapped in each other, still kissing even though the orgasms are over.

"Can we just spend the next twenty-four hours in bed?" Jackson sucks my bottom lip between his and runs his palm down my spine.

"I have this thing called work that's going to make that a challenge. And I think you probably have to do the same."

"This seems very logical and not at all what Fun London would say."

"Fun London has been on hiatus. Mopey London has been out in full force, and I think my sisters will be very happy to send her packing."

"Mmm. That's fair. I think everyone who has had the misfortune of being around me lately will agree that I'm a much happier person when you're in my life." He cups my face between his palms and gives me another long, lingering kiss. "If twenty-four hours is off the table, can I at least convince you to have dinner with me and stay the night?"

"Definitely. Let me call my sisters so they don't wonder where I've disappeared to. Then you can have me until the morning." I am fully prepared to have very little in the way of sleep tonight, and I'm okay with that.

Jackson reluctantly allows me to leave his lap and retrieve my phone. I grab his dress shirt from the floor and shrug into it, reveling in being surrounded by the scent of his cologne.

When I finally do find my phone, it's blowing up with messages from my sisters that span the last few hours. "Oh no." I slap a palm over my mouth.

"Is everything okay?"

"I missed a meeting with one of our clients and Harley had to fill in for me." I scroll through the messages, Harley's increasingly frantic requests to call, and her fear that she's going to mess up the meeting because she doesn't know enough about the account other than they're really important. "I need to go run interference. Avery had an emergency this morning, and I said I'd manage the meeting, but Selene showed up, and then . . . well, you know the rest of the story." I run a hand through my hair and blow out a breath. This isn't great. And there's no way I'll be able to enjoy my evening with Jackson if my sisters are angry with me, or if I've messed up with one of our clients.

"Can I do anything to help? Do you want me to drive you back?"

I shake my head and pick up my discarded clothes from the floor. They're wrinkly, but I need to get back to Spark House as soon as possible and smooth things over. "Can I call you a bit later? I'm hoping I'll still be able to make the sleepover work, but I need to deal with this."

"Just let me know."

Once I'm dressed and Jackson is back in his clothes—although he traded the dress shirt for a T-shirt—he walks me out to my car.

I let my sisters know I'm on my way back and that I will explain, and that I'm sorry, but based on Avery's frosty messages, I'm far from forgiven. Most of the time I don't like conflict, and I realize I've been seriously mopey lately, but Avery's wedding planning stress has been going on for months, and Harley and I have been picking up the slack, no questions asked. I miss one meeting, and it's the end of the world. Granted, it was an important meeting. But still, her personal life doesn't matter more than mine.

By the time I arrive at Spark House, I'm ready for the fight I'm sure I'm about to get. I love Avery, but she has to see that the way things are running has to change.

The second I walk through the door Avery is in my face. "What the heck happened to you? Do you have any idea how much sucking up we're going to have to do to smooth things over with the Williamsons? You were nowhere to be found when they got here! And you weren't answering your phone for hours!"

I cross my arms. "Do you want me to explain, or do you just want to continue to attack me?"

"You left Harley to manage a meeting that I specifically asked *you* to cover! If you had something else, you should have told me. What in the world could have been so important that you flaked on us!" Avery motions between her and Harley.

Harley looks like she wants to say something, but she's too afraid to.

"Selene showed up."

Avery's brow furrows. "What?"

"Selene, Jackson's ex, showed up here wanting to talk to me."

"About her relationship with Jackson?"

"Yes, and about how she had misplaced expectations, and it wasn't fair to Jackson because he was miserable without me, and she didn't want to be the reason things didn't work out between him and me."

"Wow," Harley says softly. "That takes a lot of lady balls."

"It absolutely did," I agree. "After that, I called Jackson asking if we could talk and he said yes. I forgot about the meeting and I'm very sorry for that, Avery. And even more sorry that it ended up falling on you," I tell Harley and take a deep breath. "But this is bigger than me missing one meeting."

"I get that you've been upset about Jackson. I know it hasn't been easy for you, but it sure hasn't been easy for us either."

Harley, who usually isn't hugely outspoken, makes a face. "I don't really think it's fair to put this all on London. I remember when you were going through your breakup with Declan that you weren't the easiest to be around either." Avery opens her mouth to say something, but Harley raises her hand. "It was your meeting and you dumped it on London last minute when she's already been under a lot of pressure."

"I had wedding stuff to deal with!"

"No offense, Avery, but you always have wedding stuff to deal with. It's been damn well constant since you got engaged. You're incessantly putting your personal issues before business.

You dropped a business meeting to tend to your personal issues, which is exactly what I did." I point to myself. "I know it's not the same, but you can't accuse me of being irresponsible without looking in the mirror."

"Of course you try to turn this on me!" Avery snaps.

"I'm not turning it on you. I'm pointing out the obvious. Just because you don't want to hear it, doesn't mean it isn't true. You've been MIA for months, Avery."

"I had to drop one freaking meeting. It's not like I do this all the time."

"Are you serious with this? You're turning into a control freak and it's hurting all of us," I tell her, my voice rising with my frustration. "I get it, your wedding is exciting and stressful, and you've got a lot on your plate, but we all do. Harley and I have been trying to pick up the slack as much as we possibly can, but it's becoming unmanageable, and this is just another example of that."

"We keep trying to tell you this, and you just keep shooting us down," Harley says.

"Great. And now you're ganging up on me. You're the one who messed up, London, not me."

I throw my hands in the air. "You're missing the freaking point!"

"What the hell is the point? I try to schedule my wedding stuff around Spark House. And in a few months, it will all be over, and then I'll have my time back and things will be normal again . . ." Avery seems to have lost her fight as she processes what Harley and I are telling her.

"But will they? You're going to be newly married, and I know you and Declan have lived together for years, but you're going to want time as a couple, as you should. And eventually you're going to want to start a family. Which, again, is something you have every right to want. We can't indefinitely juggle all of this on our own." I motion between the three of us.

"That's years from now though, and Declan knows how important Spark House is to me." There's panic on Avery's face, the kind that tells me I'm right, and she just doesn't want to see the truth. That we're going to crack under the pressure if we keep going like we are.

"We are busier than we've ever been. When was the last time we had a day off, apart from the anniversary of our parents' death? And what does that say about what we're doing here? I know you love Spark House and it's your baby, and I love that I get to be close to both you and Harley. You're my best friends, and I don't ever want to lose that, but I can't keep going like this."

"What are you saying? That you want out of Spark House? Is that what this whole thing with Holt Media has been about? You figuring out your exit strategy?" Avery looks shocked and horrified.

"No. That's not at all what I've been doing and that's not what I'm saying. What I am saying is that what you want and what I want, when it comes to Spark House, are two different things. And maybe we didn't talk about it like we should have before we started down this path. I love working with both of you, but you know that my role here did not come naturally to me. I've had to work hard to figure it out and be comfortable with my job. And I thought that when we started to secure sponsorships, we'd be able to hire new people to help alleviate the pressure, but *you* don't want to do that either. So we're all suffering as a result." I hold up a hand to stop Avery from interrupting.

"And I'm aware that I haven't been in good form for the past few weeks, but it's been months of this and there isn't an end in sight. We're fully booked out a year in advance. You have a wedding you're trying to plan, and I have a relationship I'm trying desperately to make work and a side job that I love that I can't spend any time on. I want a life. I want balance, and right now I have none of those things."

"Spark House is where it is because it's a family-run business," Avery argues, but there's fear lurking in those words.

"Spark House is where it is because we've worked hard to make it happen. I understand your connection to this place, and I know what it means to you. It means a lot to me too. But I can't keep up this pace indefinitely, and I don't think you can either."

Avery props her fists on her hips. "So what does that mean? Are you bowing out? Gonna give your two weeks' notice?"

"You know what. Screw you, Avery. Just because *you* want to live and breathe Spark House doesn't mean that Harley and I want to for the rest of our lives."

"You're unbelievable, you know that, London. You made a mistake and now you're putting it all on me."

"You're not even listening to what I'm saying. I want to be part of Spark House, but I don't want this to be the only thing I get to do. I can't keep going like this. I'm feeling burned out as it is. The Teamology initiative is just getting started and look how much busier we are already. If we're going to keep expanding, we have to bring people on board who can help us, otherwise I'm going to have a nervous breakdown. And then what are *you* going to do?"

"London's not wrong, Avery. We don't have any real time off. None of us have taken a vacation in two years, and you're going to go on a honeymoon for a week, which you should, but that means it's going to be us running the show." Harley motions between herself and me. "We're already spread too thin. I know you don't like the idea of hiring people outside the family, but we have to find a compromise. I might not be in a relationship right now, but part of that is because I don't even have time to pursue one. Or anything else, for that matter. As it is, London and I are tackling her Etsy projects together. I love both of you, but every other relationship in my life isn't getting any airtime." She sighs. "I want some balance too."

Avery glances from Harley to me and back again. "You both feel this way?"

"We've been trying to tell you this for a long time, Ave. You didn't want to hear it," Harley says.

I take the seat across from my sister. "Look, it's not that either of us wants out. We just need to find something that's going to work for all of us. We're growing, which is what you wanted, so we need the manpower to grow with us."

"But Mom and Dad were always so proud of the fact that we'd be the third generation of Sparks to run this place."

"I understand that's the way you interpret it. But Spark House wasn't doing a third of the business back then as it is now. If Mom and Dad were here, do you really think they'd be doing all this themselves?" I ask. She can't keep fixating on how things were and expect that it can stay the same. "I think Mom and Dad would be proud of everything we've accomplished here and how far we've come. Especially the fact that we had to bring in new people because we'd done such a great job."

"But Grandma Spark put me in charge of making sure we stayed a strong family unit."

"That's not going to change. It will still be the three of us running Spark House," Harley says.

"And I don't think Grandma Spark meant that we should bury ourselves in work to keep it just the three of us," I add.

"No. We can't bring in nonfamily members. Then it's not Spark House anymore," Avery snaps. "I'm voting no. It's not unanimous, so it can't happen."

"The only thing that rule accomplishes is giving you the final say about everything," I snap back. "Looking back at all the times we've had a vote, how often have Harley and I made a suggestion only for you to veto it?"

Before Avery has a chance to answer, I keep going. "The answer is almost always. It is always you against us, which indirectly means you have final say." I didn't realize how long I've been keeping my frustration inside.

"I understand you don't want things to change, Avery, but we have to start planning long-term. We should have started as soon as Holt Media added us to their Teamology initiative. It's been months now, and we're growing faster than we know what to do with. Something has to give. If we don't hire someone outside the family soon, this is going to cause a rift between us, and then it *really* won't be Spark House," Harley says in an effort to back me up.

Avery pushes out of her chair and storms out of the office.

I wilt in my chair. "That did not go over well."

"No. But give her some time to cool off and think it through. She's more upset because she knows we're not wrong. She just doesn't want to face it."

28

TEND THE FIRE YOU BUILD

LONDON

arley and I finish setting up for tomorrow's event before Jackson picks me up. I'm the last one to leave Spark House, Harley already having gone home. We're not going to solve any problems tonight. Emotions are running way too high and Avery is upset. I'm not angry at her, but I'm tired and frustrated, which isn't how I want to be when I'm spending the night with Jackson. I think we all need to be alone right now, at least for the night.

"I'm not sure I'm going to be the best company." I step into him and his arms encircle me. It's hard to believe I woke up this morning feeling resigned to the fact that Jackson was no longer going to be part of my life, and now here he is, the comfort I need.

"Things didn't go well with your sisters?" The concern in his voice tells me that I made the right decision in talking to him today, despite the problems it's caused.

"Avery is upset, and I understand why, which is probably the most frustrating part about the whole thing."

"Because you'd like to be upset as well and you're too compassionate to do that?" He smiles down at me and tucks my hair behind my ear.

"I don't know if I'm that compassionate."

"I do. Instead of going after Selene when you overheard that conversation, you immediately put yourself in her shoes, which is why you reacted the way you did, and rightfully so. With Avery, it's even more complicated. She's your sister, she loves Spark House, and you love her, but you also need some of your time back. You look beyond exhausted, and I know that coming home with me tonight means you're sacrificing time you need for other things. She needed to hear it even if it was hard for you."

I nod, aware he's right, but still hating that my sister is upset and our conversation is the reason why. Jackson takes me back to his place, and we order takeout. We set everything up on the coffee table and sit on pillows on the floor. I love that he's so refined, yet still loves greasy takeout.

"What's the biggest issue for Avery?"

"Losing control, I think. Or losing the connection with me and Harley? I don't really know, to be honest, but I never thought Spark House would take over my life the way it has. And I'm so, so grateful for everything you've done for us, but at the same time, the growth has been so quick, we're just struggling to keep our heads above water, especially when she doesn't want non-family coming in."

"It makes sense on both sides. I understand wanting to keep control of things. It took longer than it should for me to realize I wasn't Superman and I couldn't do everything on my own. Avery is just a little behind figuring that out. And she's had you and Harley juggling all the balls she's been dropping. Sometimes we need a little crisis so we can reevaluate our efforts."

"I think you're exactly right. As bad as I feel about missing the meeting, Harley and I have been doing double time trying to make things work and that's not a long-term strategy. And I want time with you. I want to be able to come see you in New York. Hell, I want a weekend off once in a while."

"Those are all reasonable things to want, and I highly approve of all of them, especially the part about spending time with me and coming to New York. I've spent a lot of years burying myself in work, and I feel like that's going to change now that you're in my life. There's no point in having all of this if I don't get to enjoy or share it with the people I love the most."

"I hope Avery can see it that way."

"I'm sure once she's had some time to think it through, she'll see that you're right." He takes my hand in his and kisses the back of it. "I wish I could take this stress for you."

"Well, there is one thing you could do that might help." I bite my lip.

His expression is earnest. "Whatever you need, London. Just tell me."

"I need you." I pull my hand free from his and lift my dress over my head, leaving me in a lacy bra and panties.

Jackson's eyes spark with lust as I climb into his lap. He settles his hands on my hips. "I'm yours to command. Where would you like me to start, London?"

"A kiss, right here." I tip my head and drag my finger along my throat.

His lips brush the edge of my jaw and sweep down my neck. He slips a finger under my bra strap, pushing it over my shoulder as he trails open-mouth kisses along my collarbone.

I undress him slowly, and he rids me of my bra and panties, and all the while, we kiss and touch, an unhurried exploration, the perfect distraction. He brings me to orgasm with his mouth before he settles between my thighs. And when he enters me, I feel that connection everywhere. We kiss and move together, a slow spiral up, finding comfort in each other and this love we share.

Jackson spends the rest of the night distracting me from my worries. I'm definitely sleep-deprived the next day, but I can't really find it in me to feel bad about it. I was right to voice my concerns, even though I'm not entirely sure the fallout is going to be something I like.

But I can see what the next few months are going to look like. Nothing is slowing down. Avery's getting married, and I don't want to be shackled to Spark House. I want time to enjoy my life and my sisters and my boyfriend.

I can only hope that she had time to sleep on it and has come to realize the same thing.

Jackson drops me off at Spark House just before eight. I'm surprised to see Avery's car already there. She usually doesn't roll in until closer to eight thirty. And often she stays later than me and Harley, so it all balances out in the end.

Jackson gives my hand a squeeze. "I'd ask you if you want me to come in with you, but I think I already know the answer."

"It's just fear of the unknown. I'm not actually scared of Avery. I don't want the conflict, but I know it needs to happen."

"Will you call me later, let me know how things go this morning?"

"I will. I promise. But send me your meeting schedule so I'm not interrupting anything. I don't need Mitchell on my bad side because his boss is taking off in the middle of more meetings."

"At least leave me a message if I'm in a meeting, or I'll be distracted."

"I feel like I'm a bad influence."

"Absolutely untrue. You're the best influence."

"I don't think Mitchell agreed with that yesterday when you left."

He chuckles. "Mitchell is used to me being a micromanaging workaholic. He's unaccustomed to me wanting time away from work, but he'll adjust."

He kisses me goodbye, and I head into Spark House, unsure what I'm about to face.

I'm surprised to find not only Avery and Harley, but also Declan in the office. They're clearly waiting for me.

"What's going on?" I glance at all their faces, trying to read the tone of the room.

"Come have a seat." Harley pats the chair next to hers.

I give Avery the side-eye. "Are you going to get on me again about the meeting I've already apologized for?"

"No." She looks appropriately chagrined. "I'm really sorry I laid into you like that. I had some time to think about how I reacted. It wasn't fair of me to dump that meeting on you, especially not with what you've been going through with Jackson. You never would have done that to me. It was really shitty of me, and I feel like a huge jerk. I bailed on work when I shouldn't have, and that's on me. We have a proposal for you."

"And coffee and cinnamon rolls," Harley adds.

"This isn't some kind of ambush, is it? You aren't going to ply me with coffee and tell me nothing is going to change."

All three of them shake their heads.

I take the chair next to Avery, who nods to Declan.

"I've been looking at your finances over the past couple of months, and I've projected your potential revenue for the coming year based on the increase and potential stabilization of growth." He manages our financial portfolio and has ever since he graduated from college. He spins his laptop around so I can see the growth chart. "And based on what we're seeing, it looks like Spark House is going to double profits from last year. And that's being conservative."

"Which means we should be able to hire someone else to help?" I ask, hopeful that this is where this conversation is going.

"You will definitely be able to hire someone to help. Multiple someones, actually."

Avery gives him a look. "Can we ease into things, please?"

"Absolutely, babe. Easing into things is clearly my strong suit since it took me a decade to ease into asking you to marry my stupid ass." Declan turns back to me when Avery rolls her eyes at him. "I already knew Avery was under a lot of pressure, but I didn't realize how hard this was on the two of you. There's nothing wrong with realizing that you need extra support and hiring the right people to provide that. So if you're in agreement, we thought it might be a good idea to bring me in to handle the business administration of Spark House."

"You want to work for Spark House?" I lean back in my chair, taking in Avery's, Harley's, and Declan's expressions. It doesn't look like they're joking.

"Declan has mentioned it a bunch of times over the past few months, and I kept putting him off because . . . well, it scared the crap out of me. I didn't want it to mess with this." She motions to the three of us. "But I can see how me stonewalling the two of you every time you brought it up has been making your lives impossible. I don't want either of you to hate working here, and I can see if we keep going down this path, that could happen. We're all overworked. I see that now. We don't have a work-life balance, and that's not good for any of us. I've been really selfish about all of this. I didn't realize *how* selfish until last night, and I'm really sorry it took me so long to finally stop and listen to what you were both trying to tell me." She looks like she's on the verge of tears, which isn't something that happens often with Avery.

"Anyway, an apology is just words if it's not followed by any kind of action. Declan and I talked about it last night, and I ran it past Harley. If you're in agreement, Declan can take over managing the finances and business administration, which would leave you free to work on the creative side of things, if that's what you want."

I sit there for a few long seconds, absorbing what I'm hearing. "But that doesn't take the pressure off of you."

"We're going to work on that too. I know I need to hire an assistant, so we can see if anyone on our current team would be a good fit, or we can interview. But no matter what, we're going to hire more staff. You're right, we're growing too fast, and we all deserve to have lives outside of Spark House. I'm really sorry. I shouldn't have flipped out on you the way I did last night. It was unfair and totally my fault."

"What about the unanimous vote rule?" I ask.

"I think we should change it to majority rules between the three of us. It's the way it should've been from the get-go."

"I agree," Harley says with a smile.

"I'm really sorry," Avery says again, still looking like she's about to cry.

"It's okay. We get it. Spark House is your baby, and it's our family legacy. I get that you want to keep it family-run, and that's absolutely what it will be, just with a little extra help."

Avery, Harley, and I stand at the same time and wrap our arms around one another in a tight hug. I glance over Avery's shoulder at Declan and mouth *thank you*.

He nods and winks, grinning widely.

My heart is so full of love, for my family, for Declan, who will soon join us, and for Jackson, who I know will be just as happy as I am about this new, wonderful step forward.

Epilogue

BE MY LIGHT IN THE DARK

LONDON

FOUR MONTHS LATER

"Hey, what are you doing in here? Harley's been looking for you." Jackson startles me, and I nearly drop my clutch on top of a platter of tarts.

"I'm just checking on the food."

He gives me a look I'm very familiar with. It's a half smile with an arched eyebrow. It makes his gorgeous face that much more panty-melting. And he really doesn't need help in that area. He wraps an arm around my waist and pulls me away from the table of appetizers. "Stop working and just be a sister for a day."

"I wanted to make sure we have the right appetizer assortment. Avery was very clear that it should be classy pub chic."

"Uh-huh. For someone who's been pushing to hire more people to manage stuff for you, you're pretty deep into the micromanaging."

"Says the biggest micromanager I know." I poke him in the chest.

He grabs my finger and raises my hand to his lips, kissing my knuckles. "I know. I'm working on it, but your sisters are looking for you and your presence has been requested. She's walking down the aisle in half an hour and freaking out a little."

"Avery is? She doesn't have cold feet, does she?"

"I don't think so, just struggling with the whole dress situation and talking about walking down the aisle in her soccer jersey."

"Oh my . . . no. That cannot happen. The pictures would be horrendous." I try to push away, but Jackson's hold on me tightens.

"Before you go, I wanted to tell you that you're stunning, and I cannot wait to dance with you later."

"I'm not even wearing my dress."

"Really? I didn't even notice." He glances down and skims the lapel of my shirt. "Huh. Is this my button-down?"

"Maybe." I give him a coy smile.

"I like that you didn't even ask to borrow it. It tells me everything I need to know about where we stand."

"Which is where?"

"Exactly where I want us." He presses his lips to mine, but doesn't deepen it.

Instead, he releases me on a quiet sigh. "Please go help your sister with your sister."

"I'm going. No stops or detours." I leave him in the dining hall and rush off to find Avery and Harley.

I left them for what I thought was only a few minutes so I could grab us all bottles of water, but then I stopped into the reception room, and I needed to check on the decorations and one thing led to another. Apparently, I've been gone a lot longer than a few minutes.

Not ideal on my sister's wedding day, especially when I'm one of her two maids of honor.

A lot has changed at Spark House since Declan has come on board. With him working with us full-time, it's freed me up to be more hands-on with the decorating side. It means I get to do what I love creatively, and it also means I enjoy my job that much more. I even have time for my Etsy shop and my boyfriend. It's been amazing and gratifying to see all of our hard work paying off.

I don't think I realized exactly *how* unnatural it was for me to handle all the administrative work until Declan took over the role. I could manage the finances, but the other stuff took up so much of my mental and emotional energy. I had to spend hours preparing for things that take him minutes.

It wasn't an effective use of my time or my skill set, and I'm a bit embarrassed that I didn't realize that sooner.

I find Avery and Harley in her dressing room. She's not freaking out about her dress, though. Avery isn't even wearing her dress. She's currently wrapped in a robe, and so is Harley. They're both lounging in chairs, drinking mimosas.

"Jackson said there were dress problems."

Avery waves a hand in the air. "That was just to get you back here."

"Let me guess, you were checking on the decorations," Harley says.

"No. I was checking on the appetizers. Shouldn't you put your dress on?"

"It'll take five minutes. Sit down and have a cocktail." Avery points to the empty chair with her toe.

There's already one poured for me. I take the empty chair. "I can't believe this day is finally here."

"I am so ready to get this whole ceremony over with so I can enjoy the party." Avery chugs what's left in her glass and reaches for the champagne bottle.

Harley grabs it before she can, though. "You need a glass of water and a trip to the bathroom. And you need to eat at least three crackers before I'm letting you have another glass of champagne. You can't get drunk until after the ceremony. And preferably not before the speeches are done either."

"That's . . . irritatingly reasonable."

We send Avery to the bathroom, and Harley and I get Avery's dress ready.

As promised, we make Avery eat crackers and cheese and drink a glass of water before she's allowed to have another glass of champagne, which Harley dilutes with a generous shot of white grape juice behind her back.

"Have you been doing that all along?" I ask.

"Yup. You know how much she likes those sickly sweet wines, and this keeps her from getting sloshed before she walks down the aisle."

"So freaking smart." I give her a side hug, and we deliver a drink to Avery and then slip into our own dresses before Gran comes in and we help Avery into hers.

"I have a little something for you." Gran takes a small velvet bag out of her clutch and passes it to Avery.

"What is it?"

"It's your something old." She smiles and winks.

Her something borrowed is one of my clutches, something blue is the ribbon around her soccer ball-inspired bouquet, something new is the dress, and Gran said she had something old taken care of. I'd forgotten about that until now.

Avery carefully opens the bag. Inside is a single ornate hair clip encrusted with sapphires. "Oh, this is beautiful, Gran."

"I gave that to your mother on her wedding day as her something blue, and I know that she would want you to have it for your special day."

"Oh!" Avery waves her hand around in the air. "I think I'm going to cry."

"Your mascara is waterproof, so you're safe to shed some tears." I pass her a tissue.

Avery takes a seat and lets Gran fasten the hair clip.

And then we're all hugging, Gran telling us how proud she is and that our parents are looking down on us from heaven, feeling the same way.

And then it's time to walk down the aisle.

Harley and I are Avery's co-maids of honor, and there aren't any other bridesmaids because her other closest friends are Mark and Jerome, who also happen to be Declan's closest friends and his best men.

I've been paired with Jerome, so he meets me at the end of the aisle and holds out his arm. I slip my arm through his, and we wait until the wedding march starts playing before we head down the aisle.

I spot Jackson close to the front. His eyes shift briefly from me to Jerome and darken slightly before they return to me and soften. For a moment I think about what it might be like to walk down the aisle with him waiting for me at the end, before I refocus my attention on the wedding officiant.

We take our places, and Harley and Mark come next, then Declan appears and walks his mother down the aisle. There were a few threats that he would uninvite her if she continued to create drama, so she's been subdued the last couple of months.

Gran takes the place of our father and walks Avery down the aisle. She's been home for the past month, and she brought her beau from Europe with her. They're madly in love, and I wouldn't be surprised if there were wedding bells in their future too.

The ceremony is beautiful, and despite Avery being very much a yoga pants and T-shirt kind of woman, she looks stunning in her dress. I'm grateful for waterproof mascara because I can't quite keep my emotions from taking over when they say their vows, which they wrote themselves.

Afterward we head out to the barn for photos. Selene is here with another photographer, taking pictures for a social media piece she's running on Spark House. Her date happens to be Trent. It wasn't long after she stopped by Spark House asking me to talk to Jackson that the two of them ended up together.

I guess they'd long held a torch for each other, but circumstances prevented them from acting on it. At least until it became clear that Jackson's heart was taken, and Selene's was free for the taking. Jackson is surprisingly totally fine with them dating, which helped make his friendships with them both even stronger. I'm glad she found her happily ever after, especially after putting her own heart on hold for so long.

It isn't until later, after the ceremony and the speeches are over, that I find myself in Jackson's arms, floating around the dance floor.

"Has today been fun for you?"

"It has. Not nearly as stressful as all the planning was." Today has been almost perfect. Only the tiniest of hitches when there was a slight mishap with one of the dessert trays. But it's only something I would have picked up on, and I managed to get it fixed before anyone else could notice.

He spins and dips me, bringing me back up so we're chest to chest again. "What would you do differently for your wedding?"

"I wouldn't have any kind of obstacle course. Not great with heels and dresses."

"Unless you're wearing shorts under your dress and the bottom half detaches." Jackson arches a brow.

"That was a real showstopper, wasn't it?" I chuckle.

"It was something. I thought this wedding was taking a seriously X-rated turn for a moment there. I was concerned about all the people over eighty, and also glad that there are very few of them. Although, my worry was for nothing. I've never seen an obstacle course as part of the wedding party entrance at the reception."

"Avery isn't big on conventional, as I'm sure you're aware."

"I've noticed. I'm very glad your dress is a solid color."

"And also not a jersey."

"No obstacle course, no shorts under your wedding dress, no jersey-style bridesmaid dresses. I'm getting a good picture of what you don't want, but not much of a picture of what you do."

You, I want to tell him. Standing at the end of an aisle, with his hair looking like it's due for a trim, dressed in a tux, smiling just the way he is right now. "I don't know exactly. I don't have a traditional family unit, so I don't think traditional truly fits."

He nods pensively. "This is also true."

"What about you? What kind of wedding do you want?"

He smiles softly and brings my knuckles to his lips. "Whatever you want."

I don't get a chance to react because the music changes tempo and the bride and groom are called to the dance floor for the bouquet toss. Harley, who usually isn't big on competition, elbows two people out of the way and manages to catch the bouquet.

At the end of the night, we take a car back to Jackson's place. Whenever he's in Colorado, I spend my nights there with him, and I've been flying to New York for long weekends at least once a month, so we're finding a system that works for us. And when Avery returns from her honeymoon, I'm going to spend a week in New York with him. But he's been talking about Trent taking over in New York so he can manage the Colorado branch full-time, so we'll see what the next few months bring.

As soon as the door closes, I tackle his lips with mine.

"Someone's ramped up on the wedding high."

"I'm ramped up on you in a suit."

"I'm always in a suit."

"Not true. Sometimes you're in jeans."

"Rarely." I try to slide my tongue past his lips, but he takes my face in his hands and gently pulls me back. "Slow down, my love, we have all night."

"I've been waiting all night."

"Patience is a virtue."

"It's also overrated."

"I have something I want to give you, and after that, you can get me naked and have me any way you want me."

"Can't you give me whatever it is *after* I have you any way I want?"

He smiles and shakes his head. "I'm afraid not."

I blow out a frustrated breath. "Fine. I guess I can wait if I have to."

He chuckles softly and runs his nose along the column of my throat, his lips following. "Have I told you how much I love it when you get surly over having to wait for sex?"

"Is that why you're making me wait?"

"Maybe." He threads his fingers through mine and pulls me toward the stairs.

The hall is dimly lit, and a path of candles and rose petals are sprinkled on the floor.

"What is this?"

"I wanted tonight to be special because I know today was a big day for you and your sisters. Come. There's more."

I keep step with him, and we make our way to his bedroom. More candles decorate all available surfaces, and on the ottoman at the end of the bed is a tray of fruits and a bottle of champagne chilling, two glasses waiting to be filled.

We stop just shy of the end of the bed and Jackson turns to face me. His fingertips skim my cheek. "I love you so much."

"I love you too."

"Good. That's good." He nods and exhales a slow breath.

"Is everything okay?"

He gives me a small smile. "It should be." He holds both of my hands in his. "I've spent a lot of years avoiding love because

I've been afraid of what I stand to lose. And I know that we haven't been together that long, but I also believe that when you know, you know. My parents loved each other so much, it was . . . hard to watch them losing each other. And for a very long time, I never wanted to love someone that much. It seemed too painful. But what I've learned is that loving you is the easiest thing I've ever done in my entire life. I've already lost you once, so I know I don't want that to happen again. But more than that, I don't want to spend another day without you. I'll take all the ups and downs that life throws my way, and I want nothing more than to have you at my side." He drops to his knee, pulls a small box from his pocket, and flips it open. Inside is a beautiful star-shaped diamond set in platinum. "I promise to love you with my whole heart, for as long as it beats. Please, marry me, London."

I bend and cup his cheek in my palm. "There is no better home for my heart than with you. Of course I'll marry you."

He slips the ring on my finger as our lips meet, that spark we share igniting and burning brighter than ever.

"Any kind of wedding you want, London, you can have. If you want to be princess for a day, you can, as long as you're my queen for this life and whatever comes after."

Acknowledgments

It takes an entire team of people to take a book from first draft to readers' hands. Hubs and kidlet, thank you for being there for me, for ordering pizza when I'm on a deadline, for celebrating the wins, and giving out hugs during the lows.

Deb, so many years, so many books, and so much friendship. I'm lucky to have a person like you in my life.

Kimberly, thank you for all you do, for the phone and Zoom calls, the planning, the pep talks, and ironing out the fine details with me. You're an incredible agent and I'm blessed to have you in my corner and on my team.

Eileen, it's always a joy working with you. Thank you for helping me shape this story, and making it sparkle. To my team at SMP, thank you for making this series such a joy to write. You're amazing and I'm glad the Spark sisters have a home with you.

Christa, thank you for having my back and for always being real and giving me perspective. You're invaluable and I adore you.

Jenn and my SBPR team, thank you for being awesome, and for getting my stories into the hands of readers. You're amazing and all deserve Wonder Woman awards.

Sarah and the Hustlers, I can't do this without you. Thank you for being my team.

My ARC crew, my SS girls, and my Beaver Den, I adore you. Thank you for always celebrating with me and for being the most amazing readers.

Kat, Angela, Krystin, Marnie, Julie, thank you for being such wonderful friends and amazing women.

To my bloggers, bookstagrammers, and booktokers, thank you for your love of romance and happily ever afters. I couldn't do this without your support.

New York Times and *USA Today* bestselling author HELENA HUNTING lives outside of Toronto with her amazing family and her two awesome cats, who think the best place to sleep is her keyboard. She writes all things romance—contemporary, romantic comedy, sports, and angsty new adult. Some of her books include *Meet Cute, Pucked,* and *Shacking Up.* Helena loves to bake cupcakes and has been known to listen to a song on repeat 1,512 times while writing a book, and if she has to be away from her family, she prefers to be in warm weather with her friends.